Promised Valley Conspiracy

RON FRITSCH

For Lee Ann, David, and my family

ISBN: 0615739253
ISBN-13: 978-0615739250

Front cover photograph © iStockphoto.com/Brett Charlton

Back cover photograph © John Moll

For information address:

Asymmetric Worlds
1657 West Winona Street
Chicago, IL 60640-2707

www.promisedvalley.com

Notes

A **character list** appears at the end of this novel, beginning on page 261.

The "**tellers**" referred to in the Promised Valley series of novels perform several functions. They remember and retell their ancestors' stories. They preside at full-moon and change-of-season holidays, as well as at mating ceremonies and funerals. In place of the king they hear and decide disputes among the people. They're mostly persons who "go with" members of their own gender.

The "**valley people**" are prehistoric farmers who live in a fertile river valley. They believe the gods had long ago promised it to them in return for their good behavior and obedience.

The "**hill people**" are the hunters who roam the mostly barren hills beyond the mountains surrounding the valley. They believe the gods promised the valley—with the abundance of prey in its mountain-side forests, lake, and river—to them.

The **"river people"** live in a seacoast kingdom south of the promised valley and travel up and down the river on rafts to trade with the valley people.

Chapter 1

Blue Sky, for the valley people, and Long Arm, for the hill people, had brought an end to the most recent warfare between their peoples.

They'd accomplished the cessation of fighting even though neither was his people's ruler. Blue Sky was the son of the valley people's regent. Long Arm was the chief warrior of the hill people's king.

They made their peace agreement at the end of the day of the last battle of the current war they both knew their peoples had unwisely decided to fight.

Blue Sky and Long Arm had no choice, though, but to leave out of their accord the fates of Rose Leaf, the hill people's princess, and Morning Sun, the valley people's prince.

*****

Rose Leaf, having been abducted from her own people in her infancy by Blue Sky's and Morning Sun's fathers, had spent her childhood among the valley people as Blue Sky's sister. Neither Rose Leaf nor Blue Sky had known they weren't siblings. Neither had Morning Sun.

Even though Blue Sky was, and Rose Leaf appeared to be, the children of farmers, they were the best friends of Morning Sun, the valley people's prince. In the previous war with the hill people, Blue Sky's father, Green Field, the man who later held himself out to be Rose Leaf's father as well, had saved the life of Morning Sun's father, Tall Oak.

The life saved was that of the valley people's prince who became the valley people's king later in the war, when the hill warriors killed his father in battle.

After Tall Oak reluctantly assumed the duties of a king, he and Green Field—who "whispered instructions in his ear," their people liked to say—led their people to victory.

They and their comrades killed or chased away every hill warrior who'd dared enter their valley.

With the promised valley intact and safe once again from their enemies, the people soon regained their prosperity. They farmed fertile land, and the rain goddess, if she existed, was especially kind to them, providing just as much water as they needed for abundant crops and well-fed livestock—cattle, sheep, goats, and, for those fortunate few who had them, horses—year after year.

Meanwhile their enemies, eschewing agriculture as unnatural and therefore ungodly, hunted and gathered in the barren hills surrounding the valley and often starved to death in winter.

Blue Sky and most of the valley people wished, condescendingly perhaps, that wasn't the truth of the matter.

By the time Morning Sun and Rose Leaf came of age, they'd decided to marry, raise children as beautiful and happy as they were, and live the remainder of their lives together.

Blue Sky, who'd fallen in love with the prince for the same reasons Rose Leaf had, became their champion nevertheless.

He and others among the valley people chose to defend Rose Leaf and Morning Sun's right to marry and have children together, even after it became known that Tall Oak had forbidden their mating because Rose Leaf was the hill people's princess.

Many of the king's highest officials would've liked nothing better than to see Blue Sky dead. He was the son of a farmer, and yet he freely told the people those officials were corrupt and therefore didn't need to be obeyed.

All the valley people knew he could do that only because he was Green Field and Gentle Brook's son—and it didn't hurt that the prince favored him.

Rose Leaf, Morning Sun, and Blue Sky's rebels, who ultimately included Gentle Brook and Green Field, succeeded. They did so by persuading the farmers the hill people were as human as they were.

Consider, they argued, Rose Leaf herself—and her intellect, beauty, and compassion.

*****

The most recent war between the valley people and the hill

people arose after Long Arm, leading his brothers and cousins, cleverly abducted both their own people's princess and the valley people's prince.

The hill people's king, Lightning Spear, held them among his people, against their will.

The persons Rose Leaf and Morning Sun lived with, though, were Long Arm's family—who quickly came to love them as much as Blue Sky and the valley people did.

*****

At the end of the last battle, fought on sunset pass, Blue Sky had given himself up to Long Arm, who was free to kill him if the valley people reneged on their promise to let the hill people's warriors drag their dead down the slope on their side of the mountains.

The valley people were the victors in that day's battle and in the previous battle in the upper gorge. Both had been defensive battles they'd fought to salvage at least their upper valley—and prevent the genocide the hill people's king had promised them if they didn't leave it.

The valley people had lost the war, though, in the first battle on the hill people's plain. Their unimaginable defeat that day forced them to give up their lower valley. Its farmland and pastures were twice the size of the upper valley's.

The valley people's current chief warrior, Many Numbers, had asked every family he encountered, with as much sympathy as one chosen to achieve the aims of the god of war could muster, and as often as possible with Green Field at his side, how many of their family had perished in the battle.

Based upon their answers, Many Numbers concluded that one-fifth of their people who were alive before the battle were now lying on the plain, unburied. That one-fifth comprised almost all of the valley people's able-bodied men.

*****

As the hill warriors went about their work after their defeat on sunset pass, carefully keeping the severed limbs and heads of their dead comrades together with their bodies for fitful burial, Long Arm, using his foot, had forced back into its proper shape the arm Blue Sky had broken at the end of the fighting.

Long Arm also tied splints around his enemy's arm, using the clothes and spears of his dead comrades, to hold it in place until it had a chance to heal.

Despite the many cups of pod-tea Blue Sky had drunk, he passed out from the pain.

But after he came to his senses again, he made his truce with Long Arm: the hill people could have the lower valley, and the valley people would keep the upper valley.

They knew their peoples—their rulers as well as their ruled—would readily assent to those terms. The huge numbers of able-bodied men on both sides killed in the three battles up to that point had horrified their peoples into wanting no more killing, no matter what its justification might be.

Blue Sky and Long Arm therefore did what they did knowing they could get away with it.

They also knew they were only buying time before the next warfare between their peoples. But during that time, they and others among their peoples would be free to imagine the renewed hostilities might not be fought as previous wars between their peoples had been waged.

In those wars the valley people and the hill people simply killed one another for being the other—and nothing else counted.

*****

"Here's what a broken arm in a war does," Blue Sky said to the older men he was working with the morning after he incurred his injury and brought the fighting to an end.

Some of his co-workers were the same age as his father, Green Field, now the regent of their people, whose laws had elevated him to his position against his will.

The older men could clearly see on Blue Sky's face evidence of the physical pain he suffered.

"It puts me," Blue Sky said, "in the company of the heroes of the previous war."

"We aren't heroes," one of the older men responded, spitting out his words. "Heroes aren't merely people who do what they're expected to do. Wounds in a war don't make a person a hero. Everybody who fights in a war suffer some kind of wound. You found that out yourself."

"I agree," Blue Sky said, looking the man in the eye. "But that and perseverance, like your own, do make you heroes. You received your wounds in the war you fought when I was an infant. Despite them, you lived on. And you, along with the women, older children, and surviving able-bodied men of this most recent war, brought it to an end. Thanks to you, our people still exist."

The older men looked at one another and rolled their eyes. The regent's son often made strange remarks.

This time it was obvious he was doing it to avoid the truth. Nobody in his kingdom had imagined he'd kill as many hill warriors in the battles at the upper gorge and on sunset pass as he did. Nobody had imagined so much of what happened in those battles he'd calculate in advance—relying upon the persons who had the most useful knowledge and insight as to how they might accomplish their victories.

Surely nobody had imagined he could persuade his cautious father to go along with his radical arguments—especially that their people needed to give up, for the shortest while possible, their lower valley, and save themselves in their upper valley.

Despite his people's abundant praise for what he'd done, he couldn't admit he was their hero. That was because he didn't believe he was.

He'd done what he did without giving thought to what he otherwise knew was true: killing other humans—and the hill people were unquestionably humans—always raised the question whether the person who did it had done so with a self-serving intent peoples other than his own might well consider evil.

In that view, since Blue Sky's purpose in killing so many hill warriors was merely to save himself and his people from extinction, he was as guilty as he was innocent.

The people, though, wished to believe the father and son who'd saved them from that fate were heroes.

And the more the father and son insisted they weren't, and had only done what they had to do in the story their people would later tell about the time they lived in, the more their people became convinced they were.

*****

After their victory in the early-autumn battle on sunset pass, which resulted in Blue Sky and Long Arm's armistice, the valley people had one important task to perform before they returned to the valley floor.

Most of the tree trunks they'd rolled down the slope maiming and killing the hill people's warriors had ended up wedged among boulders in the uppermost band of the rough terrain below. They needed to get them back to the ridge in case a hill people's king should ever decide to march his army up his side of the pass again.

If there was a next time, the farmers might not have more than two days to assemble their army. They had to have the timbers already in place.

As soon as they were certain the hill people's army was leaving, they began their work. They wanted Lightning Spear, the hill people's king, and Thunder Hunter, the brutal chieftain of their second most powerful tribe, to see what the hill people could expect if they chose to mount another attack on sunset pass.

It didn't hurt that the two hill people the valley people had come to admire—Long Arm, Lightning Spear's chief warrior; and Wandering Star, Lightning Spear's bastard son and the hill man Blue Sky loved—could also see what the valley people were doing.

The hard work was looping ropes around the tree trunks to extract them from their resting places. With his arm broken at the end of the previous day's battle—and set back in place by Long Arm as both of their peoples watched—Blue Sky couldn't help much with that.

Leading his father's stallion pulling timbers up the slope, though, was something he could do.

The slope on the hill people's side of the ridge line was too steep for the horses. So the valley people tied long vine and leather ropes to the trees and pulled them up the hill people's side of the slope by leading the horses down their people's side.

They ran the ropes over the stony ridge line where it was relatively smooth and rounded. They avoided its more jagged sections.

The youngest boys and girls Green Field had allowed coming up to sunset pass as auxiliaries with the army stationed themselves on the ridge line. They liberally coated the ropes with tallow the valley people otherwise would've used for cooking food or making candles. The youthful lubricators with their good eyes could also tell when they had a rope so frayed no amount of grease would keep it from snapping before they saw it again.

Blue Sky's horse-leading comrades that day were mostly the oldest men among the auxiliaries. They'd fought alongside his father and Tall Oak in the previous war and survived it, but their injuries had precluded their fighting as warriors in the present one.

The day Tall Oak's army set out to rescue Morning Sun and Rose Leaf—or, failing that, the king and Sturdy Limb, his brother and chief warrior, had promised, to "teach the hill people a damned good lesson"—Blue Sky saw several of these men in tears.

Now, leading his father's stallion, listening to their stories, he could imagine how they must've felt being left behind. Their sons, nephews, cousins, neighbors, and even some of their brothers, were going off to fight their people's eternal enemy, who'd abducted their beloved prince and his mate-to-be. They, though, were staying home with the women and children—as if they were cowards.

For all the good they could do the kingdom then, they later told Blue Sky on sunset pass, they'd thought they might just as well already be in their graves.

Their injuries in the previous war, though, had also saved them from almost certain death on the hill people's plain and given them the chance—along with a number of women, older children, and survivors of the battle on the plain—to defend their people on the cliff-top above the upper gorge, and later on the ridge at sunset pass, with fatal trees, tree limbs, and boulders aimed at their eternal foe.

They'd also lived to see horses pulling the missiles up to the places where their people needed them, and to be among the first to realize they could never survive as a people without the assistance of those creatures.

Blue Sky knew he and his able-bodied warrior comrades, with their simple-minded and blood-soaked finishing-off of wounded and trapped enemy warriors, had done less to keep their people alive than the women, children, healing warriors, old men, and horses had.

And yet, due alone to the great number of enemy warriors Blue Sky had killed—as if he were crazed, even though he'd had no wish to so abruptly end his opponents' lives except to save his own and his people's—the valley people considered him a hero.

Blue Sky believed that was a mistake and often said so.

But every time he did, his people merely laughed—as if he'd once again said something so extraordinary its only possible purpose was to amuse.

*****

The farmers who lived in the valley their gods had promised them had blundered into a war with their enemies, the hunters who roamed the hills beyond the mountains surrounding the valley.

The farmers' king and his officials, who ruled from their bluff-top town above the river, had incited their people into sending their army out of the valley to attack the hill people. The valley people's army consisted of all the able-bodied men in the kingdom—except the four of those who'd openly made their opposition to the war known.

The hill people had monstrously abducted the farmers' prince—as well as the woman he loved. The farmers had agreed he could marry and have children with her—even after they'd belatedly learned the woman he wished to marry and have royal children with was the hill people's princess.

Her ostensible father and mother, Green Field and Gentle Brook—who were Blue Sky's father and mother—as well as the king and queen themselves, had kept it a secret. They'd done so to guarantee that Rose Leaf remained alive in a time of revenge—a time when killing their enemy's princess would've made great sense and given them profound satisfaction, even if she was an infant who shared

12

none of her father's or her people's guilt.

The valley people and the hill people imagined their gods—who appeared, to those among their peoples who cared to notice, to be the same gods for both peoples—had given the valley to their people alone, to the exclusion of their eternal enemy.

The hill people hunters believed their gods forbade farming. And that was all that mattered to them.

Although the valley people thought their belief in gods who permitted farming made them superior to their enemy in every way that mattered, the hill people had handed them a military defeat even the valley people's most disturbing dreams hadn't prepared them for.

Only a small fraction of the valley people's army, all of them severely injured, had survived the opening battle of the war and returned to the valley.

The vast majority of their warriors still lay unburied on the hill people's plain where the battle was fought. Wolves, vultures, and ravens had feasted on their flesh.

So fared the army that included all but four of the valley people's able-bodied men.

One of those able-bodied men opposed to the war was Green Field, the farmer who'd saved the life of Tall Oak, then the prince, in the previous war with the hill people. Another was Green Field's son, Blue Sky, the prince's boyhood friend who'd been led to believe that Rose Leaf was his sister.

The other able-bodied men opposed to a hasty use of force against the hill people were Many Numbers and Spring Rain, two of the tellers the people respected and admired the most, the orphans Fair Judge had raised in the home the valley people provided for children whose parents were dead and whose relatives declined to raise as their own children.

The four dissident men and their three women allies—who were Gentle Brook, Blue Sky's mother and Green Field's wife; Fair Judge, the teller the people insisted upon calling by a name she never would've chosen for herself; and Rainbow Evening, the queen no less—had argued that means other than an all-out attack on the hill people should've first been employed to gain the return of the prince and the woman he loved.

Tellers memorized and retold the stories their people's gods and ancestors had handed down to them. Tellers additionally heard and decided, in place of the king, disputes among their people. Spring Rain, Many Numbers, and Blue Sky were tellers. They were also men who spent their nights with men.

In the face of the dissidence of the four able-bodied men, Tall Oak and Sturdy Limb had decided to leave them home. The chief warrior then chose to say in court, knowing all their people would soon learn of his remark, "We've always left out of our battles and wars the older men unable to fight, the women, the children—and the cowards."

*****

The people had forgiven Green Field and Gentle Brook for pretending that Rose Leaf was their daughter, not the hill people's kidnapped princess.

During the previous war with the hill people, she, Morning Sun, and Blue Sky were still infants. Green Field and Tall Oak, having been captured by the hill people, escaped and took her with them, intending to kill her. When they realized they were incapable of killing an innocent child, they could only take her home with them and keep her identity a secret. If the valley people had known who she was, they would've instantly killed her.

The valley people had willfully taken almost no interest in the hill people beyond keeping them out of their valley, and killing as many of them as they could, including those who only encroached in search of food. The valley people therefore hadn't realized their enemy greatly outnumbered them. Nor had they known that if the hill people's tribes stood together taking enormous losses of their own, they could destroy the valley people's army.

After the valley people's disastrous defeat on the hill people's plain, and in order to forestall their extirpation as a people, they had to abandon the lower part of the valley their gods had promised them they'd keep as long as they honored and obeyed those same gods.

Because the king and all the others except Morning Sun above Green Field in the line of succession to the kingship were killed in the

14

battle on the plain, Green Field became the regent for the kingdom in the absence of the prince. He appointed Many Numbers chief warrior and Fair Judge first teller.

The farmers still living after the battle on the plain escaped to the upper valley with an army consisting of the dissidents Green Field, Many Numbers, Blue Sky, and Spring Rain; the few survivors of the battle who'd healed enough to fight again; and the new men who'd come of age when summer ended and autumn began.

They bloodily fought off two attempts by the hill people's warriors to invade the upper valley, the first time through the gorge separating the lower and upper valleys, and the second time over the mountains at sunset pass.

The valley people nevertheless immediately began to speculate how long it would be before they'd get back all of the kingdom their gods had promised them. Many Numbers assumed, as Long Arm had, in view of the valley people's losses on the hill people's plain, it would take a generation to accomplish that.

Blue Sky's refusal to obey his people's laws, which he in the arrogance of his youth felt entitled to ignore, had brought the war on. He therefore wished not to believe it would take a significant portion of a generation for his people to return to the lower valley—or for him to see Morning Sun and Rose Leaf alive again.

*****

When they were very young, Blue Sky, as well as Rose Leaf and Morning Sun, lived in fear of the sire of the stallion Blue Sky led pulling tree trunks over sunset pass. They hadn't the slightest inclination to disobey Green Field's and Gentle Brook's strict and repeated warnings not to go near him—which specifically meant they weren't supposed to go into his stall in the barn or the horse pasture when he was present in those places.

One good kick from him, Gentle Brook and Green Field cautioned, and they'd be dead, yet another unfortunate child who never made it to the full flower of adulthood.

The rule, though, didn't apply to Green Field. Somehow, despite the horse's reputation, the two of them worked the fields together many days from sunrise to sunset, and nothing bad ever seemed to happen. Blue Sky couldn't recall being told the horse had attempted to kick his father or had misbehaved in any other manner.

Blue Sky's early childhood assumption was that his father had no reason to fear the horse because the two of them were friends. His father rubbed down the stallion at the end of a long summer day, kept him well fed and watered, and sheltered him in the winter in a warm barn with new straw in his stall as often as he needed it.

His father let the stallion share the pasture with their mares, and many of their neighbors' mares as well, when they were in heat—often as Morning Sun and Blue Sky watched in awe. No wonder the gods loved horses.

Growing older, the prince and Blue Sky found themselves trying to decide one full-moon afternoon if Blue Sky could sit on the back of that horse and ride him as he did the mares and geldings.

Morning Sun had initially shaken his head. "Your father and mother say he'll buck you off. He'll kill you."

Blue Sky refused to believe it.

"Your father and mother know what they're talking about," the prince insisted. "More than my father and my uncle do, and they're supposed to be running our kingdom."

Blue Sky hadn't yet reached the point in his life where he felt he could openly say he agreed with that last remark—even though he did.

"I'm sure he won't mind if I mount him," Blue Sky said. "The mares and geldings don't. Why would he?"

"Stallions are supposed to be different," Morning Sun said.

"We can see that. But no more different than we and Rose Leaf are different."

Morning Sun smirked.

"He likes my father," Blue Sky persisted. "You can see he does. Why wouldn't he like me?"

Blue Sky finally told Morning Sun he was going to ride the stallion. The prince could go with him and watch him do it, or he could choose not to, as he saw fit. The king, queen, and Blue Sky's parents were in the village orchard drinking wine. Rose Leaf must've been with them.

16

Morning Sun went into the horse pasture with Blue Sky. The mares and geldings raised their heads and stared at them. The boys walked among them hoping that might keep the stallion at ease.

The stallion, though, was gazing at the mountains, taking no notice of their presence.

Coming within a house-length of the horse, Blue Sky asked Morning Sun to stay back and let him go the rest of the way on his own. That would keep both of them from being killed if the horse did turn out to be as mean as people said he was.

Blue Sky walked around the stallion so the horse had to see him. Blue Sky didn't want to frighten him with a sudden appearance at his side and make him skittish. Blue Sky walked toward him, keeping contact with his eyes. He reached his arm around his neck the way his father did.

The horse, which had often seen Blue Sky, Rose Leaf, and Morning Sun riding the mares and geldings, accepted Blue Sky's embrace.

Blue Sky stroked his neck. The stallion enjoyed it as much as the other horses did.

Blue Sky took his time rubbing the horse's body, even his male parts, gently.

Blue Sky led the horse to the boulder Rose Leaf, the prince, and he had rolled down from the forest to stand on when they mounted the horses. Still stroking the stallion, Blue Sky stood on the rock with his right thigh against the horse's body.

From time to time, he slowly brushed his right foot upward against the animal's loin, sometimes getting it all the way up to his back, sometimes even letting it rest there.

At the end of one of those maneuvers, Blue Sky let his foot and leg slide over the horse.

Although the stallion was partly supporting him now, the animal wasn't making any effort to throw him off.

Blue Sky took his other foot off the mounting rock and righted himself on the stallion's back.

The horse did a kind of dance for a while, rocking forward and backward.

At the end of which Blue Sky still sat upright on his back.

The stallion whinnied and stood motionless.

17

Blue Sky stroked his neck, showing his gratitude with his hand the way his father did.

Blue Sky looked at Morning Sun and laughed.

"He doesn't care," Blue Sky said. "I told you he wouldn't."

Morning Sun didn't seem persuaded just yet. The horse could still change his mind.

"Get Rose Leaf," Blue Sky said. "I want her to see this."

"I see you," Rose Leaf called out.

She came toward them from among the mares and geldings, where she'd been spying on her brother and the prince.

"I want to ride him too," she added. "Whether the prince does or not."

She did so that afternoon. As did Morning Sun, who also chose to ride the horse into the orchard so their parents, astonished and frightened at first, could see for themselves what their three misbehaving children had accomplished.

A short while after that, though, Green Field decided Blue Sky and Morning Sun had grown too big, and soon Rose Leaf would as well, to ride the horses without hurting them. He asked the three of them to promise him from that day forward they'd no longer do it.

They made their promises honestly enough. But it didn't take them long to decide they couldn't find any good reason to keep them. They never stopped riding the horses. It was obvious they weren't too heavy for them, not even when Blue Sky and Morning Sun were fully grown.

Among the three of them, on the other hand, it was a secret strictly kept. They agreed they could tell no one else, not even Morning Sun's cousins or their friend Early Harvest, for fear Green Field would learn they were disobeying him. It gave them no pleasure to fail to keep their promises to him, of all people.

They found a clearing in the forest far removed from any farming village. They took the horses there and rode them.

They'd often watched them running in their pasture for no apparent reason. They could only conclude it was something they liked to do. In the clearing they discovered the horses liked to do it even with fully grown humans on their backs.

18

The trick was learning how to stay on. Each of them fell off a few times, but the horses, seeming to know something was wrong, almost always slowed down or came to a stop.

One day Blue Sky watched as the horse Rose Leaf was riding increased the length of her stride on her own initiative—and gracefully leapt over a prone Morning Sun, who'd unfortunately just fallen off his own mount.

The three of them agreed, despite what the incident told them about the horses, they could never let anybody else know they'd come that close to killing the prince.

*****

The hill warriors who'd stayed below the gorge during the battle on sunset pass had given the valley people no indication they harbored any desire to attack them in the gorge again. Possibly the valley people's faux warriors parading on the upper side of it had them fooled. Or the hill warriors realized limbs and rocks would've rained down on them no matter who was there.

It took a number of days for the hill warriors who'd survived the battle on sunset pass to return to their encampment below the upper gorge. Wandering Star, Blue Sky's hill-man friend and the hill king's unacknowledged son, had told them the shorter days of autumn would disadvantage the hill people's army.

Well before dark every evening, their warriors would have to be done with their hunting and traveling, and all of them accounted for in an encampment ringed by Thunder Hunter's warriors. That was in case any of the warriors of the other tribes, Lightning Spear's included, should decide, with winter approaching, to sneak away and rejoin their families.

Some of the warriors of the lesser chieftains would've been tempted the most since their families roamed the hills through which the army traveled on its way to and from sunset pass.

The hill warriors stayed in their encampment below the upper gorge only the remainder of the day they arrived and that night.

Blue Sky could see Thunder Hunter's sons Dark Storm and War Cloud and their teller cousin True Hunter, who all knew how to make their presence known, had once again survived. None of them appeared to have suffered an injury in any of their day-long fighting with the valley people in three battles in which many of their comrades died.

The next morning most of the hill warriors departed. For several days afterward the valley people watched as their evening campfires moved farther south along the river in the lower valley.

The hill people also left a contingent of warriors at the gorge.

One day Many Numbers invited Blue Sky and others who could see well to go up to the cliff-top with him. He assigned each of them a section of the landscape to count how many hill warriors they could see within it.

Based on the grand total he calculated from the numbers they gave him, he concluded the hill people hadn't left a contingent large enough to mount another meaningful attack in the gorge.

But he was certain they had more than enough warriors to keep his people from breaking out of the upper valley without a ruinous loss of warriors.

*****

The leaf-losing forest turned as crimson and gold as a sunset after a late-in-the-day storm.

The valley warriors wounded in the battle in the mountains slowly healed. The pain in Blue Sky's left arm subsided, and the appendage became as useful to him as it ever was.

A few of their warriors endured permanent injuries. Early Harvest's cousin Good Harvest always walked with a limp after suffering his wound. He often referred to it proudly, though, calling it his proof he'd fought for his people when they needed him most. It didn't hinder his ability to work his fields, tend to his livestock, or train for the next battles with the hill people, whenever and wherever the valley people would fight them again.

And, as was the case with Early Harvest, one of the few valley warriors who'd returned from the battle on the plain despite his injuries, his war-fighting wound didn't seem to diminish the number of young women who made it apparent they enjoyed his company.

20

Those valley people who'd survived their encounters with the hill people had reason to rejoice. But they could never forget their many warriors whose bones lay unburied on the hill people's plain.

Likewise, the valley people were glad to learn what Long Arm had told Blue Sky on sunset pass: that Morning Sun and Rose Leaf were well and surprisingly well-treated. It was impossible, though, not to imagine the fear they had to live with.

Rainbow Evening found it impossible to imagine anything else. She rarely came out of the house she shared with Fair Judge. When she did, it was only to sit in the autumn sun with Fair Judge, Gentle Brook, Green Field, Many Numbers, Spring Rain, or Blue Sky.

Whenever Blue Sky was with her, she questioned him about his conversation with Long Arm on sunset pass. Was he certain Long Arm was telling the truth? If Morning Sun and Rose Leaf did see one another, was it as it was on sunrise pass, as lovers? Could they in fact have children?

Or would the hill people's king force Rose Leaf to mate with a hill man she didn't want? Would that king order Morning Sun's execution for no other reason than his being the enemy prince?

*****

It was comforting for the lower-valley people to have the upper valley as a sanctuary and the upper-valley people as their hosts. But for those who'd lived all their lives in the lower valley, the only homes they'd ever have would always be there.

Blue Sky found it difficult to believe his people wouldn't go back to the lower valley—and to the safe and prosperous kingdom where he'd grown to adulthood.

He'd rather be killed in battle, even end up in a bone pile, than abandon hope of his people's speedy return.

And that would require something more than the defensive warfare Wandering Star thought the valley people were so good at.

RON FRITSCH

Chapter 2

The warriors told the people the army was hosting a special competition in honor of their missing prince and the woman they hoped would someday be his mate. It would take place during the afternoon of the next full-moon day on harvested fields near the gorge.

The warriors said Blue Sky had challenged Early Harvest to a race, and Early Harvest had readily accepted the challenge. Blue Sky, the regent's son, wasn't Morning Sun, the prince, but Early Harvest and his cousins had agreed he was a worthy opponent to compete in Morning Sun's stead.

After all, in the racing competition the summer they came of age, Blue Sky wasn't eliminated until his match with the prince, and that was Morning Sun's last race before his final match with Early Harvest. Blue Sky was Morning Sun's last opponent before Early Harvest in the spear-throwing and wrestling competitions as well.

Blue Sky once tried to explain to Noon Breeze and the other apprentice tellers in a wine-drinking session on sunrise pass his three losses to Morning Sun.

Blue Sky said he'd assumed, even as Early Harvest hadn't, that it was his duty to accept defeat since his opponent was the prince.

His drinking companions jeered in disbelief.

They reminded him of his previous excuse that the prince had more time to train for the contests than he, a farmer's son, had. Why would Blue Sky need any more time than he had to train for games he intended to throw in any event?

Noon Breeze couldn't help himself from taking a contrarian position to that of his comrades, many of whom he enjoyed going with.

"I don't doubt you deliberately lost to Morning Sun," he sneered at Blue Sky. "But you did it only because you were in love with him. And it didn't do you any good anyway. He was in love with your sister. And you were too blinded by your own lust to see it."

Blue Sky could scarcely blame his comrades for laughing at that.

The warriors announcing the race also hinted it would be like none their people had seen before—or so Many Numbers, Early Harvest, and Blue Sky had promised them.

23

One difference was obvious from the outset. The warriors had demarcated the race course with vines looped around stakes driven into the ground in an oval, but it covered well more than twice the distance of the traditional running track.

Many more people showed up for the event than the hosts had anticipated. The gods had blessed the valley people, despite their other troubles, with a bountiful supply of wine that autumn. The farmers had given the army more of it than the warriors and auxiliaries could possibly consume by themselves. The warriors had made it clear that for the race the wine would be free to any person of age.

The older children had to take care getting and drinking it, knowing they'd impose an unnecessary burden on a reluctant regent to order their punishment if they got caught. Green Field's pained announcement of their punishment would be worse than the punishment itself.

After the people had assembled, Green Field, Gentle Brook, Full Harvest, Early Harvest, Many Numbers, Spring Rain, and Blue Sky gathered at the starting line.

Many Numbers began with an announcement.

"The competitors wish to dedicate their efforts today to those most responsible for our victories in the upper gorge and on sunset pass."

The people fell respectfully silent. Before every competition, their athletes were expected to offer their endeavors to gods and goddesses of their choosing, to gain their favor and increase their chances of winning. Their ancestors supposedly made speeches praising the god or goddess they'd chosen. Now though, athletes merely recited the deity's name and skipped the time-consuming flattery.

Morning Sun was expected to dedicate his efforts to the sun god, who was as mighty as the god of war, and he always did.

Yet he'd often turn to Rose Leaf and Blue Sky and mutter, "The goddess of love, I meant to say."

"The contestants both wish to dedicate the race," Many Numbers continued, with a nice pause for everyone to guess which god or goddess they'd selected, "to our horses."

For one delightful moment more, the people remained silent.

The valley people had a law strictly prohibiting mockery of the gods.

In one of their people's stories, the god of war brought to ruin a king who, perhaps having drunk more wine than he should've, facetiously described that god as "dumber than an ox." Spring Rain and Many Numbers were convinced this was the same king who'd refused to go with a woman and provide the kingdom with an heir to the kingship—and brought on a civil war.

The punishment for the blasphemy Many Numbers, Early Harvest, and Blue Sky had committed was banishment from the kingdom. None of their people, though, could remember hearing a story in which any of the last three kings, from Morning Sun's great-grandfather on down to Tall Oak, had imposed such a punishment. The tellers weren't even certain what banishment would consist of. Did they force the offender to live beyond the guard posts? If they did, the punishment would be tantamount to execution—not by their chief warrior and his deputies but by the savage hill people. Or could the guilty person attempt to live alone in the forest?

The hill people's kings still enforced their law against blasphemy. It was the one their tellers had invoked when they convinced Lightning Spear to exile Wandering Star, who was, all the while, handing them far more evidence of his crime than they needed to convict him.

Perhaps at the thought of Green Field's attempting to banish Many Numbers, Early Harvest, and Blue Sky, the people began tittering.

The apprentice tellers, though, having fought in the upper gorge and on sunset pass without any perceptible assistance from far-off gods nobody could see or hear, openly laughed.

"Heresy!" one of them yelled, bringing on another round of guffaws.

Green Field gave his son the resigned-to-his-fate look Blue Sky had expected from him.

"For that purpose," Many Numbers resumed, "the contestants wish to have two particular steeds brought to the starting line to receive their dedications on behalf of all our horses."

The people, glad to see the charade continue, and perhaps

suspecting that Many Numbers, Early Harvest, and Blue Sky had, like the tragic king of yore, already partaken of more than their share of the day's libations, cheered.

"Bring on the horses," some of the warriors yelled.

"Bring on the horses," the people happily agreed.

"Bring Full Harvest's stallion to the starting line," Many Numbers ordered.

The horse, Noon Breeze leading him, emerged from a nearby orchard.

The first night coming home from the battle on the plain, Early Harvest was in a pod-tea delirium when he suddenly told Blue Sky he wished he had one of his father's horses to ride.

After Blue Sky insisted a fully grown man couldn't ride a horse, Early Harvest assured him one could. He further informed Blue Sky he and Good Harvest had often done so.

"It doesn't hurt the horses," he said. "Your father's mistaken about that."

He told Blue Sky he and Good Harvest had been very careful not to let his father or anybody else know what they were doing.

The crowd making way, Noon Breeze led the stallion to the starting line.

"You can mount the horse," Early Harvest said to Noon Breeze.

Green Field looked at Blue Sky as if his son had struck him a blow.

Green Field had publicly admitted he was as responsible as anyone for bringing on the most recent, and most devastating, war with the hill people. He'd refused to become Tall Oak's chief warrior. Although he'd killed a great number of hill warriors in the previous war, he could never execute his own people. His choice had led to the battle on the plain, which killed far more valley people, all of them able-bodied men, than a chief warrior could ever hope to execute.

Looking his hero, his own father, in the eye, Blue Sky smiled.

He'd arranged this drama for him.

With Spring Rain cupping his hands for a foothold, Noon Breeze quickly mounted the stallion.

26

The crowd murmured.

Shortly after coming down from the battle on sunset pass, Early Harvest, Good Harvest, and Blue Sky began teaching Noon Breeze, Spring Rain, and Many Numbers how to ride the horses. They gave their lessons deep in the forest to keep them a secret, even from their comrades.

The people, including the apprentice tellers, eyed Green Field and Full Harvest anxiously, knowing full well their strict rules against grown people and older children riding the horses.

Once again, not knowing what to say, the people wisely chose to say nothing.

Green Field separated himself from Gentle Brook and Full Harvest and drew closer to Many Numbers, Early Harvest, and Blue Sky.

"What are you doing?" he asked, but in a curt whisper only the three of them could hear. "You know this is no way to treat a horse. Why do you want the people to see this? Noon Breeze might be smaller than most men, but he's still too big to be sitting on a horse's back. Please ask him to get off that horse."

"You're wrong about the horses," Blue Sky said.

"Grown people can ride them," Many Numbers said.

"We're going to show the people that," Early Harvest added.

Green Field turned to Blue Sky.

"You're deliberately doing this in front of the people," he said. "You know I'll have to go along with it. You know I can't let the people see the three of you and me quarreling."

Blue Sky laughed. His own father, his hero, was making him out to be a manipulative Sturdy Limb.

"There's no need," Blue Sky said, "for the people to see us quarreling."

Green Field turned to Many Numbers again.

"Even you?" he asked. "My son has always been able to goad his friends into one damned thing after the other. But even you?"

The day the prince rode the stallion into the orchard unannounced, Green Field told Tall Oak and Rainbow Evening he was well aware of Blue Sky's long history of inciting Morning Sun to misbehave in open court.

"I can see what he's doing," he said. "The sad thing is,

Morning Sun and Rose Leaf go along with everything he tells them to do."

Morning Sun and Rose Leaf, who knew there was no truth in that remark, laughed.

Green Field, though, persisted with Many Numbers. "I'd hoped you'd be able to resist him. I'd even hoped you might be able to restrain him."

Many Numbers laughed. "When you couldn't?" he asked. "I've never sired a child, and yet I'm supposed to be a better father than Green Field, of all people?"

Early Harvest and Blue Sky looked at one another and smirked.

Gentle Brook, Full Harvest, and Spring Rain, the only people who'd dared draw close enough to hear the conversation, laughed for everybody to see and hear.

"Noon Breeze isn't hurting the horse," Early Harvest said. "You can see that for yourself. The horse doesn't mind his weight."

"Walk the horse," Many Numbers directed Noon Breeze.

The crowd stepped back to give the horse room.

"Does the horse's back sway?" Early Harvest, still whispering, asked Green Field and Full Harvest. "It looks as straight and strong as a tree trunk to me."

"The horse isn't displeased at all," Spring Rain interjected. "If he were, why wouldn't he simply buck Noon Breeze off his back? That would give everybody something to laugh about."

"That's a strong horse," Green Field said. "That's the horse I gave Full Harvest. I knew how good he'd be. He's my stallion's brother. My old stallion was their father. His favorite mare was the mother of both of them. They were all good strong horses."

"And my father and our family," Early Harvest said, "have always been grateful to you for this stallion. Most of the horses in the upper valley are descended from him. But you're wrong about what we can do with our horses. We adults can ride them."

Green Field turned to his son again.

"You know I won't stop you," he said, glancing anxiously at the crowd. "You'll have to go ahead with this performance you and your friends are putting on. But I'm telling you now, you'd better be

28

right."

"The kingdom is what counts," Full Harvest said, his eyes darting from Blue Sky to Early Harvest to Many Numbers to Spring Rain and back to Blue Sky again. "You're all heroes. And rightly so. You kept the hill people out of the upper valley. Our people will listen to anything you say. But you don't want them to start thinking you don't know what you're talking about."

"They won't think that," Blue Sky said, putting his hand on Full Harvest's shoulder.

The people were staring at them, waiting. Even those nearest them, the apprentice tellers and Early Harvest's cousins, were strangely quiet. None of them had seen a grown person riding a horse before, but there Noon Breeze was, and neither Green Field nor Full Harvest had ordered him to get down.

"Bring Green Field's stallion to the starting line," Many Numbers loudly ordered.

The horse emerged from the orchard. Good Harvest was riding him.

The people made way for them.

"See," Blue Sky said to his father, as horse and rider approached. "Our horse doesn't mind having an adult rider any more than his brother does. And this rider isn't a runt like Noon Breeze."

The apprentice tellers and Early Harvest's cousins, who overheard that, snickered.

One of the apprentice tellers saw fit to reveal, loudly enough so that at least the group with the regent could hear him, that Noon Breeze wasn't a runt where it counted.

Green Field and Full Harvest examined both stallions from end to end and top to bottom, even listening to them breathe.

Many Numbers motioned to Noon Breeze and Good Harvest.

"Please ride the horses among the people," the chief warrior said.

Warriors, young women, and older children crowded close to the two animals, many of them as painstaking in their examinations as the regent and Full Harvest had been. The older people behind them had to strain to see what the younger people were talking about.

After all the people present that day had a chance to view the stallions' insouciance at adult humans sitting on their backs, Noon

Breeze and Good Harvest somehow got the horses to return to the starting line.

Many Numbers asked the people to clear the racecourse.

They quickly did so, taking up positions behind the vines.

"Now," Many Numbers said, "with the riders still on their backs, the horses will run in their second gait."

"I assume," Green Field quietly said, as Many Numbers' message echoed through the crowd, "the riders have done this before."

"So have Many Numbers and I," Spring Rain confessed.

Green Field looked at Spring Rain, as if even the god of love had betrayed him.

"I also assume," he said, "my son taught you how to do it."

Noon Breeze, having heard the regent's comment, laughed.

"Your son," he offered, "is the biggest troublemaker this kingdom has ever seen."

Green Field looked up at Noon Breeze sitting on Full Harvest's stallion and sighed.

Noon Breeze laughed again. "He's your son. Don't ask us how he got the way he is."

Gentle Brook joined in the laughter at Green Field's expense.

"Proceed with the horses," Many Numbers ordered.

"Proceed with the horses," Gentle Brook, the regent's wife, loudly affirmed.

Noon Breeze and Good Harvest rode down the track.

The valley people had noticed horses moved in four distinctive gaits. The first, the slowest, was when they simply walked, lifting only one foot off the ground at a time. Even supporting a rider on its back or pulling a cart full of wheat or barley, a horse could walk all day.

In the second and somewhat faster gait, the horse ran with two feet off the ground at the same time. They were always a diagonal pair, the left rear foot and the right front foot, or the right rear foot and the left front foot. Blue Sky and his comrades had discovered a horse could carry a rider a longer distance at a greater speed than the fastest human with the most stamina could run. The rider, though, was subjected to a great deal of jostling up and down.

Now, watching as Noon Breeze and Good Harvest bounced up

and down, few men or older boys in the crowd failed to grimace.

"How in hell," an apprentice teller asked the question they all had in mind, "are they doing that?"

"They've got them tied up," Spring Rain explained, whispering so that Green Field wouldn't hear him. "Under their loincloths. Leather straps. Tied against their bellies."

That news passed through the crowd faster even than the horses and their riders.

Men and boys of all ages avidly sought an unobstructed view of the horses and their riders in the first row of the crowd on either side of the racecourse.

The women, perhaps realizing the issue at hand didn't quite so directly affect them, seemed only too happy to give the males all the room they needed.

The horses and their bouncing riders came back to the starting line.

As the crowd cheered them, Noon Breeze and Good Harvest slid down from the stallions.

"Now for the race," Many Numbers said.

*****

Early Harvest and Blue Sky mounted the stallions.

"You're racing on the horses?" Green Field asked. "In their fastest gait?"

"On the horses," Spring Rain replied, "going as fast as they can make them go."

If a horse was running in its third gait, people with good eyesight who got their heads down close to the ground could see that the animal regularly had three feet off the ground at the same time. Likewise, when it ran as fast as it could in its fourth gait, they could see it lifted all four feet off the ground. Horses could run in their fourth gait much faster than a human could run, but not as long.

As Green Field's questions and Spring Rain's replies went out to the crowd, they drew the responses Blue Sky and his co-conspirators had expected: "I don't believe it!" "That isn't possible!" "This time they've gone too far!" "They must think we're fools!"

Early Harvest and Blue Sky remained on their stallions at the

31

starting line nevertheless. They were waiting for Fair Judge to make her way through the crowd. Many Numbers had insisted only the first teller could start a race of this importance and decide who won it.

"You don't know," Early Harvest said to Blue Sky, speaking softly so that nobody else could hear, "how much I envy you. You rode horses in the forest with Rose Leaf and Morning Sun."

Blue Sky looked at him and laughed.

"If you'd thought you were Rose Leaf's brother," he said, "you couldn't have fallen in love with her."

Early Harvest sighed. "That would've been all right. It didn't do me any good to fall in love with her anyway. But I would've spent my days with them the way you did, riding horses. Don't you know how lucky you were?"

No longer laughing, Blue Sky looked at Early Harvest. Coming home from the battle on the plain wounded, Early Harvest was seldom not helping another survivor. Maybe Rose Leaf should've chosen him for her lover and mate. Rose Leaf and Morning Sun would still be in the valley. No war would've been fought to bring them back.

"Which one of you was it?" Early Harvest asked. "Which of you was the first to ride a horse running as fast as it could? You've never told me that."

Blue Sky smiled. Early Harvest and Good Harvest hadn't dared let their horses run when they were riding them. Blue Sky had to show them how to do that.

"Rose Leaf," Blue Sky replied.

Early Harvest laughed. "I'll be damned. She beat you and Morning Sun to it."

That was also when Rose Leaf decided she wanted to wrestle with Morning Sun, but he wouldn't have any part of it.

"How am I supposed to control myself?" he'd asked Blue Sky. "She doesn't understand. I'd be inside her before I had a chance to think about it."

It's possible Morning Sun didn't realize it at the time, but Blue Sky also knew temptation, and how difficult it was not giving in to it. Taking a look at the prince was all he had to do to bring it on and force himself to deal with it once more.

Blue Sky smiled at Early Harvest again.

"Rose Leaf," he said, "didn't have to bother with straps holding anything up down there."

Many Numbers was shouting above the noise of the skeptical crowd.

"The first teller has come forward and agreed to start the race," he announced.

As Fair Judge let the fact of her acquiescence in the dubious entertainment go out to the people, she turned to the riders.

"Will the horses know," she asked them, "when I give the command?"

"They'll know," Early Harvest assured her.

Unlike the self-dramatizing Law Keeper, Sturdy Limb's compliant ally Tall Oak had appointed first teller because Green Field had refused to become chief warrior, Fair Judge succinctly gave the riders her preliminary commands and got to "Go!" in short order.

The horses charged down the racecourse.

The crowd, assuming Early Harvest and Blue Sky would surely fall off—what was holding them on?— screamed.

Blue Sky and Early Harvest rode away on their horses, laughing.

And when the people realized they could stay on despite the speed of their mounts, the screams turned to cheers.

As the horses ran neck and neck, Early Harvest and Blue Sky urged them to go even faster.

The brute strength of the horses pulsing against their legs gave them their answer.

It was the closeness of Early Harvest's footraces with Morning Sun that the people couldn't forget. Now again, neither horse was letting the other get ahead, and the crowd made known its approval.

As they passed the stake that Many Numbers had said marked a quarter of the race, though, Green Field's stallion was running ahead of his brother, but only by half the length of his body.

The people loudly approved this development, too.

Blue Sky's horse increased his lead to the length of his body, not counting his tail.

The people cheered the horse on, yelling, "Green Field! Green Field!"

33

But Green Field the horse was finding it more and more difficult to increase his lead, and was soon even losing some of it.

Full Harvest the horse halved the lead, and kept coming on.

Blue Sky thought his horse could see his competitor out of the corner of his eye and, like a human or a god, cared whether he remained ahead or fell behind.

The crowd wildly cheered.

At what Many Numbers said was the halfway stake, Full Harvest's stallion was taking the lead.

And the crowd, fickle as ever, roared: "Full Harvest! Full Harvest!"

Early Harvest, passing Blue Sky—the son of the woman his father, Full Harvest, loved most—glanced at him and laughed.

"Full Harvest!" the crowd screamed.

The valley people adored, more than anything else, winners and winning.

Blue Sky wondered if that was why most of them believed the gods existed, even in some far-off, preposterous heaven no human had ever seen.

Individuals a competitor might've thought were his best friends would often desert him the moment he fell behind in a contest, and, believing no apologies of any kind were necessary, blatantly and loudly cheer for his opponent.

Early Harvest and Blue Sky had gotten a good taste of that in their coming-of-age-summer competitions with the prince. It did neither of them any good to complain. They either had to practice more and try to do better the next time, or silently and gracefully accept their lot in life.

In that autumn day's race in the upper valley, though, Green Field's stallion and Blue Sky his rider were apparently not ready to accept their lot if that had anything to do with defeat.

Blue Sky worked his legs as if he and his horse were one.

Having fallen behind by the length of his opponent including his tail, Green Field's stallion responded. As they approached the three-quarter mark, he was reducing his brother's lead.

When the finish line came into view straight ahead for both of the horses and their riders, they were neck-and-neck again.

The people cheered, many of them switching back to Green Field the stallion's side after having just moments earlier given themselves up to the four-legged Full Harvest.

It was as if Blue Sky's horse wasn't about to let his brother beat him. Making one final effort the gods undoubtedly would've loved to see, he surged into the lead.

Ahead by the length of his body from his nostrils to his shoulders, Blue Sky's horse flew past the finish line and Fair Judge with the crowd screaming, "Green Field! Green Field!"

*****

As Early Harvest and Blue Sky slowed their horses, warriors and auxiliaries broke from the crowd and sprinted toward them.

Until that late-autumn day, after the battles with the hill people in the upper gorge and on sunset pass, the valley people hadn't thought it was possible for an older child or adult to ride a running horse. Now they'd seen with their own eyes it was—even when the horse was running as fast as it could.

As Early Harvest and Blue Sky rode their horses at a walk, the warriors and auxiliaries patted the animals and smeared one another with their profuse sweat.

The riders brought their horses around until they were face to face with the two persons whose names the wine-drinking crowd that day had decided they shared.

As was the custom for the victors of their people's athletic contests, Blue Sky thanked Early Harvest for running the race with him.

"Your horse ran well today," he said, his words going out to the crowd. "He's ordinarily nowhere near as fast as this horse. He's a number of years older. That's the difference."

Blue Sky looked at his father and Full Harvest.

"He's slowing down," he couldn't help but note, "the way old people do."

The crowd laughed at that.

"If your horse is so much faster," Noon Breeze presumptuously asked the regent's son, "why did Full Harvest's stallion almost beat him?"

Blue Sky knew what was coming from that comrade.

"Maybe," Blue Sky replied, "you should answer your question yourself. The people enjoy hearing your opinions. You so often amaze them with your vast store of wisdom."

The people enjoyed hearing that said of the man who'd told Lightning Spear, the hill people's king, before the battle in the upper gorge, to go to hell.

"Maybe," Noon Breeze offered, "Early Harvest is a better rider than you are."

The people laughed at that, too, and many of the warriors and auxiliaries, especially those from the upper valley, started shouting, "Early Harvest! Early Harvest!"

When Blue Sky joined in the cheering for his adversary, so did the entire crowd, including their fathers and Gentle Brook.

Early Harvest looked at Blue Sky and took his hand.

The people laughed again. It was customary for the winner to take the loser's hand.

*****

Early Harvest and Blue Sky slid off their fathers' horses, giving them up for vigorous and well-deserved rubbings-down by the warriors and auxiliaries, many of whom were demanding they be taught how to ride a running horse, preferably not later than that same day.

"You'll all get your chance," Noon Breeze promised them.

Blue Sky and his comrades had other horses waiting in the orchard for that eventuality. Everybody might get their chance, but Noon Breeze was also promising the apprentice tellers they'd be first, the same promise Good Harvest was making to his and Early Harvest's cousins.

Blue Sky and Early Harvest could see the pointless fistfights looming.

Following Long Arm's example below the upper gorge, they walked between the quarreling groups, pointing out to them being first meant nothing and promising none of them would be overlooked. They told them a choosing of straws—chance alone—would determine when their opportunity came.

The former disputants, having no further reason to fight, embraced one another.

*****

Later, though, the two disobedient sons were alone with their parents. Everybody else was still admiring the horses.

Gentle Brook embraced both of them. Like Morning Sun, Early Harvest was, to her, as much her son as Blue Sky was. Tears ran down her face.

"I was scared to death you'd fall off," she said to them, "but I'm awfully damned glad you did what you did."

"Now do you see?" Early Harvest asked his father and Green Field. "Now do you see what our horses can do?"

"Blame the river people," Green Field replied. "They told my father he had to treat horses the way they did oxen. I only went by what they told him. Nobody rides oxen."

Blue Sky laughed. "Why would you go by what the river people told your father?"

Green Field, having no good answer, looked at his son as a pupil would an especially demanding tutor.

"The river people didn't know where the horses came from," Blue Sky said. "Why would they know what horses could do?"

"Green Field," Early Harvest interjected, "your father's horses have won two battles for us. Did the river people tell him they could do that?"

Full Harvest put his hand on Green Field's shoulder.

"Our sons and their friends," he remarked, "seem to have taken over our kingdom."

Green Field, staring at Blue Sky as if his son were a prospective lover who'd turned him down, didn't hesitate.

"They can have it, too," he said. "I'm a farmer, a mate for life, and a father, and that's all I've ever wanted to be."

That wasn't, though, all his people wanted him to be.

37

*****

The trees on the lower slopes of the mountains lost their leaves. Snow covered most of the evergreen forest higher up and deepened on the mountain tops above the tree line. One morning the valley people awoke to a dusting of snow in their fields as delicate as blossoms in spring.

Their overriding concern was the whereabouts of the hill people's warriors, other than the contingent they could see encamped along the river beyond the orchard.

Many Numbers, Blue Sky, and others went up to the cliff-top in the evenings to look for the smoke rising from the hill people's campfires. Since almost all the campfires were in the mountains, the valley people presumed they were hunting.

The few forest animals that somehow got into the valley people's farmland, most often when an entryway in the wall was thoughtlessly left open, never seemed to wish to stay for long. It normally took only a bit of yelling to prompt them to run back to the forest.

They were usually young bulls, rams, and billies that sensed the farmers nearest the forest had cows, ewes, or nannies in heat. The farmers were exceedingly careful not to let their female animals mate with the "inferior" wild breeds they saw in the forest.

The valley people believed the wild animals turned and ran so readily because, facing the challenge of a number of humans shouting at them together, they had no interest in remaining on the farmland side of the wall. They could easily see they'd have few places to hide, wrongly assuming wolves and bears must be lurking about.

In any event, Many Numbers was certain they were detecting far fewer campfires than they'd expect to see if a significant part of the hill people's army remained in the lower valley.

So the regent and chief warrior, having concluded that the hill people must've decided against mounting another attack before spring, disbanded the army. They sent new men of age to replace the old men in the guard posts in the mountains. They ordered the other warriors and auxiliaries to carry on the work of the kingdom where it most

38

needed to be done: in their villages. If the guards detected the hill people's army returning to the valley in force, the army would have sufficient time to assemble at the gorge, or wherever else Lightning Spear and Thunder Hunter might decide to attack next.

*****

The apprentice tellers, though, remained at the gorge to provide a first line of defense in case of a surprise attack from the hill warriors encamped beyond the orchard, and to keep guards posted on the cliff-top throughout the days and nights.

The apprentice tellers and their four teller comrades decided to erect a roof over the rectangular area enclosed by the house and huts they lived in. Borrowing Green Field's horses, they pulled tree trunks down from the forest and buried their bottom ends in the ground. Those became the posts holding up the roof beams. They used smaller tree trunks for the rafters. After they covered the new roof with thatch, each hut became a room, as did the original house, all of them facing a central fire area.

Now their revels would be held indoors on cold winter nights, and nobody would have to dance in the snow. Their dwelling thus became the largest structure in the upper valley. The most notorious, too.

There weren't, though, as many opportunities for revels as most of them, and not just Noon Breeze, would've desired. They had far too much work to do that winter.

The houses their people had hastily erected during their preparations for the arrival of the hill warriors needed reinforcement and refinishing. They had more granaries and barns to build as well. The grain supplies they'd transported from the lower valley required more permanent repositories than ox carts covered with hides. The livestock they'd driven north would end up sick or dead without shelter in the winter.

The evening meal around the apprentice tellers' fire was therefore far more often the prelude to a virtuous night's sleep than it was anything else.

*****

The women and older male tellers came to the house to give lessons to the apprentice tellers, telling them the stories their gods and ancestors had handed down to them.

Even Blue Sky had to concede the stories were worth knowing and retelling, whether they truthfully described actual events or not. He thought the tellers should know why they believed what they were supposed to believe—and why they should raise more questions than they did.

The occupants of the house sometimes invited the tellers to stay for the evening meal. Many Numbers insisted they comport themselves appropriately for the occasion. What might pass for a joke among themselves could easily offend their visitors.

One of the apprentice tellers—Noon Breeze might've put him up to it—once invited the older male tellers to stay for a while after the women tellers left.

The obviously surprised invitees, after conferring together, politely but firmly declined.

One of them later told Many Numbers they had no desire, after what had happened to their people, to revive memories of Law Keeper's embarrassing pursuit of Spring Rain.

Some of those older men were said to be of the opinion Law Keeper had done nothing Spring Rain couldn't have ignored.

Others of them would whisper, at least to Blue Sky, that Law Keeper had intended, if he didn't get his way, to make life difficult for both Spring Rain and Many Numbers—neither of whom had a family to fall back on.

"I knew that man his entire life," one older teller told Blue Sky. "He was evil."

Perhaps, but he'd also given his life for their people in the battle on the plain. Noon Breeze said he'd fought as well as any man his age could've been expected to fight. After receiving his mortal wounds, he laid dying a long time that day. He had no pod tea to lessen his suffering.

In any event, the older male tellers were agreed their attendance at one of "the regent's son's revels" was, under the circumstances, "out of the question."

*****

"I don't understand it," Noon Breeze complained. "Why do the people call them 'the regent's son's revels'? The regent's son just lives here like the rest of us. The revels would sure as hell go on without him."

Noon Breeze knew the answer to his question as well as anybody.

When the people told and retold the stories they'd heard concerning the revels in question, they understandably wished to aim their arrows as high as they could.

Autumn Wine did so in her own story.

"I don't give a damn," she insisted, "what the regent's son and the men he lives with do in that house they built. They saved us from the hill people. Thanks to them, my family is still alive."

That family now officially included Solemn Promise's twin sister, who'd become the mate of Autumn Wine's older grandson. The hill people had killed her previous mate on the plain.

*****

Blue Sky, Many Numbers, Early Harvest, Good Harvest, Spring Rain, and Noon Breeze traveled throughout the upper valley, stopping wherever they found work to be done. The families who needed the most help were usually those who'd lost the most in the battle on the plain.

Sometimes Green Field left Fair Judge in charge of the court and traveled with Blue Sky and his comrades. The people they visited often said they never would've expected Tall Oak to help them build or repair their houses, granaries, and barns. When Green Field reminded them he was only a regent and not a king, he could tell from the blank but not unkindly expressions on their faces they'd failed to grasp the importance of the distinction he was attempting to make.

Whenever horses were available, the band of volunteers rode them, shortening their travel time and saving their energy for the hard work ahead. They taught the regent himself how to ride. The people would come out with their children to the main pathways just to see him approaching on his stallion.

The valley people never looked forward to winter, but its arrival that year brought the solace that, for a season at least, they were probably safe.

Inextricably entwined with it, though, was a feeling utterly foreign to them: a rising dread of spring.

Chapter 3

The day fell precisely between the second and third full moons after the winter solstice. The previous night there was no moon. At sunset that evening the slender crescent of a new moon would make its first appearance above the western mountains.

Fair Judge had come that morning with the oldest tellers to the house Blue Sky lived in with his comrades to recite stories for the apprentice tellers who lived among them.

Some of the old men had grown tired of Blue Sky's pointing out the inconsistencies and improbabilities he thought should be resolved or eliminated in order to "improve," as he argued, the stories.

Unfortunately for the old tellers who insisted they had no right to do such a thing, the apprentice tellers agreed with Blue Sky. For the young people after the battle on the plain, it was difficult to justify a position simply because it was one their people had long since approved.

Ordinarily, the older tellers could've shut the apprentice tellers up by reminding them who'd fought in the last war. The old men had seen the killing—the spurting blood, the spilled guts, the bared bones—and the young men hadn't.

But the older tellers no longer had that advantage. From a discreet distance late one autumn afternoon, they'd watched the younger men frolicking naked in the river, washing off the blood of hill warriors they'd killed. The younger men were therefore free to question whatever they wished.

*****

The alarm came down from the cliff-top that afternoon: hill people were approaching.

All the warriors and auxiliaries near the gorge raced to their positions.

They saw two groups of hill people running in their direction across the snow-covered fields. A woman and three children, all of them screaming, were nearing the lower-valley entrance to the gorge from the east. Warriors, brandishing bows and arrows, were running toward them from the encampment beyond the orchard.

43

The warrior in the lead, having come within range of the woman and children, stopped to aim his arrow at them.

Before he could get his shot off, an arrow deeply pierced his belly, and he dropped to his knees.

One of the valley people's archers on the cliff-top had precisely aimed and shot the arrow.

The stricken warrior's comrades froze, hastily raised their shields, and renewed their chase.

The woman and children, still screaming, dashed headlong into the gorge.

The hill warriors in the lead, who were themselves approaching the entrance to the gorge, suddenly came to a halt, pointing with their spears at the valley people on the cliff-top above them.

"No farther!" they were yelling in their language to their comrades. "No farther!"

The woman and children, seeing the warriors were no longer giving chase, stopped as well. The younger two children, a girl and a boy, clung to the woman. The oldest child, a boy about ten, stared at Blue Sky across the snow-and-ice-covered passageway.

Blue Sky handed Spring Rain his spear and walked toward the hill people.

The valley people's front-line warriors as well as the auxiliaries on the cliff-top had arrows trained on the hill warriors in case they should decide to drop their shields and do any further aiming of arrows in the direction of the woman and children.

"He's Wandering Star's friend," the older boy said to the woman.

Spring Rain repeated the boy's assertion in the valley people's language. It echoed out in the usual fashion to the crowd behind the warriors and to the auxiliaries on the cliff-top.

The woman and children were emaciated. Their bones were showing beneath their skin.

Blue Sky took the woman's hand and led her and the children to his people's front line, protecting them from the cold north wind blowing down through the gorge.

"Thunder Hunter's warriors," Blue Sky said, loud enough for

44

the auxiliaries on the cliff-top to hear him, "killed the grandmother of these children."

All of Blue Sky's people, having heard the disgusting story, knew what he was talking about.

"Her son was the father of these two children," Blue Sky continued, motioning toward the boy and girl clinging to the woman, and then to the woman herself, "and this is their mother. She showed us how brave a human can be. She could only hope our people would act to save her and the children with her."

Blue Sky put his hand on the older boy's shoulder.

"This boy is the woman's nephew," he said, "her children's cousin. Their fathers were brothers."

He repeated his remarks to the hill woman and the children in their language so they'd know what he was telling his people.

The woman and her children wept.

"They killed my grandmother," the boy said, pointing at the warriors who'd been chasing them. "Thunder Hunter's warriors. I saw them do it. Wandering Star saved my life."

The boy looked up at Blue Sky.

"You were there," he said. "You saw what happened."

Spring Rain, his voice breaking, translated the boy's remarks for the valley people.

The hill warriors were also repeating them in their language.

*****

The apprentice tellers brought leftover bread and meat from their midday meal.

Without bothering to dry their tears, the hill woman and children took the food and ate.

The apprentice tellers gave them water to wash it down.

"You chose a moonless night to come to the gorge," Blue Sky said to the woman.

"That was Wandering Star's idea," the older boy said.

The valley warriors were making way for Green Field, Fair Judge, and several other women she'd appointed high tellers.

Word came down from the cliff-top that the archer who'd saved one of the hill people, probably the woman, from taking an arrow in her back, was the regent's wife and Blue Sky's mother, Gentle Brook.

It was one of the days she and Full Harvest spent on the cliff-top with other auxiliaries, making certain the hill warriors could see them there, some of them posing as the younger people who'd won the battle in the upper gorge the previous autumn.

Autumn Wine's grandsons, the older one having healed by then from his wounds on the hill people's plain, had taught Gentle Brook and a number of other women, including Solemn Promise's sister, East Land's niece, and her companion, how to use a bow and arrow.

The auxiliaries took bows and arrows with them to their watch days on the cliff-top, using the time for practice.

As soon as Gentle Brook saw the leading hill warrior drop his shield to take aim at a defenseless woman and three children, she took her own aim at him and let her arrow go. Her eyesight was apparently still as good as her son's.

"We know," Green Field said to the hill woman, "what happened to your children's father and grandmother. I'm sorry. We're all sorry."

Blue Sky repeated in her language what his father had said.

"Where's your father?" Blue Sky asked the boy.

The boy turned and pointed toward the hill warriors, who were still repeating all the remarks the hill woman, her son, and the valley people were making.

"Down there," the boy replied.

"With them?" Blue Sky asked.

"Those are Thunder Hunter's warriors," the boy answered, curtly.

"His father," the boy's aunt clarified, "is buried down there."

"Wandering Star told us," the boy added, wiping his face, "your warriors threw him in the river. He floated downstream with the others."

Spring Rain had a difficult time repeating those remarks, and the valley people were so quiet then they could hear every quiver in his voice.

Blue Sky and his comrades in the gorge looked at one another, a number of them letting their tears fall. They'd killed this boy's father in the same place where they now stood with his son and his brother's mate and children, all of them starving. They'd dropped a tree limb or a boulder on the man's head. Somebody had slit his throat. Perhaps Blue Sky had done it himself.

"And your mother?" Fair Judge, her own voice unsteady, asked the boy in his language.

Spring Rain had been teaching her how to speak it.

The boy shook his head, covering his eyes with his hand.

"She died," his aunt said. "She was my sister. During the last full moon, she died."

"I'm sorry," Fair Judge said. "All of our people are sorry."

The hill woman wept.

Fair Judge embraced her.

"She starved to death," the boy said. "That's why we came here."

Green Field put his arm around the boy.

"We had no men to hunt for us," the hill woman said.

"This damned war," the regent muttered.

The hill woman looked at him quizzically.

"This damned war," Spring Rain whispered to her in her language.

Then, making no attempt to hide his own tears, he looked past her.

"This damned war!" he yelled at Thunder Hunter's warriors, using their words.

"Wandering Star," the boy said, "told us your people never starve."

Blue Sky turned to the boy's aunt.

"Did Wandering Star," he asked, "tell you to come here?"

"He told us," she replied, "your people have no obligation to help any of our people."

"Did he tell you," Blue Sky asked, "we'd take you in and help you anyway?"

"He told us if we got past them," the boy replied, nodding in the direction of Thunder Hunter's warriors, "your people would never send us back. You'd know they'd kill us if you did that."

"It's treachery," the hill woman said, "to come here and beg your people for food."

Consorting with the enemy was treachery for the valley people as well. Blue Sky became a traitor the moment he entered the gully to get a closer look at Wandering Star. Long ago, the king would've had him killed if he'd been caught doing such a thing. By the time Blue Sky did it, though, his people's only real punishment for the crime was to leave the wrongdoer to his fate.

"Do you wish to live with us?" Fair Judge asked the woman.

"It's either that or die," the hill woman replied.

"That leaves us no choice," Fair Judge said to Green Field. "We have to take them in."

"We have to find them shelter," Spring Rain said.

A number of people mentioned an old person who'd died recently. None of his relatives or neighbors had made any claim to his house.

Several of the women tellers closest to Fair Judge led the hill woman and children through the ranks of the valley people's warriors and the crowd behind them.

"Death to traitors!" Thunder Hunter's warriors began yelling at the woman and children.

Blue Sky and Spring Rain told the people what the hill warriors were saying.

"Death to Thunder Hunter's warriors!" Noon Breeze yelled back in their language.

The apprentice tellers and Early Harvest's cousins loudly joined him.

Most of them didn't pronounce the words quite right, but Thunder Hunter's warriors got the message anyway. They brandished their spears in the direction of the gorge, even as they retreated to their encampment, carrying their wounded comrade with them.

They'd seen the auxiliaries on the cliff-top poised to rain rocks and limbs down on them if they'd made any attempt to enter the gorge.

One horrific day the previous autumn they'd watched the valley people do it.

*****

"The question isn't one starving woman and three starving children," Green Field said. "I'm sure we'll take good care of them. I'm sure we can all agree they've suffered enough."

He, Many Numbers, Fair Judge, Gentle Brook, Spring Rain, and Blue Sky were sitting at the fire with their hosts in Full Harvest and Early Harvest's well-constructed house.

Guests and hosts alike nodded their heads in agreement with the regent's remarks.

"The question," the regent continued, "concerns the people who come next."

"Having been assured by Wandering Star," Blue Sky added, "the kindly farmers won't turn them away."

"He simply told them the truth," Early Harvest said. "As he would."

Coming home from the plain, Wandering Star had insisted Blue Sky's people would be much more likely to agree to fall back to the upper valley if Early Harvest told them they had to do it.

"It was one thing," Blue Sky offered, "keeping hill warriors out of the valley—even when they were only hunters who appeared to be warriors. It would be something else to turn away starving women and children and watch their own people kill them."

"We can't do that," Spring Rain said. "It isn't possible. We have to take them in."

"We do," Blue Sky said, having acquired one more reason to justify his obsessive love of Spring Rain, the mate of Many Numbers from their boyhood. "Especially since they're starving only because we killed so many of their husbands, fathers, and uncles."

"But how many hill people will show up here?" Green Field asked.

That was, of course, the ultimate question.

Wandering Star knew it would be, too. He also knew what Blue Sky's answer would be.

Green Field turned to Fair Judge. "What do the gods tell us to do?"

A king or regent with a decision of great importance to make was supposed to ask the first teller such a question.

Assuming, Blue Sky thought to himself, it mattered.

49

Fair Judge shook her head. "I can't think of any story where the question has arisen."

"Nor can I," Many Numbers agreed.

"We sometimes let an enemy live and go home," Spring Rain added. "But we never let them stay with us. I think we have to decide this question on our own. The gods are calling upon us to make the right decision."

Spring Rain, who'd chosen to believe gods existed, had just admitted, Blue Sky realized, those gods were so powerless they had to let humans decide their own fate. Those gods were disclaiming responsibility for any disaster that might result. They could always blame it on human stupidity.

"Whatever our ancestors might've done," Fair Judge said, bringing Blue Sky and the others back to reality, "we can't turn these people away."

Her predecessor and his high tellers would've spent the rest of the day debating what their people's stories told them, and they still would've reached no decision concerning the matter at hand.

"If we did," Gentle Brook interjected, "we'd have to turn away Rose Leaf herself. Even with the warriors chasing her. She's a hill person. And look how we love her."

Spring Rain took Gentle Brook's hand, the hand that had inflicted that day's single wound.

"I can't imagine," Blue Sky said, "what good it will do to worry about how many of them show up in the gorge. A great number of their women, children, and old people must be starving now. Four or five of their warriors died on that damned plain for every one of ours they killed."

His mother took his hand.

She and the others present looked at Blue Sky the way their people did when he returned from the plain and told them their sons, fathers, lovers, and brothers were dead—and the way his comrades and opponents did in battles.

They could all see something had happened to his mind.

"Go on," his mother said.

"How surprising will it be," he asked, "if the mates, children, and feeble fathers and mothers of those warriors show up here asking us to save their lives? There's only one thing we should or can do. We open our arms to them and welcome them all."

Blue Sky said that knowing the question it raised.

His people's new men traditionally spent the first year of their adulthood in their encampments heroically keeping the hill people out of their promised valley. Did they suffer deaths, injuries, and other hardship for nothing?

"I don't know why we should care," Blue Sky added, "if they all come to live with us. Who'll Lightning Spear and Thunder Hunter have to attack us with then? I've noticed they don't do any of the fighting themselves."

Early Harvest placed another log on the fire.

In the winter the valley people fell in love with their fires.

The god who supposedly gave fire to their ancestors first had to steal it from the hell-gods. He was one of the few gods Blue Sky admired—more so because the king of the gods in their bizarre heaven had punished him severely for what he'd done.

"I hope all the hill people show up here," Blue Sky said, "asking to live with us."

*****

The hill people who'd come to the upper valley hadn't seen a house before.

The older boy said the one they were in, the one the tellers had given them in Full Harvest's village, seemed to him to keep the cold wind out as well as a tent did, and probably kept out the rain and snow as well, too. On the other hand, he added, it would be a lot more difficult than a tent to move.

Earlier that afternoon the children in the village had enticed him and his cousins to get into an ox cart and go for a ride. The hill people had never seen an ox or cart either, but they'd heard stories meant to make them believe the farmers had animals that somehow pulled large wooden containers with circular tree trunk parts, held together with vines and leather, on both sides of them.

The "wheels"—the farmers' word for them—rolled along the ground but remained in the same position relative to the container as it moved.

No less than Wandering Star and Long Arm claimed to have seen them.

They had no words of their own for many of the things the valley people couldn't live without. They referred to houses, granaries, and barns—their warriors having seen them up close in the last war—as "the hell-gods' handiwork in which the farmer thieves and their captive animals live." The boy readily agreed the valley people's words—"house," "granary," and "barn"—would be much simpler to use once one knew what they meant.

The boy said his name was Deer Tracker. His aunt said that had been his father's name, and after the man's death in the gorge, the boy had insisted on taking it for himself.

The boy and his aunt were sitting at the fire with Green Field, Many Numbers, Fair Judge, Gentle Brook, Full Harvest, Early Harvest, Blue Sky, and Spring Rain, who was interpreting.

The two younger children had fallen asleep.

"I'm sorry," Gentle Brook said to the hill woman whose life she'd saved that day, "for what my husband, our people's regent in place of a king, needs to say to your nephew. But this boy can never forget what Green Field is going to tell him. Please don't let him forget it."

The hill woman looked at Green Field. "Say whatever you need to say," she responded.

Green Field turned to Deer Tracker.

"As long as your people and our people are hostile," he said, "you can't go back to your people."

Fair Judge nodded her head in agreement.

"Even if there are people out there you wish to see again," she said, "you have to stay here with your aunt and cousins."

The boy looked at the regent and first teller without blinking his eyes.

"Sometimes," Many Numbers said, "our warriors do things we don't want your warriors to know about."

Deer Tracker looked as steadily at the chief warrior as he had the regent and first teller.

"The falling rocks?" he asked. "The trees?"

"You know what we're talking about," Many Numbers replied.

"Your people's warriors," Green Field said, "might torture you to find out what you've learned after living with us."

"You might have to tell them," Fair Judge added, "even if you didn't wish to hurt us."

"I understand," the boy said.

"So if you do try to go back," Green Field said, "our people will stop you."

"After that," Fair Judge said, "we'd have to put you in a much smaller house than this one. You wouldn't be able to live with your aunt and cousins. You'd be all by yourself in what our people call a 'hut.' Our people would bring you food to eat, water to drink, hides to wear, and wood to burn, but you wouldn't be able to get out of the hut whenever you chose."

"And we don't want to do that," Green Field added. "Please don't make us do that."

There was a strong north wind that evening. The belongings of the man who'd lived in the house—his crockery, hides, boots, even his spear, perhaps the very one he'd used to kill hill warriors in the previous war—were still where he'd left them when he died. He was lying in his oldest hides under a pile of snow, waiting for a thaw for the tellers to bury him.

Wandering Star had told Blue Sky and his comrades his people didn't wrap in hides those who died in winter. They left them naked under the snow.

Spring Rain and Blue Sky quickly condemned that particular practice as barbaric, even if they were more than ready to agree the hill people in general weren't.

Many Numbers sighed and patiently pointed out to his comrades Wandering Star's people might not have as many old hides to spare as the much more wealthy farmers had.

He agreed with Wandering Star it made no difference whether the dead were wrapped or not, as long as their family and neighbors packed enough ice and snow on top of them to keep the wolves and vultures away.

That was the night Many Numbers and Wandering Star briefly considered going together but chose not to in view of the restraint Blue

Sky and Spring Rain had exercised in response to their desires for one another.

"We realize," Many Numbers said to the hill woman, "you might know things about your people's warriors we'd like to know. There might be things your nephew knows. But we want to make it clear you and he aren't required to tell us anything about them."

"You might know some of the warriors out there," Blue Sky said, motioning in the direction of the gorge. "You might not want to see us hurt them."

Deer Tracker blinked his eyes at the end of those remarks.

"Those warriors aren't ours," he said.

"Why aren't they yours?" Blue Sky asked. "Because they're Thunder Hunter's?"

"Yes," the boy replied, shouting his answer loudly enough to cause one of his cousins to stir from the exquisite sleep young children enjoy.

Spring Rain had no need to interpret that answer. By then most of the valley people knew the hill people's equivalents for such simple words as "yes," "no," "one," "two," "in," and "out," sometimes even using them in place of their own words for emphasis, especially if the speaker wished to convey the menace of a Lightning Spear or Thunder Hunter.

"All the warriors in the valley are Thunder Hunter's," Deer Tracker continued. "He doesn't trust our warriors. He says they'd give the valley back to your people."

"Are Thunder Hunter's warriors hunting in the forest?" Blue Sky asked.

"They won't let us hunt there," Deer Tracker replied.

"Even when we're starving," his aunt said.

"Thunder Hunter says our warriors don't want to fight anymore," Deer Tracker added.

Blue Sky turned to the boy's aunt. "Is that true?"

"Maybe it is," she replied. "Many people agree with Wandering Star. He insists the war is pointless, and we should leave you people alone."

"How many agree with that?" Blue Sky asked. "Do most of

54

your people?"

"There's no way to know," the hill woman replied. "Wandering Star can speak freely. He's the king's son. Lightning Spear won't let anybody touch him."

"Not even Thunder Hunter," the boy said.

"It's different for other people," the hill woman said. "Our cousin told people he agreed the war was stupid. Thunder Hunter's warriors found out about it. Some of them went to his tent one night and killed him, his mate, and one of their children."

Spring Rain's lips trembled as he interpreted the woman's last remark.

"We thought they'd be coming for us next," the woman added.

"They kill children?" Fair Judge asked.

"Our cousin had three children," she replied. "The two younger children ran away. The warriors caught the oldest, who was attempting to help his mother escape. He was twelve years old. They killed his mother. Then they killed him too."

"Where were the gods?" Spring Rain demanded to know before he began his interpretation.

Sturdy Limb had taken two sons not yet of age into battle. It had to be said in his defense, though, neither he nor anybody else expected them to fight. The warriors they were with had promised the people they wouldn't let the boys go near the front line.

Valley Defender told Blue Sky they were killed at the end of the day, when their people's warriors had nothing left but a front line—and Valley Defender himself was past the point where he could protect them.

"We told Wandering Star what Thunder Hunter's warriors did to our kin," the hill woman continued. "He went to see his father. Lightning Spear was outside his tent holding court. In front of all the people there, Wandering Star screamed at him. They say the king let him go on for a long time, almost as if he enjoyed seeing him so angry. But finally, to shut him up, he asked Long Arm's people to take him away."

Blue Sky stared at the hill woman while she described what his lover had done.

"Lightning Spear knew," the hill woman continued, "Wandering Star wouldn't fight with Long Arm's family. He's forgiven them for abducting him and two of his farmer friends. Long Arm's family has taken a liking to Rose Leaf and your prince. Nobody dares say anything against either of them in the presence of members of Long Arm's family. They immediately let the speakers know, in one manner or the other, they don't agree."

Long Arm had told Blue Sky the truth on sunset pass.

"My sister and I," the hill woman continued, "decided we had to leave. We didn't want Thunder Hunter's men coming for us."

"Thunder Hunter tried to kill Wandering Star," Deer Tracker added.

Blue Sky and the other valley people present turned to stare at the boy.

"Wandering Star was in the mountains above sunset pass," the boy said. "He was watching the battle with your people from a high ledge. Five of Thunder Hunter's warriors tried to sneak up behind him and push him off it."

"They wanted his death to appear to be an accident," Deer Tracker's aunt explained.

"Your people stopped making any noise," Deer Tracker said, "to see if any of your warriors were missing. It was so quiet Wandering Star could hear Thunder Hunter's men coming up the path behind him. He hid waiting for them. He had the high ground. He speared the first three. The other two ran away. The three men he'd wounded admitted what they were trying to do. They said Thunder Hunter himself gave them their orders. Then Wandering Star kept his agreement with them. He slit their throats. He finished them off."

The boy's story left the valley people at the fire that evening speechless.

"Was Wandering Star hurt?" Blue Sky asked, finally.

Deer Tracker laughed. "Not Wandering Star," he replied. "They never touched him."

"When Lightning Spear found out about it, he was furious," the boy's aunt said. "He made Thunder Hunter agree not to resume the war until spring."

"We want Thunder Hunter's warriors to go back to the land they roam," Deer Tracker said.

"Our people didn't know what we were getting into," his aunt said. "We always thought your warriors were ruthless. They killed our hunters just for getting too close to your people's guard posts. Even when our people were only looking for food for their families."

Six of the ruthless warriors she'd described, each of them having slaughtered a goodly number of her people's men, were sitting at a fire with her and her nephew. Two women who seemed to be pleased they lived with the ruthless warriors were also with them.

"But Thunder Hunter's warriors are much worse," the hill woman continued. "Wandering Star says your warriors were only protecting your people. He says you thought our hunters were warriors. And how could you tell the difference? But Thunder Hunter wants our land, your land, everybody's land. And even Lightning Spear isn't as brutal as he is."

"Even Lightning Spear?" Spring Rain asked at the end of his interpretation.

The woman turned to Blue Sky. "You saw that for yourself. Before the battle on the plain. Thunder Hunter and War Cloud begged him to let them kill you. Lightning Spear let you go."

Gentle Brook looked at Blue Sky and shook her head.

He'd had a difficult time explaining that part of the story to his mother and father. Nobody else would talk about it with them until he did.

All the survivors of the battle on the plain had assumed Blue Sky's death would be the first.

"We wish that battle had never happened," the hill woman said. "We wish our king had never captured your prince. Though we're glad the princess is back. Our people adore Rose Leaf."

The wind was rattling the dead man's crockery. In his declining years he hadn't been able to keep his house in good repair, and he was too proud to ask his neighbors to help him.

"My family," Full Harvest said to the woman, "will fix this house for you tomorrow."

*****

The valley people subsequently learned the hill warrior who took an arrow in his guts that afternoon died several days later.

Thunder Hunter had refused to let his warriors drink Wandering Star's pod tea, whether it relieved their suffering or not.

He'd decreed imbibing it was something only the weak and cowardly farmers would do.

The warrior who took the arrow was said to be in horrific pain the entire time he lay dying.

He had two people—one of them the hill people called Thunder Hunter from his birth, the other the valley people knew from her birth as Gentle Brook—to thank for that.

*****

Deer Tracker and his aunt told the valley people Wandering Star had described for them the obstacles they faced if they attempted to go over to their well-fed and benevolent enemies in the upper gorge. The primary one was the contingent of warriors Thunder Hunter had left behind to keep the farmers imprisoned in their upper valley.

Wandering Star nevertheless believed it was possible those who were skillful enough could elude the warriors. They'd have to approach the gorge from the forest on the eastern side of the valley, traveling during the night, making no unnecessary noise, and carefully avoiding contact with any of Thunder Hunter's warriors out on a hunting expedition.

Between the forest and river there was no cover. Thunder Hunter's warriors would surely see them. They'd therefore have to run from the moment they left the forest and not stop or even hesitate until they got to the upper gorge.

As in the upper valley though, the distance between the forest and the river near the gorge wasn't great. In fact, Wandering Star said, the edge of the eastern forest was closer to the lower-valley entrance to the gorge than the encampment was.

But even as Wandering Star was telling Deer Tracker and his aunt what they had to do, he was also reminding them, over and over, he thought Thunder Hunter's warriors would probably kill them. The two younger children would fatally slow them down.

"That's the only thing he was wrong about," Deer Tracker said.

58

"He wasn't wrong," Early Harvest quickly countered. "He just wanted you to pay close attention to what he was telling you."

The hill woman and Deer Tracker also told the valley people Wandering Star had similarly instructed other hill people in the forest. Some of them were waiting to see what happened to Deer Tracker, his aunt, and her children.

"Now," Early Harvest said, "knowing you made it, they'll try to do what you did."

"They'll do it, too," Deer Tracker replied.

*****

Between the new moon and half moon at least one alarm came down from the cliff-top every day. And even though most of the groups attempting to reach the valley people included children, all of them got to the gorge before Thunder Hunter's warriors could stop them.

The valley people took them in and went about their business. For Blue Sky, Spring Rain, Noon Breeze, the apprentice tellers, Early Harvest, Good Harvest, and their cousins, that included building houses for the newcomers.

Two of them were brothers only a few years shy of coming of age. They'd lost their father in the battle on the plain. They'd lost their mother long ago when she was giving birth to a stillborn sibling. They informed the valley people as soon as they arrived in the gorge they'd continue living in their tent. They'd carried the hides for it on their backs, and they'd still outrun Thunder Hunter's warriors. They also wished, they said, to hunt in the forest rather than depend upon farmers for food and whatever else they needed.

Green Field agreed. If the boys didn't violate the rule handed down to Deer Tracker and made no attempt to return to their people, they could live in the upper valley however they wished.

When the boys brought back their first kill, a buck, some of the valley people traded bread and grain for parts of it. Many of the men remembered occasionally sharing roast venison with their comrades around an encampment fire while they were bravely keeping the hill people out of their valley—and how good it tasted.

Deer were so easy for them to kill. Maybe the animals couldn't imagine humans on the farmers' side of the mountains, who rarely took any interest in their doings, would seize the best of them from time to time, slit their throats with a sharp blade, roast them over a blazing fire, and eat them.

*****

The valley people were seeing fewer campfires in the lower-valley forest. There were appreciably more of them, though, in the encampment beyond the orchard. Then one day there were none at all in the forest.

The next morning, in the glare of the sun on new overnight snow, the valley people learned why Thunder Hunter's warriors had called their comrades back from hunting.

They were taking down their tents and moving their encampment closer to the gorge—to within, it appeared, the same distance from the gorge as the edge of the forest. In order to place their encampment so near to the farmer-thieves, who weren't stupid even if they were evil incarnate, they needed more warriors to fight off any surprise attack those demons might attempt.

They didn't know the strictest order Many Numbers had given his army concerning the defense of the gorge was to never attack, never break out of the gorge to pursue the hill warriors, and never give up the protection of the cliff-top above them. They couldn't accept the loss of any of their fighting people, not even if the trade-off was the killing of every hill warrior in the encampment they'd come to despise as much as they did war itself.

Green Field said that wasn't merely the chief warrior's order. It was the regent's as well.

That day and the next none of the hill people dared outrun Thunder Hunter's warriors.

*****

The alarm came down from the cliff-top late in the afternoon of the third day.

60

Four hill people were running toward the gorge.

Thunder Hunter's warriors were pursuing them.

The people seeking the farmers' help that day appeared to be two women, a man, and a child. The valley people could soon see the child was a boy about the same age as Deer Tracker.

But the man and one of the women were undoubtedly the oldest people who'd so far attempted to outrun Thunder Hunter's warriors.

The valley people, horrified, could also see the proximity of Thunder Hunter's warriors, the depth of the snow, and the lack of youthful agility on the part of the two older people meant they weren't going to make it.

Individuals among the valley people cried out. Then, like a conflagration consuming smaller fires in its way, the agitation in all their voices rose to become one collective scream.

Falling farther and farther behind the young woman and boy, the older man and woman made no calls to them for help.

The older woman fell. The man stopped and knelt down to pick her up.

The valley people's screams echoed off the walls of the gorge.

Thunder Hunter's warriors surrounded the older couple.

The younger woman and boy, unaware of what was happening behind them, kept running toward the gorge.

Two of Thunder Hunter's warriors were closing to within a spear length behind them, unwisely separating themselves from their comrades despite their shields, and tempting more than one of the valley people's warriors to ignore their chief warrior and regent's order, give up the safety of the gorge, and kill them.

The warrior chasing the younger woman raised his spear preparing to make his thrust.

The warrior pursuing the boy, reaching the gorge entrance, suddenly broke off the chase.

"Stop!" he yelled to the other warrior, pointing with his spear toward the cliff-top.

Both warriors, realizing they'd put their lives in jeopardy, turned and sprinted back to their comrades.

The younger woman and boy, having reached the safety of the gorge, themselves turned to see why the valley people were still screaming.

The old man, staring at the hill warriors who had him surrounded, stood above the old woman, the look in his eyes one of profound disbelief.

The warrior facing him thrust his spear.

Blood spurting from his belly, the old man fell to the snow, next to the woman.

The younger woman and boy screamed.

The valley people in the gorge and on the cliff-top echoed their screams.

The killing of a defenseless old man who'd committed no real crime was evil. The valley people—so beguiled by the illusion of optimism that some of them named their children Gentle Brook, Green Field, Rose Leaf, Full Harvest, Early Harvest, Blue Sky, and Morning Sun—were incapable of seeing it any other way.

Another of Thunder Hunter's warriors, his spear aimed at the older woman, ignored her plea for mercy and thrust it through her body.

"Hell-gods!" the valley people screamed in the hill people's language. "Hell-gods!"

That was the ultimate insult for both peoples.

The younger woman and boy screamed again. The boy was ready to go back to confront the warriors. The woman was attempting to restrain him.

Blue Sky and Spring Rain dropped their spears and ran forward.

The boy broke free from the woman.

Running behind the boy, Blue Sky reached out with his healed left arm and grabbed the flimsy hide the boy was wearing for a coat. This slowed the boy down just enough for Blue Sky to reach out with his right arm and maneuver it around the boy's neck, bringing him to a stop.

"They're killing my grandma!" he screamed in Blue Sky's ear. "My grandpa!"

Blue Sky wrapped his arms around the boy and lifted him off the ground.

He was much lighter than the survivors of the battle on the plain he'd carefully laid in ox carts—but they hadn't put up any resistance.

The boy struggled to kick himself free of Blue Sky's grasp.

Spring Rain, taking several blows to his ribs he paid no attention to, grabbed the boy's feet.

Many Numbers didn't dare let any other warriors go out to help Blue Sky and Spring Rain. They were almost within range of any arrows Thunder Hunter's warriors might decide to send their way.

Blue Sky wriggled out of his own coat and covered the boy's face with it so he couldn't see what Thunder Hunter's warriors were doing to his grandparents—taking turns thrusting their spears into their bodies in the snow.

"Hell-gods!" the valley people screamed.

Blue Sky and Spring Rain carried the squirming boy, Spring Rain holding his legs, Blue Sky grasping the rest of him, back to their front line. The boy was still struggling to break free when they handed him off to the apprentice tellers and Early Harvest's cousins, who quickly subdued him.

Turning and seeing the younger hill woman had fallen to her knees in the snow, Spring Rain and Blue Sky ran to her and lifted her to her feet.

At first she seemed surprisingly light. Then the reason became obvious to them: she was starving. All four of the hill people running toward the upper gorge that day were starving. If the boy hadn't been, he might've escaped Blue Sky's grasp.

"My mother," the hill woman wept. "My father."

Thunder Hunter's warriors, using the new snow to clean the blood off their spears, were done with that hill woman's mother and father.

Spring Rain, his face as streaked with tears as the hill woman's, embraced her.

The valley people fell silent. As did Thunder Hunter's warriors. As did the boy.

They could only hear the river rushing by and the hill woman weeping.

The gods had apparently chosen to take to their beds early that winter day. The valley people had screamed themselves hoarse—and gotten back no indication of any kind they'd been heard in heaven.

There were two intersecting circles in the sunlit snow around the drifts where the woman's mother and father had fallen, in what was for them a time of extreme hunger and far too little mercy.

The circles were the color of sunset in winter: crimson.

*****

If Thunder Hunter's warriors had meant to show the farmer-thieves how brutal hill warriors could be—by killing two defenseless elders who posed no threat to the warriors killing them—they'd fully succeeded.

They'd put to death the old starving people only because they were fleeing to the upper valley for food and shelter the farmers were more than willing to share with them.

Catching and forcing them back to the hills to resume starving would've been bad enough. Killing them was unpardonable.

The valley people reverted to the way they'd conducted themselves in the days following the battle on the plain: without a single occasion for even the most restrained form of levity arising.

If they lived in a world where people could do what Thunder Hunter's warriors had done without suffering the slightest punishment for doing it, more than a few valley people—including the regent's son and the kingdom's chief warrior—had the temerity to ask, why was hell said to be somewhere else?

Chapter 4

For three days after Thunder Hunter's warriors killed the old couple as the valley people watched helplessly—crying out to gods who'd proved once again, assuming they existed, they took little if any interest in the matter—no hill people attempted to outrun Thunder Hunter's warriors.

On the morning of the fourth day, a reduced trickle of them started again—but this time without any young children or old people. These refugees tended to be mothers with older children, the valley people having recently killed, in one or the other of their recent battles, the mates of the former and the fathers of the latter.

They were also older children who arrived without adults, a number of them boys within a year or two of coming of age who'd decided they didn't wish to fight and probably die as what they chose to call "Lightning Spear's gift-slaves to Thunder Hunter."

They told the valley people Wandering Star had made them practice running in a meadow across melting snow and mud patches while he assessed their chances of outrunning Thunder Hunter's warriors. Some were making the attempt without gaining Wandering Star's approval, but they, along with those he did approve, were succeeding in any event.

"He was being careful," Early Harvest once again insisted, "for your own good."

"And you knew that," Many Numbers agreed, "and came anyway. We welcome you all."

The valley people hadn't imagined hill people, even starving hill people, would wish to live peacefully with them.

It was equally clear their guests hadn't given any thought to the possibility their eternal enemies would take them in and provide them shelter, food, and clothes, even furs thick enough to give them comfort when they slept—not until Wandering Star let it be known the farmers would.

And Gentle Brook's well-aimed arrow proved to them how right he was.

*****

One morning the valley people took up their positions in and above the gorge and saw two people they didn't wish to see attempting to outrun Thunder Hunter's warriors: a grandfather and his grandson they assumed—correctly, they learned later.

The grandfather looked as if he'd suffered an injury to one of his legs almost as debilitating as the one a hill warrior in the last war had inflicted upon Noon Breeze's father. His grandson appeared to be seven or eight years old.

After the previous night's rain, the most direct route from the edge of the forest to the gorge was entirely mud. If the ground had been dry that morning, it's possible the grandfather, despite his age and injury, and the grandson, despite his youth, might've outrun the warriors.

That wet morning, though, the grandfather fell, his bad leg buckling under him.

A number of the valley people in the gorge and on the cliff-top screamed.

As understandable as their reaction was, it was also a mistake.

The grandson turned, saw his grandfather on the ground, and slowed his pace.

The valley people, suddenly realizing what they'd done, fell silent.

"Keep going!" the grandfather yelled to the boy.

Thunder Hunter's warriors were surrounding the old man.

"You promised me you'd do it!" he implored his grandson. "Go on!"

The boy, as conflicted as he was, resumed running toward the gorge.

Three of Thunder Hunter's warriors, though, had broken off from the main group to chase him.

One of the warriors standing over the grandfather raised his spear with both hands and drove it straight down, piercing the man's belly.

This time, all the valley people in the gorge and on the cliff-top screamed.

The three warriors chasing the boy were closing the gap

between him and themselves. When they came within range of the cliff-top archers, they wisely dropped their weapons so they could hold their shields in front of them and still have a free hand.

A second warrior in the main group thrust his spear through the old man's upper body.

One of the warriors chasing the boy lunged forward and caught him by his shoulder, making him stumble in the mud.

The valley people screamed again.

The three pursuing warriors grabbed the boy by his legs and arms and started dragging him through the mud back toward the main group of warriors.

The boy, though, was making it as difficult for them as he could. Since they only had three hands among them available to grasp him, the boy always had at least one foot or hand free for kicking and punching.

And since the valley people had their sharpest-shooting archer-auxiliaries—including Autumn Wine's grandsons, the older grandson's mate, East Land's niece and her wife, and the regent's mate—standing in a row on the cliff-top taking aim at them, they had to exercise extreme care to keep their shields between their bodies and any farmer arrow that might come their way.

The valley people were no longer making any attempt to conceal their fury. The old man, knowingly taking his chances—no doubt having incurred his wound in the last war with the thieves, no doubt having killed a number of farmer warriors before he did—would soon be dead.

His grandson, struggling to stay alive, too young to have inflicted harm on anyone in his brief life, was an entirely different matter.

Having finished off the old man by rupturing his throat, comrades of the warriors struggling with the boy, dropping their weapons and hoisting their shields, came to their aid, dragging the boy through the mud beyond the range of the cliff-top archers.

The valley people in the gorge, on-lookers and warriors alike, angrily pushed forward. Those in the front lines could feel them pressing against their backs, yelling in their ears in the hill people's language as best they could, again and again, "He's a boy! Don't kill him!"

Thunder Hunter's warriors dropped the boy in the mud, standing over him and giving him a kick whenever he tried to get up.

"Don't kill him!" the farmers and the hill people living with them screamed.

They were on the verge of breaking through the army's front lines in the gorge.

Many Numbers, Early Harvest, and Blue Sky exchanged glances.

They were losing control of their people. And if they, having presumed to lead their people, failed at that, they'd lose everything.

One of Thunder Hunter's warriors was attempting to aim his spear for a thrust, but the boy, writhing in the late-winter mud, wasn't giving him a stationary target.

"Hell-gods!" the valley people yelled in the hill people's language. "Hell-gods!"

The front-line warriors, unable to withstand the pressure of the crowd behind them, were approaching the entrance to the gorge. Once they got beyond it, though, they'd lose the protection of the cliff-top. They'd be inviting an open battle with Thunder Hunter's warriors.

The valley warriors could win such a battle. But even if they did, they'd lose so many warriors the upper valley would be the hill people's for the taking.

The valley people and their guests, though, weren't the only people protesting.

"Don't do it!" one of the hill warriors in the main group yelled in the direction of the boy and his captors. "Don't! Stop!"

The valley people had seen this man before, loudly ordering the other warriors around.

"Stop!" Blue Sky shouted to his comrades and the people behind them. "Stop!"

Many Numbers and Early Harvest took up his cry.

The hill warrior in command ran toward the boy.

Blue Sky, Many Numbers, and Early Harvest turned to face their own people, yelling in both languages, "Go back! Go back!"

Glancing behind him, Blue Sky could see the commanding hill warrior had reached the boy and the warriors holding him down.

He picked the boy up by the collar of his coat and, muddy as the boy was, threw his arm around him.

Having been reduced to silence again, the valley people and their guests scrambled back up the passageway incline, but they kept their eyes trained on the hill warriors.

Thunder Hunter's warrior who'd rescued the boy turned toward the gorge.

"He'll go back to his cousins," he yelled. "My warriors won't harm him."

Spring Rain immediately repeated those remarks in the valley people's language, shouting them almost as loudly as the hill warrior had, letting them echo off the canyon walls.

The valley warriors took their usual positions in the gorge, staring at the hill warriors.

The lead hill warrior walked the boy back to their encampment, taking care to shield him from the sight of his grandfather's mutilated body.

If Thunder Hunter's warriors had killed the boy, the valley people would've gone for them. Their archers would've come down from the cliff-top and shot every arrow in their quivers at them. Nothing in their world, not even the gods in their heaven—and certainly not one of their chief warrior's too numerous rules, however well thought out it might be—could've stopped them.

*****

"He was at the battle on the plain," Blue Sky heard himself say, through his tears.

His comrades turned to him.

They'd watched the hill commander barking orders to his subordinates. They'd decided he was unbearably arrogant. They never would've put up with such a person for their leader. Sturdy Limb was a lamb compared to him. The hill commander personally beat his men for making trivial mistakes. The valley people could hear their screams.

Blue Sky, who sometimes regretted possessing eyesight as keen as his, had always known who the man was. But he hadn't previously revealed that fact to either his people or their guests.

He'd thought the truth would ruin the story for them all. Now he realized it was the story.

"He's the hill warrior," Blue Sky said, "who saved Deer Tracker's life."

*****

"He's the one," Early Harvest asked, "who held his hand over Deer Tracker's mouth?"

"Thunder Hunter must not hate him for it," Blue Sky said, nodding. "He wasn't giving orders then. He was taking them."

"But look where Thunder Hunter put him," Many Numbers scoffed.

The chief warrior had a point. The upper-gorge encampment probably wasn't an assignment many of Thunder Hunter's warriors would've volunteered for.

After all, it required them to chase down and kill their own people.

Blue Sky began to wonder if the man who couldn't stomach killing children was so ill-tempered and loud because he hated what he was doing.

Thunder Hunter's warriors were digging a grave for the old man where they'd killed him. After the ground had thawed, they'd done the same thing for the older couple they'd killed. Their graves were apparently supposed to serve as warnings to the next people choosing to run past them.

Some of the hill people living in the upper gorge confirmed what the valley people had assumed. The grandfather was a hero in the last war, and the farmers had given him his wounds.

But in this subsequent war, in which his people turned on their own, his bravery in the previous conflict did him and his grandson no good whatsoever.

*****

Noon Breeze and the apprentice tellers, along with Good

Harvest and the upper-valley cousins, were at the front line, leading their people in taunting Thunder Hunter's warriors, getting the right words for their sport from Spring Rain and Blue Sky.

No true warrior, they were yelling, would kill an unarmed war hero too old to pose any possible threat to them.

Couldn't they see, some of them loudly inquired, how much their own people hated them?

At the same time, Fair Judge and a number of the other female and older male tellers made their way down the gorge through the crowd.

When they reached the apprentice tellers and cousins, the first teller asked them if they'd please step aside.

The apprentice tellers and cousins promptly quit their yelling and did as Fair Judge had requested them to do.

Spring Rain said Fair Judge proved the gods weren't at all displeased their people's first teller was a woman.

"The people do what she asks them to do," he said to his godless companion and lover.

Blue Sky declined to disagree.

In many ways Fair Judge ruled the valley people's kingdom more than the regent, the chief warrior, and the regent's son did.

Fair Judge and the tellers stood where the valley army's front line had been. The first teller took a step forward and turned to face the others. She led them in singing, in the hill people's language, the songs the valley people's tellers ordinarily sang in a funeral ceremony. Except for the pronunciation of the words, they were the same songs the hill people's tellers would've sung.

Reading Fair Judge's lips and having by that time some knowledge of the hill people's language, the tellers and apprentice tellers sang with her. Some of the tellers had brought instruments and were passing them out to those among themselves and the apprentice tellers who could most skillfully play them. Spring Rain and Blue Sky turned to face the people so that all those singing could read their lips as well as the first teller's.

The hill warriors weren't conducting a funeral ceremony. Under their laws as well as the valley people's, a traitor wasn't entitled to one, even if he was a wounded hero of a previous war.

Many of the hill people living in the upper valley added their voices to the songs.

After Thunder Hunter's warriors finished their digging, they surprised the people singing in the gorge and on the cliff-top. They waited to lay the man in his grave and cover him up until the singers got to the proper places in the ceremony for them to perform those rituals.

Their leader was standing next to them.

Blue Sky wondered if he'd asked them—quietly, for a change—to do that.

*****

The killing of the grandfather and capture of the boy didn't stop the hill people from attempting to reach the upper gorge. Most of them met success.

Occasionally, though, the hill warriors did catch some. Since many of those captured were children, who were merely sent back to wherever they came from—a number of them only to begin another trek through the forest and chase across the fields—the captures the valley people usually observed caused them sorrow but not unbearable anguish.

But the few hill adults who failed to reach the upper valley, and suffered the same fate the three grandparents had borne, were often the mothers and grandparents of children who were present to watch Thunder Hunter's warriors slaughter and bury them where they fell.

The valley people cried out to the gods every time they saw it happen, but that only exposed the true horror of their situation. They were forced to witness the pointless killing of other humans, and they weren't able to do anything about it but scream to the gods.

Who were choosing—as they could, being gods—not to listen or care.

*****

It was also true, though, most of Thunder Hunter's warriors didn't appear to take any pleasure in chasing down and killing their

72

own people.

They often seemed to be going through the motions, running nowhere near the speed one might've expected from men so young and robust. Despite the season, they'd found game in the lower-valley forest and fish in the lower-valley river to roast for their supper almost every evening.

Blue Sky noticed the same few men always did the killing of the people they caught. When they were done, they'd yell, laugh, and embrace one another, covered once again with their own people's blood, making no effort to conceal their glee in slaughtering humans.

As they raced in screaming for a kill, their comrades, their commander included, would step aside for them, as if they were gratefully letting the usual killers do what they all knew had to be done but had no wish to do themselves.

Their leader also seemed to punish the men who did the killing far more often than he did the other warriors. He personally delivered their punishment with a whip. He always drew blood.

The valley people decided Thunder Hunter's encampment, whose only true purpose now was to keep their own people out of the upper valley, was hell itself.

*****

The orchard beyond the entrance to the gorge was in bloom. On the cliff-top, Blue Sky and Green Field could see all the orchards in the lower valley were in bloom.

"I'd rather die," Blue Sky said, "than give up hope of living in our village again."

The sun was rising over the eastern mountains, and Green Field and Blue Sky were at the end of a night of guard duty—even the regent and his son did guard duty— sitting together staring at the lower valley.

The auxiliaries who were to spend the day on the cliff-top were climbing the path behind them, already complaining about one insignificant thing after the other, as their people liked to do.

In that season, though, even the most indolent among them would've rather been planting the fields than watching and waiting for the daily chase and hoping they'd see no killing that day.

And yet many of the valley warriors and auxiliaries had to remain near the gorge. They had no choice but to help the hill people coming to them. They had to make sure Thunder Hunter's warriors knew just how far they could go.

Blue Sky turned and looked at his father and noticed he was in tears.

"I thank the gods you're still alive," his father said. "Despite all your attempts to get yourself killed."

"Are the gods," Blue Sky asked, "responsible for such a slight thing as my still being alive?"

Green Field ignored his tears and stared at his son. "You might be slight to the gods," he replied, "but you're everything to your mother and me."

"If they're responsible," Blue Sky said, pretending not to hear what his father had said, "they've got a lot of other things, more important things than me, to be ashamed of."

At least the regent's son hadn't made that comment in front of the people.

"You know," Blue Sky continued, "I'm not waiting for any help from the gods. Whether they exist or not, we've always had to figure out for ourselves what to do. And right now what we've got to figure out is how we're going to get ourselves home."

Green Field stared at the lower valley.

"We're safe here," he said. "Our people can live quite well here. Even with the hill people coming. They work just as hard as our people do. They contribute. The boys and some of the women wish to become auxiliaries. The boys will someday become warriors. Many Numbers and Early Harvest think we can hold off Lightning Spear and Thunder Hunter forever."

"Maybe they're right," Blue Sky said. "But maybe that isn't enough. We've got to go back. That land we worked was ours. I want to see us there again in our village and our fields. And our horses, cattle, sheep, and goats in their pastures. And no stupid war with the hill people going on. I'll never give up hoping for that."

"Some day," Green Field said, looking at the lower valley. "Some day."

74

"Some day soon," his son amended. "I don't want Lightning Spear and Thunder Hunter thinking they can keep us penned up—not even in our blessed and bountiful upper valley."

"Some day," Green Field repeated.

"Killing their own people," Blue Sky spat, "and making us watch."

He gestured toward the lower valley, orchards in bloom as far as they could see.

"I'm willing to die for it," he said.

There was a reason none of their people's tellers or apprentice tellers except one had survived the battle on the plain. They'd taken a vow to always be willing to die first for the kingdom, ahead of the men who were fathers, even ahead of the men who weren't yet but might still become fathers.

"I'm not willing to see you die for it," Green Field said. "I don't care if I am the regent of this kingdom, I'd much rather have you alive. You're my son. You're your mother's son. We love you. More important than that, the people love you."

Blue Sky felt he had no choice. He had to pretend once again he hadn't heard what his father had said.

*****

The orchards were still in bloom one afternoon when two hill people easily outran Thunder Hunter's warriors. They were grown men as far past coming-of-age as Spring Rain, Many Numbers, and Wandering Star, the valley people learned later. The warriors chasing them quickly gave up, without even bothering to yell a single "death to traitors" in their direction.

The hill men, who carried no weapons and had no beards, came to a stop between the entrance to the gorge and the valley people's front line. They stood in the afternoon sunlight staring at the people who were supposed to be their enemies.

"You don't look as if you're starving," Many Numbers said in their language.

"We're not," one of them agreed, using the valley people's words for his reply.

The valley people in the gorge and on the cliff-top murmured.

"We didn't come here for food," he added, again speaking the valley people's language.

The two hill men's dark brown curls fell only as low on their foreheads, ears, and necks as the valley men's did, which was the style Blue Sky had introduced in his coming-of-age summer. Before that, few valley men let their hair cover any part of their foreheads, ears, or necks.

Among the hill men, only Wandering Star—who, being Lightning Spear's bastard son, could get away with it—cut his hair or shaved his beard.

"Did Wandering Star teach you how to speak our language?" Blue Sky asked, using his people's words so that Thunder Hunter's warriors wouldn't know what he was saying.

"He did," the second hill man replied, using the valley's people's words.

Wandering Star had taught them the rules for going from their language to the valley people's, but they still didn't pronounce or use the words exactly the way the valley people did. It no longer mattered. Those of the valley people in daily contact with hill people could understand most of what their guests said, and make themselves understood as well.

"Why did you come here?" Green Field asked.

He'd made his way to the front line with Gentle Brook, Fair Judge, and Full Harvest.

"To fight on your side," the first hill man answered.

He was a head-length taller than the other man.

"Against your own comrades?" Many Numbers asked.

"You've killed most of our comrades," the second man quickly shot back.

"We came here to fight them," the first man said, pointing in the direction of the lower-valley encampment. "Thunder Hunter's warriors."

*****

Noon Breeze handed Blue Sky his spear and went out to

welcome the hill men by giving each of them a long embrace.

Walking between them, with one arm around each of their midsections, he brought them to the valley people's front line.

Then he put to them the next question his housemates and he couldn't help but have for two men their age coming to live with their enemies, for whatever their reasons, with no women or children in sight: "Are you tellers?"

"Yes," the taller man replied.

"I told you," Blue Sky overheard one of the apprentice tellers say to a comrade.

The shorter man, who was only as tall as Noon Breeze, looked at Blue Sky and smiled.

"We saw what you and Wandering Star did before the battle on the plain," he said. "We were certain we were going to see War Cloud kill you. Instead, the king let his son's friend live, even though he was a farmer."

"We were amazed," the other man added.

Hearing those remarks, Green Field shook his head, and Gentle Brook closed her eyes.

"We fell in love with you," the shorter hill man said.

The taller hill man looked Blue Sky up and down and smiled.

"You must've fought that day," Blue Sky said to the hill men.

"All day that day," the taller man replied.

"Both of you," Blue Sky said, "must've killed a number of our comrades."

"We had to," the other man confirmed. "Otherwise, they would've killed us."

"Or Thunder Hunter's warriors would've," the taller man said.

"Did you fight us here?" Blue Sky asked. "And up in the mountains?"

"We fought in all three battles," the shorter hill man replied.

"We buried a lot of our friends," the other man added.

"We were helping carry away our dead when our chief warrior set your arm," the shorter man said. "We saw you pass out."

The apprentice tellers had gathered around the hill men closely, crowding out the other warriors and auxiliaries, even Green Field and Gentle Brook.

"Any of us in any of those battles," Blue Sky said, "could've killed you."

"I'm thanking the gods we didn't," Noon Breeze quickly added.

"One of your trees down there almost got us," the taller man said, pointing toward the lower-valley entrance to the gorge.

"Two more up in the mountains," the other man added, "came awfully damned close."

After hearing those remarks repeated, the valley people once again had nothing to say.

Blue Sky embraced the hill men, taking his time with each of them.

"Wandering Star misses you," the taller man said to Blue Sky, whispering in his ear in his language so that nobody else could hear him.

"He told us that himself," the other man added during his embrace, speaking as softly in Blue Sky's ear as his companion had. "He'll never forget the night you and he laid your spears down together."

Those were the words Wandering Star had asked Blue Sky, during their last night on sunrise pass, to wait to hear.

*****

The taller hill teller called himself Evening Shadow. The other man was known as Night Whisper.

Noon Breeze and the apprentice tellers were taking them to the closest and largest house in the upper valley. The newcomers had briefly seen the valley people's houses, barns, granaries, and court in the lower valley before they and their fellow hill tellers, following the orders of Heaven's Voice and his high tellers, had put them to the torch.

"Those aren't your birth names," Noon Breeze quickly and correctly guessed.

Wandering Star had told the valley people that name-changing was as common among his people as it was among the farmers. He, Lightning Spear, Thistle Dew, Thunder Hunter, and his sons hadn't changed theirs. But Dancing Song, Heaven's Voice, and True Hunter weren't born with those names. Before the battle on the plain, the cousin next in line after Thunder Hunter's sons, Dark Storm and War Cloud, took the name Dark Cloud.

Long Arm's family renamed him in his late boyhood, when his body was reshaping itself to become a man's. They realized he'd be taller than most hill people, as many in his family were. But they also saw that his arms were conspicuously long in proportion to his body. As a result, he was already winning spear-throwing contests against the best spear-throwing men.

And after Long Arm captured Rose Leaf and Morning Sun and took them to Lightning Spear, his tall, long-armed younger brothers, who'd assisted with the abductions, took new names, the older of the two becoming First Brother, and the younger, Second Brother.

Evening Shadow and Night Whisper had to wait until they came of age before they could rename themselves. Their families had refused to permit the changes, claiming to be embarrassed by their choices. What did those names have to do with hunting or fighting wars?

*****

As soon as Blue Sky and his housemates reached the upper-valley entrance to the gorge, they ran into a number of hill people. In fact, most of the hill people living in the upper valley then were streaming in their direction.

Evening Shadow and Night Whisper had fought in and survived three horrific battles. They were heroes to the hill people even if their adversaries in those battles had become their forgiving hosts.

The hill people asked them what had happened to their beards.

Some of the older hill boys, who'd started to grow their own, loudly asked them why they wanted to look like farmers, even as they knew the farmers present could hear them.

"Won't the farmers," Evening Shadow asked, "make you shave off yours?"

"Their king told us we didn't have to," the older of the two brothers who'd insisted on hunting replied, referring, as the hill people living in the upper valley always did, to the regent. "Only if we choose to fight in their army do we have to. That's what he told us."

Long ago, that was the rule for all the valley men. They were free to grow beards if they wished—and their mates and companions let them—but they had to shave them off when they were serving with the army. Beardless, they wouldn't be mistaken for enemy warriors.

Blue Sky saw Good Harvest motion, for the benefit of his cousins, toward the apprentice tellers and Blue Sky's other housemates.

"They shaved off their beards for them," he said of the two grown men who'd come over to the valley people's side.

He and his cousins snickered.

Green Field and Early Harvest, who'd observed what was quickly becoming a celebration among the hill people, approached Blue Sky, Many Numbers, and Spring Rain.

"Our guests seem to like them," Green Field said. "I thought you said hill people hated their tellers."

Blue Sky explained the hill people despised their first teller, the high tellers, and the many lesser tellers who sought to keep or obtain their favor. Those tellers didn't believe they should have to provide for themselves. Having direct access to the gods, they argued, they were entitled to live off the people's tribute. That was why they were always demanding more and more of it. They wouldn't perform ceremonies for the people, not even funerals, without getting their tribute in advance. And Lightning Spear went along with them.

On the other hand, Wandering Star and the tellers not in the first teller's favor, including most of the younger tellers, opposed teller tribute as much as the people did. Those tellers would sit down and eat a meal with the people after a ceremony, but that was all they'd expect to get out of it. They often brought game with them for the people to roast for the meal.

They wanted their people's admiration, not their scarce supplies of food, leather, furs, and firewood. If they had their way, the king's bastard son would be the hill people's first teller.

Green Field and Early Harvest stared at Evening Shadow and Night Whisper.

Fair Judge's tellers had performed the ceremonies for the hill people living in the upper valley expected of their own tellers. As they did, the valley people's tellers used the hill people's words.

The valley people's regent, or "king," supplied the food for the meal that followed.

Early Harvest shook his head. "How do we know these two aren't just posing as Wandering Star's friends? They can find out a lot from those apprentice tellers. Wine loosens their lips just as much as it does mine. My cousins aren't the only people who can see what's going on here. How can we stop two grown men if they try to sneak back to their people with our secrets?"

"Confront them," Blue Sky said. "Tell them why you're worried. I'm sure they won't be offended. They'll understand. But I'm not worried about them at all."

Many Numbers and Spring Rain stared at Blue Sky. Having observed their most recent hill guests whispering in his ears in the gorge, they remained silent.

*****

Noon Breeze and the apprentice tellers promised the hill people they'd hold a feast for Evening Shadow and Night Whisper the next evening, after all the people had proper time to prepare for it. Every hill person would be invited. Those of age who wished to do so could drink wine. The tellers and apprentice tellers would supply music for dancing throughout the evening. If the hunters among them wanted to bring a deer or two and other game to roast, the valley people would trade them grain for the meat at the going rate.

Many Numbers, Fair Judge, Gentle Brook, and Green Field, with Blue Sky and Spring Rain urging them on, gave their assent.

Blue Sky and his comrades finally got the two hill tellers to their house.

Wandering Star had explained to them as best he could how the farmers built them. What he'd been able to tell them about that and a number of other odd things the valley people did, such as castrating young bulls and training them to become oxen, had left them with an endless supply of questions by the time they reached the upper valley.

Noon Breeze and the apprentice tellers, preparing that

81

evening's unanticipated revel, which they'd chosen not to mention to the hill people, were only too happy to dazzle their guests with their witty answers.

Many of the apprentice tellers who'd never met Wandering Star were also curious to know how hill tellers lived. The hill people did indeed have Law Keepers who used their positions to gain access to younger men.

The most notorious, the newcomers assured them, was Heaven's Voice, their first teller, Wandering Star's nemesis. They'd like nothing better than to see him dead.

Chapter 5

Fair Judge left to Green Field and Early Harvest the task of giving Evening Shadow and Night Whisper the warning she and the regent gave all the other hill people who'd come to live in the upper valley: as long as the hostilities with their people continued, they couldn't go back.

Green Field and Early Harvest came to the regent's son's house. Despite the intense chatter in the background the preparations for the revel required, they gave the new arrivals the requisite warning.

"There's something else you need to know," Green Field said to the hill tellers.

Early Harvest glanced at Blue Sky and nodded his head.

"Your coming to the upper valley," the regent continued, "worries some of our people."

The apprentice tellers fell silent.

Green Field and Early Harvest repeated the complaints they'd heard.

Unlike the hill children and mothers who'd previously reached the upper valley, these two latest arrivals had been warriors among their own people, and two spears, two bows, two shields, and some arrows were all it would require to make them warriors again. Lightning Spear and Thunder Hunter could've sent them to cause the valley people harm. Maybe as spies. Some had gone so far as to question why Thunder Hunter's warriors had so readily given up their chase.

The hill tellers looked at one other uneasily.

Spring Rain laughed. "I would've given up too," he said. "Why would I want to wear myself out doing something as hopeless as chasing down these two men? And making a fool of myself, once again, in front of my enemies?"

"You're damned right," one of the apprentice tellers said, loudly enough for the regent to hear him. His comrades quickly let the regent know they agreed.

Blue Sky was aware his father didn't wish to do what he was doing or say what he was saying.

"I'm sorry," Green Field said to the hill tellers. "But we'll have to watch you carefully until we get to know you better. We certainly wish to believe you're no longer our enemies, but we can't simply go by what you tell us. I hope you understand our position."

The apprentice tellers, having stopped their preparations, stood around the fire staring at the regent without saying a word.

Blue Sky looked at his father. He suddenly wished to do whatever it took to get him and his mother back to their village and the kingdom safely in the hands of somebody else.

"I know," Noon Breeze said to the regent, "what you can do with these two men."

Only he had nerve enough to speak to Green Field in that tone of voice.

"You can order them," he continued, "to live in this house with us—and see how they like that."

The apprentice tellers snickered.

Evening Shadow and Night Whisper looked at Noon Breeze and laughed.

"I promise you," Noon Breeze said to Green Field, "we'll keep a close eye on them. And if we see anything funny going on, we'll put a stop to it as quickly as Gentle Brook's arrow reaches its target."

So Noon Breeze, who'd fought in all three battles with the hill people the same as Early Harvest, showed how easy it was to mock the kingdom's regent and get away with it.

Green Field turned to the hill tellers. "Do you wish to live here with my son and his friends?" he asked.

Noon Breeze stood between Evening Shadow and Night Whisper with his arms around them.

"It'll be all right with me," Night Whisper replied, his smile having for some reason faded. "But I don't understand why you'd stop us from going on our hosts."

Both Noon Breeze and Green Field stared at him.

"What's he talking about?" one of the apprentice tellers asked.

"Wandering Star told us he did," Night Whisper continued, speaking to the regent. "When he was with your people, he did. He told us he and your own son did."

Spring Rain, who'd figured out what the problem was ahead of everybody else, laughed.

"In our language," he said to Night Whisper, putting his hand on his shoulder, "'going on' doesn't mean the same thing as 'going with.'"

It turned out that the hill people had no "going on" expression in their language.

Noon Breeze and the apprentice tellers howled.

"Nobody's going to stop you from doing that," one of the apprentice tellers said.

"I'm ready to go on you," another said, "whenever you are."

"And I'm ready to go on your friend," a third offered. "whenever he is."

"And I'll go on you both at the same time," a fourth added.

Green Field looked to Many Numbers and Early Harvest as if for help, but even Early Harvest was too amused listening to the banter to be of any assistance.

Blue Sky put his arm around his father's shoulders.

Night Whisper, visibly relieved, embraced Spring Rain and Noon Breeze.

Then he turned to the regent. "I had no idea your people would receive us so warmly."

"And now you know," Noon Breeze said, laughing.

He gestured toward Green Field.

"And you can thank this man for coming here and making it known," he added.

Green Field had never truly understood Noon Breeze—even though the younger man's story could bring tears to his eyes, especially the part where Autumn Wine's grandson reached his family with the news that Noon Breeze had survived the battle on the plain.

"If this man," Noon Breeze said to his new friends, "had been our king when Long Arm abducted Rose Leaf and Morning Sun, we never would've tried to kill you in three battles—and luckily fail to do it in each of them."

"If he'd been our king," Spring Rain said, "nobody would've tried to kill anybody."

"I'm not a king," Green Field protested once again. "I'm a regent."

"Whatever you're called," Noon Breeze said, "you're in charge of the kingdom, and we're all damned grateful you are."

"That's right!" one of the apprentice tellers yelled.

"That's damned right!" the rest of them, by then having touched cups to lips more than once, loudly affirmed.

"It might be time for us to go," Blue Sky heard his father mumble to Early Harvest.

Early Harvest, laughing, took the regent by his arm and led him away, hopefully to attend to some business of the kingdom more urgent than what his son's friends had on their minds.

*****

Noon Breeze found out Wandering Star had introduced Evening Shadow and Night Whisper to wine. Wandering Star and Dancing Song had surreptitiously made a quantity of it the previous autumn following the instructions Blue Sky had given him.

Noon Breeze promised he'd bring them all the wine they wished to drink—but not so much, he insisted, it would keep anybody from "going on" anybody else.

Evening Shadow turned to Blue Sky.

"Can we speak with you alone?" he asked, so softly only Blue Sky could hear him.

Blue Sky walked with him and Night Whisper to the far side of the fire.

They could hear Noon Breeze tell the others he couldn't believe Blue Sky would insist on being the first to go with both of the hill tellers. Couldn't he be satisfied being first with just one of them? Did he need to be so greedy?

"Who in hell does he think he is?" Noon Breeze asked, loudly.

Spring Rain laughed. "Do you suppose," he asked, "he thinks he's the regent's son?"

"I assume," Blue Sky said as softly as he could to the two hill men who'd whispered in his ears, "you have a message for me from Wandering Star."

*****

Evening Shadow and Night Whisper had learned from their allies that Wandering Star was looking for a teller or tellers willing to go over to the valley people's side. Whoever did so needed to know beforehand that neither their own people nor the valley people would let them come home again.

Evening Shadow and Night Whisper, who were boyhood friends and cousins like Spring Rain and Many Numbers, volunteered for the mission.

The most difficult part of it wasn't outrunning Thunder Hunter's warriors at the upper gorge. As tellers, with no children or mothers of children to feed, shelter, and clothe, they had no good reason for leave from the army. Lightning Spear often denied it even to fathers of starving children—lest he provide more evidence supporting Thunder Hunter's accusation that the king's warriors, and those of the lesser chieftains, were cowards.

If a hill warrior departed the army without leave, he was a deserter, and Thunder Hunter's warriors, who surrounded the main encampment, were free to kill him on sight. When a man deserted, either his comrades soon heard he was dead, or they learned nothing more about him, letting them hope he'd reached safety and could keep himself hidden as long as it might take.

Evening Shadow and Night Whisper followed Wandering Star's instructions, crawled on their bellies in mud, slept in caves without fires, and washed their clothes in a brook in the forest on the valley people's side of the lower-valley mountains. That's where Wandering Star met them—and gave them the information he wanted them to take to the valley people.

"He says your people should think it comes from Night Whisper and me," Evening Shadow said. "You and your father and the others running your kingdom should deny it came from him."

Wandering Star wanted Blue Sky to reveal him as the source of the information only to those of the valley people who needed to be aware of it. He said Blue Sky would know who those persons were, and they and he would understand why the bastard son's part in the matter shouldn't be revealed to anybody else.

Suppose, he said, one of the hill boys living in the upper valley misbehaved—put his hands on a girl, say, where they didn't belong— and the valley people punished him, and he succeeded in running back to his people. He might wish to let them know Wandering Star was a spy for the farmer thieves who'd meted out his punishment. Thunder Hunter would surely win the next argument with Lightning Spear concerning the fate of the king's treacherous bastard son.

Thunder Hunter had already accused Wandering Star of sending hill people to live with the farmers in the upper valley. Lightning Spear dealt with that by telling Thunder Hunter he absolutely refused to believe Wandering Star would do such a thing.

Lightning Spear knew how to lie. Why should he care, he'd supposedly asked his lesser-chieftain cronies in private, if starving women, children, and old people went begging among the farmers—or if the farmers were foolish enough to take such useless people in and keep them alive? He couldn't see why Thunder Hunter's warriors wasted so much of their time and effort trying to stop them—and so often failed.

He told Thunder Hunter it was his warriors' responsibility to keep their people out of the upper valley, and if they weren't up to the job, Lightning Spear would put his own warriors in the encampment at the entrance to the upper gorge.

He knew Thunder Hunter would never agree to that and would therefore continue to suffer the humiliation of not being able to stop most of the turncoats from reaching the upper valley. And Lightning Spear's own warriors, and those of the lesser chieftains, wouldn't have to endure the hatred accruing to those who killed their own people for nothing more than making a desperate attempt to stay alive.

Wandering Star was well aware many of the valley people would nevertheless suppose he was the one who'd sent Evening Shadow and Night Whisper to live with them.

"They'll figure out why it's best not to know for sure," he told his messengers. "They'll go along with a denial from Green Field."

Blue Sky looked at Night Whisper and Evening Shadow and nodded his head.

"Our people will do that," he agreed.

Evening Shadow and Night Whisper would be the only known traitors in this part of the story. But since they'd also be living with the farmers, treachery wouldn't matter to them any more than it did to the

88

other hill people living in the upper valley. All of them were traitors subject to summary execution if only Thunder Hunter's warriors could get their hands on them—those who'd come of age, at least.

"What is it," Blue Sky asked, "Wandering Star thinks we farmers should know?"

*****

The revel that evening started long after the apprentice tellers had intended it would.

When Blue Sky, Many Numbers, Spring Rain, and Noon Breeze left the house with Evening Shadow and Night Whisper, the apprentice tellers loudly complained how unfairly their four teller housemates, to whom they'd been so accommodating—to Many Numbers and Noon Breeze in any event—were treating them.

Noon Breeze had to promise them—even asking the gods to kill him instantly if he shouldn't be telling the truth—there'd be no "going on" the hill guests until they returned and chose, among all those who made themselves available, the one or ones they wanted.

Green Field, Gentle Brook, Fair Judge, Early Harvest, Full Harvest, and Good Harvest met them on the cliff-top.

Green Field readily agreed those ten plus two individuals were the only persons who needed to know Wandering Star was giving them information.

Noon Breeze went down to the house and brought back an apprentice teller whose family had lived in the village behind the first orchard they could see from the gorge.

Those on the cliff-top asked him question after question.

Spring Rain and Blue Sky remained on either side of him, often embracing him, in order to assure him he wasn't on trial, and all the people who ruled the kingdom wanted or needed was the truth concerning nothing more incriminating than the lay of the land he'd grown up in.

"We've got to do it," Early Harvest was the first to insist, after the apprentice teller answered the last of their questions and returned to the home he lived in with the regent's son and chief warrior.

They all knew Green Field, no longer allowed to fight, would never, on his own initiative, order his warriors to do what Wandering

Star had proposed.

They also knew, as the regent did, a decision from him wasn't needed.

The warriors and auxiliaries who might be killed or injured—and the people who might suffer because of their deaths or wounds—would decide.

*****

The apprentice tellers made up their minds before the revel began that night, and woke up the next morning as Blue Sky did—without having changed them.

Their people's warriors and auxiliaries who were at home working in their fields started arriving that afternoon, bombarding Evening Shadow and Night Whisper with questions.

A few of them did at first inquire as to the possibility of Wandering Star's involvement in the matter. But Evening Shadow and Night Whisper told them Wandering Star had nothing to do with it. They insisted on their own motivation to kill as many of Thunder Hunter's warriors as it took to make the rest of them go back to where they came from.

Evening Shadow and Night Whisper pointed out they were very much in the middle of what happened the day Long Arm stopped the fighting at the upper gorge. They'd positioned themselves to be the warriors who'd first thrust their spears in the bellies of War Cloud and Dark Storm if that proved necessary to keep Wandering Star alive. And if they failed, they'd be the first to die.

They would've started the civil war between their people that surely would've followed their thrusts.

Blue Sky had recognized them as soon as he saw them running to the upper gorge. They were who they claimed to be.

Spring Rain also quietly noted that as long as Wandering Star was still living with his people, he'd hardly wish to be known as a traitor to them.

Some of whom, Many Numbers just as quietly noted, were living in the upper valley.

The answers, such as they were, must've passed rapidly among the people. Soon nobody saw fit to raise that particular question again.

*****

The valley people spent the next day repairing every raft they had and tying them together to make what would become one long and narrow chain of rafts.

The incoming warriors and auxiliaries brought confirmation of a trend some of the people—Fair Judge and her high tellers foremost among them—found alarming. A number of younger women were with child despite their never having participated in, or even anticipated their participation in, a ceremony blessing their union with the men who'd impregnated them.

Some of the women were mothers whose children had lost their fathers in the battle on the plain, and clearly the children in their bodies and their older brothers and sisters couldn't have the same fathers.

Rumors passed among the people naming the men involved, all either survivors of the battle on the plain or men who'd come of age the previous autumn. Some people said Early Harvest would be the father of at least six of the children and his cousin or half-brother Good Harvest three more.

Fair Judge and her associates paid Full Harvest, Early Harvest, and Good Harvest a visit in their village.

Early Harvest supposedly insisted the women had told him they wished to have his children.

"They told us that, too," Fair Judge conceded. "But you could've refused anyway."

"I admit that," Early Harvest replied. "I'm guilty. I didn't have any will power. I'd been drinking. I found the women pleasing to be with. And we were either getting ready to fight a battle, or we'd just fought one. I couldn't send them away. I'm sorry, but I couldn't. And I didn't. You're right. All the blame is mine."

"I'm equally guilty," Good Harvest said.

And once Early Harvest and Good Harvest started going with the women, there was no reason to stop. Not until the women got too big, at least. And even then accommodations could sometimes be made.

"The gods," Early Harvest was also supposed to have remarked, "surely must want more children in our kingdom. Someday they'll have to work the fields, tend the livestock, cook the food, haul the water and firewood, and learn to fight and kill hill warriors."

The people were busily passing those remarks around, some thinking them brazen, others saying the only trouble with them was their honesty.

Gentle Brook, who was present during the confrontation, confirmed to Blue Sky and Green Field that Early Harvest did make the statements people said he'd made.

Full Harvest had to come to the rescue of Early Harvest and Good Harvest. He told Fair Judge and her associates he knew the families of the women involved. He gave his promise that no grandchildren of his—or their brothers and sisters and mothers—would ever go hungry or lack for whatever else they needed.

Blue Sky supposed it didn't hurt that Gentle Brook sat at the fire between Early Harvest and Good Harvest that rainy spring day. She testified she considered them as much her sons as Blue Sky was, and she was quite certain they'd do for any children they fathered, as well as their families, whatever needed to be done. She, as a matter of fact, would see to it they did.

"Those children will be a hell of a lot better off growing up than I was," Noon Breeze said.

Fair Judge fretted that the other men, who'd clearly followed Early Harvest's example, might not be so concerned about their bastard children.

Full Harvest told Fair Judge he would give as much as one-tenth of his family's harvests to the tellers, for as long as necessary, to give to any mothers with children who lacked food, clothing, or shelter. He was confident, he added, tellers led by Fair Judge and the young teller the people liked so much, Spring Rain, would know where it was most needed, and therefore he'd give it to them to dispense. In the meantime, he'd take care of any children Early Harvest, Good Harvest, and their cousins, or half-brothers, might father.

92

That was the deal Fair Judge made with Full Harvest during her visit. Many thought she got the better end of it. Others—and Blue Sky was one of them—believed Full Harvest had only agreed to do what he would've done in any event. Despite that, the regent's son went out of his way to thank the first teller for insisting the children be provided for.

Many Numbers noted that one of Early Harvest's children could become king. It would only require the deaths of Morning Sun, Green Field, Blue Sky, and Full Harvest, without any of them producing another male heir "to stand in the line," as the tellers put it, for that to happen.

Although the hill people's tellers insisted no bastard could ever become their king, one of the best-loved kings in the valley people's stories clearly was. In the hill people's version of what appeared to be the same story, the person in question was simply "the previous king's son."

"In any event," Spring Rain noted, "those of us who live in this house are in no position to criticize Early Harvest and his cousins for what they might've done."

Spring Rain said that softly—and yet loudly enough for him to be heard by all those who lived in the house, the apprentice tellers included, sitting around their campfire.

All of them fell silent when he spoke.

"Is that what you said to Fair Judge?" Blue Sky dared to ask.

Spring Rain looked at Blue Sky as if he'd enjoy giving his lover a good slap across his face.

"You know damned well I didn't say that to Fair Judge," Spring Rain replied instead.

"What did you tell her?" Blue Sky asked.

"I told her," Spring Rain replied, "I wished an Early Harvest or Good Harvest had been my father, even if my mother and I didn't live with him. If I could've at least gone to see him and be with him once in a while. If I'd known he was in fact my father. If I could've hugged him."

Only Blue Sky, now the regent's son, could break the silence that followed those remarks.

"Is that what made Fair Judge cry?" he asked.

*****

The day after that, with Many Numbers in full command, the warriors and auxiliaries practiced—doing the same things over and over as only Many Numbers could make them do, reducing them to beg openly for the end of practice and the blissful coming of the real battle.

Evening Shadow and Night Whisper, spears in hand, practiced with the warriors and auxiliaries all day.

The revels that evening continued until dawn. The following day, as the warriors and auxiliaries had planned, even if it was spring, they slept.

*****

And in the evening twilight that day on the cliff-top ten plus two people saw the smoke from Wandering Star's campfire where Evening Shadow and Night Whisper had said it would be.

Wandering Star was letting them know nothing had changed and they could proceed.

"You can tell the army and the people," Green Field said, "I'm giving the order they want me to give."

He and Blue Sky embraced.

"I beg you," the regent whispered in his son's ear, "don't do anything foolish. You've got to survive. If you don't, your mother and I won't survive. Neither will the kingdom."

*****

Many of the hill people knew rafts existed, but they had no word for them in their language. They also didn't know farmers had any need for them.

The hill people knew only that the river people used them to transport themselves and their possessions on the river between their land and the valley, oxen on either side of the river pulling them upstream, and walking behind them holding them steady as they

94

floated downstream.

Since Thunder Hunter's people roamed the country between the lower gorge and the land where the river people came from, most of his warriors had no doubt seen their rafts.

Wandering Star himself had once traveled to the land Thunder Hunter's people roamed. Walking along the river, he saw for himself the traders from the south, their oxen, and their rafts laden with goods for the farmers in their valley.

Thunder Hunter supposedly allowed the river people to ply their trade through his people's land because what they were doing could only be detrimental to the farmers, who were giving up their valuable livestock and grain in return for such useless things as pottery they could just as easily make themselves and a clothing material that couldn't possibly keep them warm. He liked to say the farmers' dealings with the river people proved just how bright they were.

Before Wandering Star met Blue Sky, he had no idea that the valley people used the river traders' salt to make brine and preserve meat and roots, that their livestock for some reason thrived on licking blocks of it, or that the valley people sprinkled it on boiled food to revive its taste. Most of the year hill people preserved meat by drying and smoking it. In the winter they froze it.

Wandering Star and Many Numbers agreed the hill people had no use for salt because they didn't ordinarily have much surplus food to preserve, and of course they had no livestock to tend.

It was also true the valley people didn't have to have the traders' linen and pottery, or even their salt. They liked possessing those things anyway—the pottery was much sturdier and lasted far longer than the farmers'—and to get them they only had to give up animals and grain they didn't need anyway.

Wandering Star told Blue Sky his people had no stories in which their gods had said anything about the river people and the goods they traded to the farmers. Their tellers, though, insisted all those things were as unlawful for the hill people to have as the animals and crops that the farmers—as if they were the gods themselves—raised and planted. Possession of any such item was heresy, requiring the death of anyone so foolish as to want what the enemy farmers wanted.

The prohibition didn't leave out the floating platforms the river people used to transport those forbidden goods up and down the river.

*****

The raft train the valley people constructed extended well back into the upper valley. The warriors boarded it as they'd practiced, taking their positions one after the other in strict order, recreating the line that stretched across the slope on the hill people's side of sunset pass.

At the rear end of the train the individual rafts were separated some distance from one another. Carefully selected auxiliaries rode those rafts. They were to pass hand signals back and forth between the warriors on the rafts and the other auxiliaries, most of them standing on either side of the river in the upper valley, holding onto ropes attached at one end to the train and draped at the other end around their people's horses.

Those thought to be the ablest auxiliaries of them all—including Autumn Wine's younger grandson, Noon Breeze's brother, Solemn Promise's twin sister, East Land's niece, and her companion—rode on the rafts with the warriors, most of them working guide poles.

The riverbank auxiliaries were letting the ropes play out. The auxiliaries in charge of the horses were walking them backward. If the auxiliaries and horses hadn't held the train steady, it would've swept through the gorge so fast those riding it would've been thrown off.

As in their practices, though, the train slowly and noiselessly slid through the gorge.

Almost all the valley people were in or near the gorge that night, working the ropes, tending the horses. Evening Shadow and Night Whisper had asked the hill people living in the upper valley to sit with their hosts' young children and their elderly and ailing.

The warriors and the auxiliaries with them were on their knees and haunches, keeping themselves low above the water but still ready to do whatever they might need to do.

Although Thunder Hunter's warriors had pitched their tents near the river, Wandering Star had realized they couldn't see any part of it from their encampment. The banks were so high all the way to the gorge that a person could look across the fields and not know a river was there.

The apprentice teller who'd grown up in the village behind the orchard said children living in the area all had a moment when somebody, usually an older brother or sister or cousin, showed them how walking only a short distance away from the river made it disappear.

Thunder Hunter's warriors posted guards who kept watch throughout the nights for a possible surprise attack by the farmer thieves. What they mostly watched was the gorge to the north and the fields between the gorge and the encampment—where they'd assumed an attack would have to come. They knew that an attempt by the farmers to march their army over the mountains and come at them through the forest to the east of their encampment was no more feasible than it was for the hill people to attack the farmers over the same mountains.

Wandering Star had discovered the guards paid no attention to the terrain to their west because that was where the river was. Thunder Hunter's warriors assumed the river, still fairly deep and swift at their distance from the gorge, was a barrier. They also disregarded the fields to the south of them. They thought the farmers had no way to get around the encampment to attack them from that direction.

Even if the cleverest of Thunder Hunter's warriors could've imagined the farmers had rafts, it's not likely he would've envisioned them passing slowly and silently through the gorge in the middle of the night, transporting an army of warriors with spears and shields.

The night was cloudless. Spring Rain lay on his back on the command raft, in the middle of the chain, staring at the full moon.

He was watching where it was relative to the fixed stars.

Many Numbers wanted to begin the battle when all of Thunder Hunter's warriors except the guards would be sleeping, and yet the wakefulness of dawn would still be a safe distance away.

The lead raft crept past the encampment and didn't stop until the command raft was due west of it.

Spring Rain raised his spear, letting Many Numbers know the moon was where they wanted it to be. The auxiliaries poled the raft train to the west side of the river, where most of them got off, holding ropes attached to the rafts, clambering up the bank, and hiding themselves in the grass growing at the top of it.

The rest of the auxiliaries remained on the rafts. They and the warriors poled the train to the east side of the river, where the warriors got off.

The warriors also hid themselves in the grass at the top of the riverbank. The auxiliaries remaining on the raft train held it in place.

On Many Numbers' signal, waving his spear in the light of the full moon, his warriors climbed over the top of the bank and ran toward the nearest tents.

They'd told themselves to remember the defenseless women and old people the men in the tents had killed, as the valley people and their hill guests had watched, screaming to the gods to make them stop.

Some of those warriors had guffawed at their meaningless rage, their shameful impotence, their inability to do anything but cry out to their useless gods.

The valley warriors had practiced in groups, half of them pulling a tent apart, the other half thrusting their spears into the bodies of the warriors sleeping inside.

Thunder Hunter's warriors in the westernmost tents hadn't a chance—startled awake, hopelessly outnumbered, impaled, impaled again, triply impaled, many of them with their throats mercifully slashed.

Two of the warriors Many Numbers, Spring Rain, Noon Breeze, and Blue Sky killed had been sleeping with their arms around each other.

The screams of the wounded men woke their comrades, who burst out of their tents like bees from a fallen hive.

Spotting the valley warriors in the light of the full moon, they came running, spears raised.

On Many Numbers' signal, the valley warriors retreated, turning tail and running as they had on sunset pass.

"The river!" they could hear the hill warriors yelling to one another. "The river!"

Thunder Hunter's warriors thought they had the valley warriors not only on the run but also trapped.

But the valley warriors leapt over the riverbank, and sprinted down to the rafts.

Thunder Hunter's warriors made the error the valley people had hoped they'd make: they leapt over the edge of the riverbank behind the valley warriors without looking first.

The last of the valley warriors were jumping aboard their rafts when Many Numbers gave the signal for the auxiliaries on the opposite shore to pull on their ropes. It was also the signal for the pole wielders, with blood-soaked warriors assisting them now, to push the rafts away from the shore and into the middle of the stream, well beyond the reach of their opponents' spears.

All the valley warriors and auxiliaries on the rafts got down on their knees behind their shields, in case any of their opponents had thought to bring their bows and arrows.

Many Numbers raised his spear again. This was the signal for the valley warriors and auxiliaries visible to Thunder Hunter's warriors to curse them as loudly as they could, every word of it in the hill people's language, calling down their own gods on them for killing defenseless mothers, grandmothers, and grandfathers—who were their own people, too.

Thunder Hunter's warriors stood at river's edge screaming back at them, calling them hell-gods, children of hell-gods, and progenitors of even more hell-gods.

That was the second blunder the valley people had hoped Thunder Hunter's warriors would make.

There was perhaps one of them for every one of the valley warriors on the rafts facing them. But they didn't know the farmers were about to outnumber them three to one.

Amid all the cursing and screaming—and all the loud, rancorous, and righteous invocations of beings who never deigned to appear in the human world—they had no notice of the other valley warriors running along the river bank, after the river made a sharp turn to the east, south of their encampment

Many Numbers gave his next signal, and the valley warriors and auxiliaries on the rafts all fell silent.

The auxiliaries on the shore behind them let their ropes play out. The auxiliaries on the rafts poled them toward their opponents.

Thunder Hunter's warriors, having fallen silent themselves,

turned to see valley warriors lining the riverbank above them.

In that direction they faced at least two warriors for every one of theirs, and the valley warriors held, once again, the upper ground.

And for every one of Thunder Hunter's warriors, the valley warriors had another one in the other direction riding a raft back to do battle with his spear raised.

Wandering Star had figured out that the valley warriors greatly outnumbered Thunder Hunter's in the encampment. Every evening, in an attempt to conceal their vulnerability from their enemy, they were starting many more campfires than they needed.

Fierce as Thunder Hunter's warriors were, even some of them had left the hill people's army—some with permission, some without—to feed, clothe, and shelter their children, the mothers of their children, and even perhaps, when they could, the people in their families too elderly or otherwise unable to care for themselves.

Thunder Hunter had kept most of his remaining warriors to guard Lightning Spear's warriors and those of the lesser chieftains. In the face of their doubts as to how many warriors would return in the spring if they were allowed to go home for the winter, the king and his most powerful chieftain had agreed their army should be kept intact.

And that fateful decision had left the encampment at the gorge woefully undermanned.

Still, Lightning Spear and Thunder Hunter must've considered, what difference would it make? After the battle on the plain, the farmers knew they couldn't suffer any additional loss of their warriors. The hill people had agreed with Long Arm: the farmers wouldn't dare come out of their upper valley for at least another generation, no matter how busily their survivors of the battle on the plain and their new men of age occupied themselves with the new women of age and the women who'd lost their mates on the plain.

The battle resumed. The silence gave way to screams.

It was as if the valley people had insanely decided to slaughter a whole herd of livestock without giving any thought to how much pain they were causing animals that had served them well, or how bruised and mangled and mixed with dirt and mud their meat and skin would become.

*****

The heartless endeavor—the valley warriors were covered once again, hideously, head to toe, with hill warriors' blood—seemed to Blue Sky to be taking far too long.

He was doing the killing his comrades couldn't bring themselves to do. He wondered if he was any different from Thunder Hunter's warriors who killed other humans simply because they could. Was he was as much to blame for the world they lived in as they were?

Reaching the worst part of it, the finishing up—making certain every enemy warrior's throat was slit—almost came as a relief.

Spring Rain had predicted they'd be glad they did their killing by the light of the full moon and not in darkness.

Spring Rain and Fair Judge were the only valley persons who'd agreed with Green Field the valley people shouldn't fight this battle. Not even Gentle Brook chose to ally herself with the dissenters this time.

Blue Sky looked up from his gruesome work and saw two apprentice tellers approaching a fallen warrior who was lying face down in the mud.

He could also see something was wrong.

The man was lying too still. He wasn't writhing in pain.

But he couldn't be dead. If the valley warriors had already finished him off, he'd be lying on his back.

Then Blue Sky saw the man's arm move.

"Watch out!" he screamed, running toward the apprentice tellers. "He's getting up!"

His warning came too late.

The fallen hill warrior did rise up, swinging his spear, scarcely pausing as his spear-point sliced through his one opponent's throat on its way to slitting the other's.

"No!" Blue Sky screamed the word he despised. "No!"

His nearby comrades, seeing what happened, took up the cry as well.

This wasn't a dream anybody could comfort Blue Sky out of. This was real.

He caught the hill warrior's spear with his own and flung it

101

over the heads of the auxiliaries on the rafts and into the river, leaving the man defenseless.

Early Harvest, who'd come running as soon as he'd heard Blue Sky's warning, thrust his spear into the man's belly. Good Harvest gave him a second thrust.

Noon Breeze leapt forward and slit the man's throat.

"No!" Blue Sky couldn't stop screaming the word he least wanted to hear. "No! No! No! No!"

The wounded apprentice tellers lay on the riverbank holding their hands to their throats, hoping they could staunch the bleeding.

But of course they couldn't, and all those present knew that.

Blue Sky knelt next to them.

The regent's son and his comrades who lived with them had favored them. One was from the upper valley, the other from the lower. They'd met just before they'd come of age, when the valley people were driving their herds north after the battle on the plain.

Blue Sky remembered seeing them on the rafts splashing one another.

When the regent's son was delirious with his arm broken after the battle on sunset pass, one of them had intuited all Blue Sky really wanted to do was sleep next to Spring Rain. That man had lost his father in the battle on the plain.

The other had assured Many Numbers they'd get the regent's son down to the valley floor alive. That apprentice teller had lost two older brothers on the plain.

During the revels the two of them mostly kept to themselves or drank wine with Spring Rain and Blue Sky as if the four of them were brothers.

Then on the riverbank the two younger men, hope visibly fading from their eyes, stared at the regent's son, the god of love, the chief warrior, and their comrades, from Early Harvest to Noon Breeze, kneeling helplessly around them in tears.

They turned and reached out for the other one last time.

Chapter 6

Blue Sky looked closely at the hill warrior who'd killed his young friends.

He couldn't condemn the man for doing what he'd done. He'd attacked armed enemy warriors. True, he'd done so after the battle had been decided, and after their deaths could bring him no benefit except his own immediate death.

But so had Tall Oak, Sturdy Limb, Solemn Promise, and all the other valley warriors in the battle on the plain. And their people rightly honored them for what they'd done.

Nor could Blue Sky or his people—having chosen the time, place, and manner of the battle themselves—object to witnessing the death of comrades, no matter how much those men, just coming of age, had earned their love.

Watching how Blue Sky did it, they'd together killed as many hill warriors as he had.

Blue Sky nevertheless questioned those beings who were supposedly responsible for setting the terms of human existence in the first place, prominently featuring irrational hatreds and horrific wars among peoples. Why was he supposed to imagine they were beneficent gods?

Was it possible—if the truth were known, behind all their empty promises of land, love, and compassion—they were hell-gods in disguise who detested all humans?

Blue Sky recognized the dead hill warrior who'd killed his young comrades. He was the loud and arrogant lead warrior. He was the man who'd kept Deer Tracker alive at the battle on the plain.

He was the man who'd promised the valley people his warriors wouldn't kill children they captured below the gorge but would only send them home. From which most of them came back a second time to attempt to gain entrance to the upper valley—without one of them failing.

The dead hill warrior was the person who'd saved the valley people from themselves.

The valley people, Blue Sky in the lead, gave him his reward for that. They killed him.

*****

To be sure, the valley people had won the battle and achieved their purpose. It was never beyond their expectation that misfortune alone might account for the deaths and injuries of some of their warriors.

The tellers knew of no stories in which their people had won a battle without any loss of warriors, let alone two such battles in a row. Three battles with only two deaths were equally unheard of.

And yet it seemed to Blue Sky as if he and his people had won nothing—as if, even, they'd suffered an incomprehensible defeat.

It possibly appeared that way to all his people that night. He couldn't detect the slightest hint of victory in their faces, or hear a whisper of it on their lips.

*****

The army took the dead apprentice tellers back to the upper valley in silence.

The valley people's horses pulled the raft train home in the first light of the new day.

All the rafts were empty except for the lead raft, now the last raft, bearing their two fallen comrades.

The valley people's warriors and auxiliaries lined the east side of the river all the way to the gorge and into the upper valley beyond. The regent's son and his housemates, wading in the water, heedless of its spring chill, guided the raft, all of them openly weeping.

When they reached the upper valley and secured the last raft, the army and the people, still in total silence, kneeled down one after the other like shafts of grain in a late-summer breeze, and kissed the two dead warriors.

*****

On the path next to the river later that morning, Green Field's and Full Harvest's stallions pulled the cart.

The court people didn't have to tell Blue Sky it was his duty to lead the horses. They didn't have to tell the boys who'd hitched the horses to the cart to hand him the reins.

He was the regent's son. He was also the person who'd done the most to convince the people they should fight the battle in which the two young men had died.

Green Field, Gentle Brook, Fair Judge, Many Numbers, and Full Harvest walked behind the cart. Spring Rain, Noon Breeze, Evening Shadow, Night Whisper, and the apprentice tellers followed them, as did Early Harvest, Good Harvest, and their cousins, as well as the remainder of the army and the people.

Their kingdom was no longer a place, no longer even a people with the exclusive right to live in it.

It was the way they looked at the world they lived in: as a world of facts and logic.

Full Harvest led a pregnant heifer, Green Field a young bull.

Long ago, their ancestors would've sacrificed the animals to the gods, killing them and letting the vultures and wolves feast on their carcasses. Not so long ago, the tellers and court people would've replaced the vultures and wolves at the feast.

By the time, though, Green Field's generation came of age, the animals were meant to remain alive, gifts to the dead men's families. In the present case neither of the families was considered well-off, the one having too few cows, the other lacking a bull.

The families of the dead apprentice tellers had agreed they should be buried in a single grave in the village orchard of the family living in the upper valley.

And that was where the families of the dead youths met the funeral procession.

Heaven and hell met there, too. The orchard was in full bloom, and the spring sun was pleasantly warming. But the two men lying on the cart, having come of age less than three quarters of a year earlier, were dead.

The regent and his son declined any assistance in digging their grave.

When the time came for them to place the dead men in the grave, the soloists' parts of the funeral service began.

Many Numbers and Spring Rain had decided to omit the god of

105

war in this ceremony. Spring Rain alone sang the goddess of love's songs.

And as the regent and his son shoveled the last of their piles of earth back into the grave, the army and the people joined the tellers in singing the final chorus of the song they sang for persons killed in battle.

They all knew the words:
"We gave the warriors one last kiss
"And sent them off to fight a war.
"When they fell dead their lives to miss,
"We begged the gods: 'No more! No more!'"

*****

Many of the warriors and auxiliaries remained at the village after the funeral and finished the family's spring planting. The others went to the village where the lower-valley apprentice teller's family had relocated and finished their planting.

They spread out from those villages to neighboring villages where the absence of warriors and auxiliaries for the last several days threatened to delay planting past the optimal time. They stayed in the fields beyond sunset working in the moonlight.

Blue Sky and his housemates labored through two days and nights without sleeping.

At dawn on the third day, they went to the encampment below the gorge and dug a grave for Thunder Hunter's warriors. They left the tents where their adversaries had pitched them. The comrades of the dead warriors could eventually come and do as they pleased with their possessions.

The regent, his mate, the court people, the tellers, and the rest of the army, having learned what Blue Sky and his comrades were doing, came to help them.

Fair Judge and the tellers conducted a funeral ceremony for the dead men, using the hill people's language. As much as the hill people living in the upper valley despised Thunder Hunter's warriors, many of them came and added their voices to the singing.

106

Maybe some of them had seen what Blue Sky had: almost all of the warriors in Thunder Hunter's encampment hadn't wished to kill their own people.

That same day the army recommenced helping the farmers finish their planting. They sent warriors and auxiliaries far into the upper valley, many of them riding horses. For the next several days, they had neither the desire nor the opportunity for any kind of amusement.

Only the need to rest the horses and oxen put a limit on what they could do.

They went to sleep each day at sunset—some of them, Blue Sky included, quite drunk. They got up well before dawn and began working again by the light of the waning moon.

The inescapable fact of the needless deaths of their two comrades—"The battle was over!" Blue Sky screamed more than once, waking—wouldn't let them rest even if they'd wanted to.

*****

There was another reason for their working long days with little sleep.

The purpose of the battle on the riverbank was to incite Lightning Spear and Thunder Hunter into sending their dispirited, declining army back into battle, perhaps to suffer another loss on the order of the last three.

Or perhaps—as Wandering Star, Evening Shadow, and Night Whisper hoped—to fall apart, with Thunder Hunter's outnumbered warriors squared off against all the others, and Long Arm this time unable, or maybe unwilling, to separate them.

It hadn't taken long, they learned, for news of the battle on the riverbank to reach Lightning Spear and Thunder Hunter.

Before the battle, the valley people had imagined their victory would open the way for the starving hill people to come to the upper valley without fear of being slaughtered.

One argument Fair Judge, with Green Field and Spring Rain concurring, had raised against the proposal to attack Thunder's Hunter's warriors was that the valley people weren't prepared to properly provide for the number of new arrivals they anticipated a victory would bring.

Nobody, not even Blue Sky, had argued that wouldn't be a problem.

The moon was well past full, though, before any hill people showed up. The first who did were three siblings, two older boys and a girl. They strolled from the eastern forest to the gorge, the look-outs on the cliff-top said, as if they did it every day.

Having learned that the farmers had slaughtered every warrior Thunder Hunter had posted to guard the gorge, Lightning Spear and Thunder Hunter had said the only proper conclusion their people could draw was that the thieves had decided to kill all the hill people.

The brothers and sister, having found and spoken with Wandering Star in the eastern forest, had decided what their leaders were saying was only the latest of their many lies.

The three siblings continued their journey and found out who was right. The boys would come of age in the next two autumns.

Their people's army, they said, wasn't far behind them.

The valley people knew that. They'd seen the campfires, first on sunrise pass, then coming down through the forest, and now following the river up the lower valley.

*****

The hill warriors began arriving below the gorge the next afternoon.

The valley warriors and auxiliaries, having brought the spring planting up to date throughout the upper valley, had already returned to the gorge.

Noon Breeze and his brother had ridden the regent's and Full Harvest's stallions all the way home to their family's village beyond the lake. The family reacted with horror to the story of the two apprentice tellers killed at the battle on the riverbank.

They insisted Noon Breeze and his brother stay home. They'd already done more in the way of risking their young lives than a kingdom could reasonably ask them to do. Some other warriors or auxiliaries working nearby, they urged, would be happy to ride the stallions back to the upper gorge.

Noon Breeze and his brother insisted they'd much rather die than desert their comrades on the eve of battle. When the time came for them to do so, they said their goodbyes, albeit not without the shedding of tears, and left, riding the famous horses they'd arrived on.

Although the valley people assumed any battle Lightning Spear had in mind would probably begin the next morning, Blue Sky and his housemates gave no thought whatsoever to a revel. They simply drank however much wine it took to let them fall asleep.

Along with the people screaming "No!" in Blue Sky's dreams came two more. These young men said nothing. They simply stared at him with hope still living in their eyes.

But not, Blue Sky could see, for long.

*****

The valley people's warriors were in the gorge, their auxiliaries were on the cliff-top, and their noncombatants were behind the warriors, some of them already brewing pod tea. They were all in their proper positions in the twilight before dawn, waiting.

The hill people's warriors were likewise all in their positions in the fields below the gorge.

Having no reason for talk, the valley people could hear, flying about above them, the first birds of the day, singing.

Both peoples' stories had it that the gods were most likely to come to earth during battles disguised as birds, the better apparently for them to see which side was winning and which might need their assistance—if the losing side was in fact the side the gods favored.

Blue Sky came close to laughing. Wasn't it marvelous? The warriors in two armies stood prepared to die horrific deaths for their people, and the gods were singing.

But why shouldn't they sing? What better entertainment could they hope for? Did their horses help fight wars in heaven? Or did those lovely beasts get to live in heaven for nothing more than going with the gods?

Lightning Spear was once again sitting in his chair at the center of the front line of the hill people's army. To his right were Thunder Hunter, his sons Dark Storm and War Cloud, their cousins Dark Cloud and True Hunter the teller, and still more cousins. To the king's left were the lesser chieftains, followed by Heaven's Voice and his high tellers, all of them standing strictly according to their rank.

Blue Sky couldn't help but admire their dedication to an order they imagined was real—even if it, like the gods, had nothing to do with the world they lived in.

For some reason, Long Arm and his two brothers were conspicuously standing halfway between their people's army and the gorge.

The hill warriors that morning apparently had nothing more to say to one another than the farmers did. Lightning Spear nevertheless raised his hand above his head asking for silence.

"Let the messenger come forward," he ordered.

The warriors behind the king made way for a person passing among them.

When he reached the hill people's front line, the valley people saw who the messenger was: Wandering Star.

He strode between Lightning Spear and the great chieftain Thunder Hunter as if they weren't present, fixed his gaze on the valley people like a man obsessed beyond reason with his beloved, handed his spear and shield to First Brother and Second Brother without saying a word, and proceeded toward the gorge alone, taking the path next to the river.

As he did so, the valley people and warriors in the gorge made way for Green Field, Gentle Brook, Fair Judge, and Full Harvest.

Wandering Star entered the gorge without casting a glance toward the cliff-top. When he came within two house lengths of the valley people, he stopped and stared at Blue Sky.

It was little more than a year since the spring night in the gully on sunrise pass when they first went together, but to Blue Sky it might as well have been a lifetime.

"Green Field," Wandering Star began, speaking the valley people's language, "Lightning Spear wishes for you to know your people can live in your upper valley in peace."

The message went back to the people in the gorge and up to the auxiliaries on the cliff-top. Nobody dared respond. Although

Wandering Star spoke those words, how true could they be?

"His tellers agree," Wandering Star continued. "He may let your people live in it."

In his monotone, Long Arm was interpreting Wandering Star's remarks for the hill warriors, who were passing them back in the usual fashion to their most distant ranks.

Wandering Star had more. "The tellers have assured our king our stories say your people took one valley from us, not two. They've decided the valley you took must've been the lower valley."

Blue Sky once again came close to laughing.

That's how the stories of the gods were. Humans—at least those in charge of things at the moment—heard in them whatever they wished to hear.

And on behalf of such weak and ineffectual gods, human beings were supposed to kill one another.

"Our people's king," Wandering Star said, "is therefore willing to grant your people the right to live in the upper valley to conclude this most recent war between your people and his."

Despite the valley people's respect for the person bringing Lightning Spear's message, they continued to give no indication they believed what he said was true.

"What about the lower valley?" Green Field asked.

"Lightning Spear's tellers tell him that belongs to his people," Wandering Star replied. "He has it now, and he'll keep it for them. He says your people will never live in it again."

The valley people murmured.

Wandering Star wasn't done. "Lightning Spear also wishes you to know he doesn't trust you or your people. He believes you'll attempt to regain the lower valley. He believes you'll attack his people to do it. He doesn't believe you'll let his people live in peace. He therefore wishes to attach one condition to his agreement to end the war with your people."

The season being spring, the birds flying above were still singing.

"That condition being what?" Green Field asked.

"Lightning Spear demands a hostage," Wandering Star replied. "A hostage who'll forfeit his life the instant your people attack his. You won't have to choose the hostage. Lightning Spear has already

111

decided who that person will be."

"Can you tell us who that person is?" the regent asked, his voice breaking.

Gentle Brook and Spring Rain closed their eyes.

As the question went back to both armies, Wandering Star stared at Blue Sky, who already knew the hill man he loved had him trapped.

When the repeaters finished, Wandering Star the messenger turned to Green Field the regent once again.

"Your son," he replied.

"Never!" Noon Breeze was the first to retort.

"Never!" the valley warriors quickly agreed.

"Never!" the auxiliaries and the people roared.

"Never!" Noon Breeze yelled at the top of his voice, in the hill people's language, aiming his answer at Lightning Spear like an arrow.

"Never!" the army and the people repeated, also using the hill people's word. "Never!"

Wandering Star saw that Blue Sky, ignoring the tumult around him, had remained silent.

The regent raised his hand, signaling for quiet.

"Wandering Star," he said, "you can tell your king that's my answer. Our people will never agree to that."

"Lightning Spear already has two hostages," Blue Sky said. "What will he do with them?"

"He doesn't consider Rose Leaf a hostage," Wandering Star replied. "She's his daughter. I don't believe anybody questions that."

"Who can't come and go as she pleases," Blue Sky said. "Who can't give birth to the children of the man she'd choose to place in her body."

"None of our people's women have those choices," Wandering Star said. "Certainly, no princess would."

Green Field extended his arm around Gentle Brook's shoulders.

"And Morning Sun?" Blue Sky asked.

Wandering Star hesitated. "Is Rainbow Evening here?" he asked.

She no longer came out of the house she occupied with Fair Judge. Her conversations had lately tended toward incoherence. She recently told Gentle Brook she regretted she and Tall Oak never had children.

Wouldn't it have been nice, she asked her cousin, if she'd borne a prince who'd been pleasing to look upon and loved by the people, and if he'd found a young woman such as she'd been, wishing to bear the prince's children, as many as he pleased, more than anything else life could offer her?

"Rainbow Evening won't hear your answer," Blue Sky replied.

"Then I regret very much to tell you," Wandering Star replied, "Lightning Spear will order his warriors to kill Morning Sun."

"No!" the valley people screamed. "No! No! No!"

Noon Breeze and the apprentice tellers once again used the hill people's word. And the army and the people once again followed their lead.

Wandering Star waited for quiet.

"Lightning Spear," he said to Green Field, "asked me to tell you your prince will die no matter what you do here this morning. He considers the present war between your people and his at its end. He promised Thunder Hunter two things at war's end: Morning Sun would die, and Rose Leaf would become the mate of Thunder Hunter's older son and bear his children."

Wandering Star stared at Gentle Brook, who openly wept.

"Lightning Spear," Wandering Star continued, "wishes me to assure you he keeps his promises. He'll keep his promise to Thunder Hunter the same as he'll keep his promise not to attack you and drive you from the upper valley, the same as he'll keep his promise to kill your son if you attack our people again—as well as his promise to keep your son alive as long as you don't attack. He also asked me to tell you your people have only themselves to blame for Morning Sun's fate. Lightning Spear promised he'd kill your prince if you didn't leave the valley peaceably. Instead of doing as he asked you to do, or even speaking with him and giving him the opportunity to agree to your people keeping the upper valley, your king chose to attack his people. As a result, countless numbers of your people and his people have needlessly died."

At that point, few if any valley people would've denied that attacking the hill people was by far the most regrettable thing they'd ever done. And the number of hill people dead as a result of it was no small part of that regret.

But why did that mean Morning Sun, who was capable of no guile whatsoever and had attacked nobody, should have to die?

"What I tell you next comes from me," Wandering Star said.

Green Field raised his hand signaling to the repeaters to remain silent.

Wandering Star had made his last statement loud enough for Long Arm to hear him, but Long Arm didn't repeat it in his people's language.

"Lightning Spear," Wandering Star said, lowering his voice so that only the valley people in the first ranks could hear him, "has no choice but to kill Morning Sun. If he gives your people the upper valley, and also reneges on his promises regarding Morning Sun and Rose Leaf, Thunder Hunter's people and his people will be at war."

Blue Sky could see Wandering Star knew Long Arm wouldn't repeat his remarks.

The valley people, though, whispered them to one another.

"What happens," Blue Sky asked, "if I refuse to be taken hostage?"

Long Arm began interpreting again.

Wandering Star smiled at Blue Sky as he often did, indulgently, as an older brother would.

"Let's first consider," he replied, "what will happen if you and your father agree."

"Never!" the valley people screamed.

Wandering Star, paying no attention to the protests other than to wait until they ceased, pointed in the direction of his people's army.

"If I go back down that path with you," Wandering Star said, "my father and Thunder Hunter will send their warriors home to feed their families. They'll leave only as many of them here as will be needed to keep your people where they belong."

The valley people were again repeating what Lightning Spear's messenger was saying.

"They'll go on killing their own people," Blue Sky asked,

114

"while our people watch?"

"No," Wandering Star quickly replied. "Lightning Spear says his warriors will capture them and take them to the tellers for punishment. None of them will be killed. If some of them still get through to your side, he'll wish them well, but he'll never let them return."

"And if you go back down that path alone?" Blue Sky asked.

"Lightning Spear will attack your people," Wandering Star replied. "He'll resume the war this morning. He and Thunder Hunter will send every last warrior they have into this gorge."

Wandering Star glanced at the cliff-top.

"They promise their warriors will walk over their own dead," he continued. "No matter how high the pile grows. They say you can't possibly have enough tree limbs and rocks up there to kill them all. They promise enough of them will get through this time to slaughter all your people. No trace of your people will remain in this world."

Many Numbers had so argued from the beginning: if Lightning Spear and Thunder Hunter were so maniacal and could actually order their warriors to fight such a battle, they could prevail. Many Numbers believed they still might be able to do so, even after their losses on the plain and in the three subsequent battles. Nobody had taken the opposing side of that argument.

"Wandering Star," Early Harvest interjected, "our people greatly respect you. You know that. But I gather you wish for us to accede to Lightning Spear's demand for a hostage."

"I do," Wandering Star agreed.

"It's impossible," Early Harvest said. "You should know that yourself, even if Lightning Spear doesn't. We'll never give him the regent's son. Whatever mistakes our people might've made in the past, putting the regent's son in your king's hands is unthinkable. He'd be as vulnerable as Morning Sun is. Tell Lightning Spear we'll never do it. Never."

Long Arm faithfully repeated Early Harvest's remarks.

Spring Rain took Blue Sky's hand. "Tell Lightning Spear the answer is no," he said to Wandering Star, not without tears in his eyes. "We're ready to fight. We're ready to die."

Staring at Spring Rain, Wandering Star looked as if he might shed tears of his own.

"I know how much you'll miss him," he said. "I know how much I have."

He hadn't lowered his voice to make those comments.

So they went out to the valley people too.

With surprising nonchalance, Long Arm repeated them to his people as well.

"Are Morning Sun and Rose Leaf," Blue Sky asked, "still Long Arm's prisoners?"

"They're in his care," Wandering Star replied. "They live with his family."

Long Arm interpreted that answer with one word in the hill people's language: "Yes."

"Would I also be his prisoner?" Blue Sky asked.

Unseen by his people, Wandering Star smiled. "You'd be in Long Arm's care," he said.

Long Arm once again used a single word to interpret Wandering Star's answer: "Yes."

Many Numbers turned to Blue Sky.

"No," he said. "No. I beg you. Don't consider it."

Spring Rain looked at Blue Sky as if he couldn't imagine living his life without the regent's son at his side.

"No," the god of love protested. "No."

And again, Blue Sky wasn't hearing voices in a dream.

Long Arm repeated those remarks to the hill people's warriors, word for word.

Noon Breeze grabbed Blue Sky by his shoulder. "You can't," he insisted.

The apprentice tellers murmured.

Gentle Brook wept. Full Harvest took her hand.

"Lightning Spear wishes to keep you alive," Wandering Star said to Blue Sky. "He asked me to tell you that. You and your father will understand, he said. If you die, he no longer has a hostage. What good will it do him if the son of your people's regent becomes food for vultures?"

Wandering Star turned to Green Field.

"Speaking for myself again," he said, holding his voice down,

"I can tell you Thunder Hunter will make every attempt to kill your son. He thinks your gods will insist you punish Lightning Spear for his death. He thinks you'll make the same mistake Tall Oak and Sturdy Limb made. He thinks you'll come out of your upper valley and attack us."

Long Arm didn't interpret any of those remarks.

"So your son," Wandering Star added, speaking to Green Field, "will need to be careful not to give Thunder Hunter's warriors any excuse to kill him. Exceedingly careful."

The valley people were whispering again.

"On the other hand," he said, "your son will be, as my father promised, in Long Arm's care. Thunder Hunter, you see, has his warriors under strictest orders not to harm Long Arm or any of his family, not even his most distant cousins."

Long Arm didn't repeat any of that.

Wandering Star continued. "Many of our people say the gods sent Long Arm to us. It's obvious he's their favorite. They led him to our people's lost princess and your prince. He captured them and took them to Lightning Spear. None of our people's stories include a hero who did what he did. And at the moment of their deepest despair. You saw him separate Lightning Spear's warriors from Thunder Hunter's. Not one of them dared disobey him."

Green Field turned to Blue Sky.

"You're my son," he said. "I'm your father."

Long Arm resumed interpreting.

"You can't make me do this," Green Field said. "You can't make me consent to your walking down that path into the hands of Lightning Spear and Thunder Hunter. I won't do it."

"Rose Leaf and Morning Sun," Gentle Brook said, "are more than enough to give up."

Blue Sky took his mother's hand.

Both peoples were openly repeating their remarks.

"But you're also," Blue Sky said to his father, "the regent of the kingdom."

Early Harvest and Many Numbers converged on Blue Sky, one on either side of him.

Noon Breeze looked at him, shaking his head.

"You don't have a choice," Blue Sky said to his father. "You have to let me do it."

"Give me your spear," Many Numbers said to Blue Sky.

Blue Sky, obeying his chief warrior's order, handed it to him.

Many Numbers laid it on the ground and ordered the apprentice tellers, as Early Harvest did his cousins, to move farther down the gorge.

They dropped their own spears and formed two lines standing shoulder-to-shoulder all the way to Wandering Star. If necessary, they'd use their bodies to keep the regent's son in the upper valley. True honorable warriors couldn't use weapons against a prince—or even a regent's son.

Watching them, Blue Sky had to laugh to himself at least.

Having fought side-by-side with them in three battles, his coming to blows with any of them for any reason was beyond his imagination. He loved them all.

"You'll have to order them to let me go," Blue Sky said to his father.

The apprentice tellers and upper-valley cousins nearest Wandering Star were all taking his hand in greeting, proud to be seen with him even if he was, officially, an enemy messenger.

He'd done nothing less, they all knew, than save the valley people from extermination. He'd done it on his own, without any expectation of any advantage to him.

"My entire life," Green Field said, "all I've ever wished to be was a farmer."

"You were never just a farmer in this kingdom, Green Field," his son said. "Tall Oak came to you with everything. You had to approve every order he gave. You even let him keep Sturdy Limb and Law Speaker in their positions. Why? Because you didn't want to rule the kingdom in their stead. Nor do I blame you for that. The only thing Tall Oak ever did without your approval was the last thing he did: attacking the hill people."

Long Arm was making certain his people heard those remarks.

The valley people murmured. They'd long suspected what Blue Sky had said was true, but it was still shocking for them to hear him say it publicly.

118

"You're my father," Blue Sky continued. "But you're also the regent of the kingdom now, whether you wish to be or not. Many lives other than my own are at stake this day."

Gentle Brook and Spring Rain had their arms around one another, both of them weeping.

"Your son is only one human," Blue Sky said to his father. "The kingdom you're taking care of is a great many more humans. The answer to Lightning Spear's demand is simply a matter of addition and subtraction. It doesn't take a Many Numbers to understand that."

"I'd much rather die in battle," Noon Breeze said, "than see you given up as a hostage."

"So would I!" each of the apprentice tellers quickly agreed.

"So would I!" each of the cousins and other warriors yelled.

Blue Sky raised his hand.

"Rather than see again what I saw one recent night," he said, "I'd gladly give myself up as a hostage to the hell-gods themselves."

Long Arm didn't repeat that.

Noon Breeze shook his head once more. "You can't do this," he insisted.

"Yes, I can," Blue Sky said. "I didn't bring you home from the plain, I didn't save your life on sunset pass, just to see you die here."

Long Arm did repeat those remarks for his people.

"If Wandering Star goes back to Lightning Spear alone," Blue Sky said, "a great number of our warriors could die this day. It's not impossible Lightning Spear and Thunder Hunter could also kill all our women and children."

Like Gentle Brook and Spring Rain, Green Field was no longer bothering to stop his tears.

"Even if we repulse them again," Blue Sky said, motioning toward the hill people's army, "consider how many of them will end up dead this day. And who will they be? Brothers, companions, and cousins of the hill people living with us—that's who they'll be. And what possible good will killing them do us? Thunder Hunter might well regain the advantage over Lightning Spear he lost in our last battle down there."

Long Arm dared to repeat those remarks. He even emphasized the last one.

Many Numbers, who was shedding a few tears of his own,

stared at Wandering Star.

"Even if we win today's battle," Blue Sky continued, speaking to his people, "what about the next one and the next one after that? How often will we send warriors to die in this gorge, or somewhere in the mountains? Who'll our farmers be then? The old and the frail? The mothers with children in their arms? Will our livestock, going without proper care, start dying?"

Wandering Star knew Blue Sky had no more choice in this matter than the regent had.

He'd observed the battle on the riverbank. Evening Shadow and Night Whisper had shown Blue Sky from the cliff-top where he'd be. He must've seen Thunder Hunter's warrior kill the two apprentice tellers after the valley warriors had won the battle. He must've seen the valley people taking them back to the upper valley on the raft.

He must've realized then, as Blue Sky did, the valley people couldn't go on. Despite their victory in one more battle, they stood defeated. They had no more stomach for fighting. It was hopeless for them to expect they could ever regain the lower valley. It would take many more warriors than they had, and most of them would be killed.

They suffered two deaths in their last battle, and realized they couldn't take one more. Why should they fool themselves? The gods had placed them, maliciously perhaps, in a world completely unsuited for the kind of people they'd come to imagine they were.

And Wandering Star was offering them his father's generous gift: the upper valley.

He must've gone to Lightning Spear and laid out the reasons for ceding it, no doubt having dreamed up the one-valley excuse for the tellers to bless the move.

Lightning Spear must've given Wandering Star his and Thunder Hunter's conditions. They must've haggled. Blue Sky could see where the line ended up. Although Wandering Star had lost Morning Sun, he'd won the lives of the people Thunder Hunter's warriors would catch trying to reach the upper valley. Thunder Hunter had traded their people's deserters—who were difficult to capture, in any event—for the farmers' prince.

Blue Sky doubted Wandering Star had opposed his being taken

hostage, knowing full well that's what it would take to make the whole thing work. Maybe he'd come up with the idea himself.

Maybe Long Arm had.

"If I leave with Wandering Star," Blue Sky said to his father, "you can send the army home. They can be farmers again. Our people can complete their field work. They can look forward to an abundant summer. They can live in peace in the upper valley for as long as they wish. Maybe even long enough to form an army Lightning Spear and Thunder Hunter will fear to see coming."

Long Arm, as Blue Sky had guessed he'd do, left out his last conjecture.

"Someday," Blue Sky said, "you might find an opportunity to strike a blow."

Long Arm chose not to repeat that remark either.

"What should your father do then?" Many Numbers asked. "Knowing you'll die if the blow is stricken?"

"He should order the blow stricken," Blue Sky replied.

Gentle Brook closed her eyes.

Blue Sky took her hand. "I'll see Rose Leaf and Morning Sun," he said. "I'll beg Lightning Spear to send Morning Sun back to our people. I'll tell Rose Leaf no matter what happens, we'll always love her."

Long Arm repeated only Blue Sky's promises to his mother.

"All three of you," Gentle Brook said, unimpressed by her son's optimism. "Rose Leaf, Morning Sun, and you. All three of you gone. All three of you prisoners of the hill people's king."

Green Field turned to Fair Judge. "Are Gentle Brook and I," he asked, "required to give up our son as a hostage? Are we required to do that for the people?"

"The people," the first teller replied, "can't ask you to give up your son as a hostage."

Long Arm repeated what Fair Judge had said.

"You and I," Blue Sky said to his father, "are the only two people who can say yes to Lightning Spear and stop the war. It's just you and I. Nobody else can tell us what to do."

And nobody disagreed with that.

Perhaps the birds flying above the gorge that morning were gods. Perhaps they had good reason to be singing. Perhaps they loved humans after all.

"Nobody," Blue Sky said to his father, "wants to hear Lightning Spear keeps his promise and kills Morning Sun. But we also know—and Lightning Spear knows—our army can't go get him. So think about it. If Morning Sun dies, I'm first in line to the kingship. If Thunder Hunter's warriors kill me, Early Harvest will probably succeed you as king."

"I'd never wish for such a thing to happen," Early Harvest quickly interjected. "I haven't been taught to rule."

"You could ask others to help you rule," Blue Sky said. "Your cousin Good Harvest. Many Numbers and Spring Rain. Rose Leaf, too, even if she is our enemy's princess."

Long Arm repeated those remarks.

Spring Rain tearfully shook his head at Blue Sky. "You can become Lightning Spear's hostage," he said, "but you can't expect any of us to be happy about it."

"Not when we have to assume," Noon Breeze quickly affirmed, "we'll never see you alive again."

"Warriors," Blue Sky said, "have always had to expect they might never see their comrades alive again. Their people's survival is simply more important than their own."

Blue Sky realized he was sounding like the god of war.

"In the meantime," he added, "they try to remain alive and hope for the best for their people, their comrades, and themselves."

Blue Sky turned to his father, who'd become what their people called the "reluctant regent."

"If I walk down that path with Wandering Star," Blue Sky said, "the kingdom has a great deal to gain. It has nothing but one insignificant person to lose."

Full Harvest could remain silent no longer. "No matter how insignificant you might imagine you are, you're everything to your father and mother. Your death will kill them."

Blue Sky turned to face the enemy army, who'd be compelled to throw themselves at the valley people in the gorge once again if Blue Sky and Green Field didn't submit to Lightning Spear's demand. Blue Sky was saving many of their lives. And he'd be living with them, too.

"Our kingdom," Blue Sky said, "would be wise to accept the great king Lightning Spear's offer and give him what he wants: the regent's son."

Long Arm repeated that in his people's language word for word.

"I see," Spring Rain whispered to Blue Sky through his tears. "I see what you're doing with Wandering Star and Long Arm. You'll get yourself killed, too."

Blue Sky realized touching his lips to Spring Rain's, perhaps never to do it again, would be the most difficult thing he'd attempt that morning. He'd do it anyway—he had no choice.

"What do we do with your son?" Many Numbers asked the regent.

Green Field stared at the only child he'd fathered who'd survived his infancy.

"No parent," the regent spat, "should ever have to do what you're asking me to do."

He looked at Blue Sky as if his son had told him he no longer loved him.

"You're right," Green Field said, punching his fist at the cloudless sky. "The gods are cruel."

And to the hill people who'd insisted the valley people's gods were the hell-gods, he was simply stating the truth of the matter.

"What do we do with your son?" Early Harvest repeated the question, gently.

And Green Field the regent gave his grudging but terse reply.

"Let him go."

RON FRITSCH

Chapter 7

"You knew I couldn't refuse."

Blue Sky said it as soon as they were out of earshot of his people.

"You could've refused," Wandering Star said, "but I knew you wouldn't."

"You knew I'd be a good little boy. Because I can't stand seeing any more people killed."

Wandering Star gave Blue Sky a derisive look.

"Don't delude yourself," he said. "You're not done seeing people killed. You're not done killing them, either. We've got a long way to go for that."

Blue Sky could only frown and shake his head the way his father did—even as he suspected events would prove, once again, his hill companion was right.

Wandering Star turned and glanced back at the gorge.

"Your people," he said, "should never forget what your mother and father are going through today. This is as painful for parents as it gets."

"But you knew, painful or not, it had to be done. Like forcing a broken bone back into place. It was either this, or a lot of people got killed today. I know. My family had to put the people first."

"Your father once told me that's what a ruling family does."

In the fields they were walking past, new clover was flourishing untended.

"When he told you that," Blue Sky said, "it was an easy thing for him to say. He wasn't in a ruling family. And he didn't want any part of ruling."

"And yet, you told everybody, he was in a ruling family, and he did take part in the ruling. And you're in a ruling family yourself. And you can't resist taking part in the ruling either."

*****

In the course of saying his goodbyes in the gorge, Blue Sky had told Noon Breeze he hoped he and their housemates would enjoy their revel that evening.

The apprentice tellers, who'd crowded around them, separating Blue Sky from his mother and father without intending to, moaned a chorus of "No!" and shook their heads.

"Without you," Spring Rain quickly interjected, "I'll sit this one out."

"Don't be silly," Blue Sky said. "You won't have to worry about dying tomorrow or the next day, or even the day after that. It's a perfect occasion for somebody as beautiful as you to celebrate. You can sing, too. Did you know some people think you're the god of love paying a visit to the human world in disguise?"

"We're giving you up as a hostage," Noon Breeze asked, "and we're supposed to celebrate? You brought some of us home from the hills. You saved our lives. Now you're going off to be Lightning Spear's hostage, and we're supposed to sing and dance?"

"Suit yourselves," Blue Sky said. "I'd have a revel, and I'd enjoy every moment of it, too. I only ask you to lift one cup to the regent's son and his pushy hill friend who made it all possible."

"You're a dreamer," Spring Rain said, wiping his eyes with his sleeve. "You dream something good can come from this. The rest of us have to live with reality. Knowing someday we'll find out you're dead. You'll be the warrior I sing about."

Wandering Star, who'd embraced Spring Rain and promised him he'd do everything he could to keep Blue Sky alive, glanced in their direction and smirked.

"I confess I didn't know," he said to the men crowding about them, "your regent's son took part in your revels. I thought he was above that sort of thing."

*****

Blue Sky turned and looked back at the gorge himself.

His people still stood where he'd left them, even the auxiliaries on the cliff-top with their piles of unused tree limbs and rocks. All of them stared down at the lower valley that sad but lovely spring morning when they found themselves reduced to trading their regent's son for what they knew, as well as Wandering Star did, would be a temporary peace.

But what was Blue Sky's frivolous pleasure-seeking life compared to the sum of theirs and their descendants'—not to mention the memory of their ancestors? If somebody had to go away and get himself killed in order to save them, why shouldn't it be the regent's childless son?

"Your two apprentice tellers," Wandering Star said, thrusting into Blue Sky's thoughts like a spear-point. "I understand why you took their deaths so hard. I don't blame you for it."

"Needless. Senseless. Like the war itself."

"They were apprentice tellers. They were supposed to be the first to fall."

"And for what?"

Wandering Star, who was shaking his head then, turned to Blue Sky.

"Why do I still have to explain these things to you?" he asked. "Your people won a great victory."

"What in hell did they win? Imprisonment in their upper valley forever?"

Wandering Star and Blue Sky knew they were making Thunder Hunter and Lightning Spear and their armies, staring at their backs, wait for them.

"Don't you see?" Wandering Star asked. "As long as your people are in your upper valley, Lightning Spear and Thunder Hunter will have to keep an army in the lower valley to stop your people from taking it back. Your people will gather strength as your boys become men—and as more of my people come up here to join you. Someday your people will break out of their prison and chase my people out of the lower valley. Then you'll send your men coming of age to the mountain encampments again. You'll have your whole valley back, just the way you had it before."

"Why can't your people keep an army in the lower valley? An army ready to kill a lot of farmers the moment they come out of the gorge?"

"Year after year? Think about it. Our warriors will eventually run away. Even Thunder Hunter's will. He knows it, too. Especially after that last battle. That's why he wants to resume the war. As soon as he can. To get it over with. And wipe all your people out."

"And my death will help him accomplish that?"

Wandering Star embraced Blue Sky.

"That's why I have to keep you alive," he said.

"My mother and father and Spring Rain will be grateful if you do."

Wandering Star laughed. "Thunder Hunter immediately agreed to your being the hostage. He even praised Lightning Spear for coming up with the idea. He saw how many of our warriors you killed in the gorge and on the pass. He tells his people you don't have human parents. He says the hell-gods must've stolen the regent's infant son and replaced him with one of theirs. They made him grow up thinking he was the brother of our princess. Then they cleverly got him to seduce Lightning Spear's foolish bastard son."

In both people's stories things like that happened—but always in the distant past.

"And it wasn't even Lightning Spear's idea," Blue Sky said. "It was yours."

Wandering Star still had his arm around Blue Sky's shoulders.

"And they never guessed I was doing it all for myself," he said. "As if I could care what happens to either of these kingdoms and their insane wars. I only wanted to go with my big, strong farmer again. And I decided I'd do anything I could to bring that about."

Blue Sky laughed. That made as much sense as anything he'd heard that day.

"Nobody can ever contend," he said, "putting yourself first didn't save a lot of lives."

*****

Lightning Spear and his army were still in the positions they'd taken up before he sent Wandering Star to present his peace terms to Green Field.

The messenger and hostage weren't yet within earshot of the hill people, but they nevertheless used the valley people's words in case some of the hill people could read their lips.

"So Thunder Hunter isn't giving up the upper valley?" Blue

Sky asked. "Any more than my people are giving up the lower valley?"

"Of course not."

"Is Lightning Spear?"

Wandering Star fixed his gaze on his father. "He told me he'd accept your people living in the upper valley permanently. He said he hopes they'll see the wisdom of staying there—and not attacking our people again."

"But he thinks my people will anyway?"

"That's why he truly wishes to keep you alive. That's why he'll make you live with Long Arm's family. The better to keep you from getting yourself killed."

Blue Sky and Wandering Star looked at one another.

Blue Sky spoke first. "I take it you and Long Arm have some kind of agreement."

Wandering Star smiled. "Rose Leaf, Morning Sun, Long Arm, and I have an agreement."

*****

The hill people's army moved south along the river, minus another contingent of Thunder Hunter's warriors left behind to keep the farmers in the upper valley and their own people out.

Blue Sky's status as a prisoner meant that he and Wandering Star walked, conversed, and ate their meals with Long Arm's brothers and cousins and helped them with their chores.

Early in the afternoon, Thunder Hunter's teller nephew True Hunter came by and demanded to know why the brothers and cousins weren't taking the thief hostage at spear-point.

Blue Sky's guards responded with silence, acting as if they hadn't heard the question above the tumult of the march, even after True Hunter asked it again, raising his voice so loudly he alarmed the comrades who were with him.

Blue Sky, who thought the man was exceptionally pleasing to see close up, tried giving him a friendly smile, but it was like throwing dry straw on a wildfire. It only intensified his anger.

True Hunter, who was so muscular he looked as if he never sat or laid down all day or night except to eat and sleep, openly announced he wanted to kill the hostage himself.

In a fair fight, Blue Sky surmised, with neither of them having the advantage of higher ground or falling boulders or trees, True Hunter might very well be able to achieve his goal.

They were headed to the bluff where the valley people's town had been. Lightning Spear had decided it would be the ideal place for him to raise his tents and rule his kingdom.

That explained why one recent evening on the cliff-top, as the farmers waited for the arrival of the hill people's army, they began to see a great deal of campfire smoke near the southern gorge.

Lightning Spear had lost the previous war attempting to storm the bluff and take the town. From spring to autumn that year, the valley people beat back waves of hill warriors coming at them day after day.

Countless valley warriors died defending the town, including the king and one of his sons, Blue Sky's grandfather and uncle, the fathers of Many Numbers and Spring Rain, and Autumn Wine's son. Noon Breeze's father suffered his wounds in the fighting. Many tellers, including Law Keeper's first companion—the only one he'd loved, he often admitted—were killed in those battles. All those lives had been lost, and wounds suffered, for nothing.

*****

When the hill people's army stopped for the first night after leaving the upper gorge, Blue Sky helped Wandering Star pitch his tent at the closed end of a peninsula the river created by making a sharp bend to the west followed by another abrupt turn back to the east. On three sides they had the river nobody could've crossed without being seen. On the fourth side, between them and the rest of the army, they had Long Arm's people.

As soon as they finished the job, Long Arm came to sit outside the tent with them. They spoke in the valley people's language. The only hill warriors who could understand them were the younger tellers who'd learned it surreptitiously from Wandering Star, as Evening Shadow and Night Whisper had, and Long Arm's brothers and cousins who'd picked it up from Rose Leaf and Morning Sun. The tellers allied with Wandering Star couldn't chance being seen with him or Blue Sky publicly and were deliberately staying away from them. In any event, Long Arm's kin wouldn't let anybody outside their family near their tent.

"We agreed the war had to be stopped," Long Arm said to Blue Sky.

"'We,'" Blue Sky asked, "being you, Rose Leaf, Morning Sun, and Wandering Star?"

"Yes," Long Arm replied, in his matter-of-fact monotone. "We agreed your people and our people must stop killing each other. One reason is, we don't want any more killing. The other reason is, if it goes on, Thunder Hunter and his sons will win everything."

Long Arm's family had raised their and Lightning Spear's tents where the valley people's courtyard used to be. Rose Leaf and Morning Sun had suggested the location.

The king's retinue—the lesser chieftains, their chief warriors, the first and high tellers and their acolytes—soon fell into line. Their supposed importance in the kingdom dictated the proximity of their tents to the king's. In the event of disputes—and there were always far too many—Lightning Spear himself, given the gravity of the matter, had to decide who should be closer and who, regrettably, more distant.

"You'll enjoy living with these people," Wandering Star promised Blue Sky.

Long Arm wasn't so flippant in his view of the matter. He told Blue Sky it was no surprise a king who concerned himself with that kind of squabbling had no time for, interest in, or energy to waste upon ordinary people.

"I notice," the hostage said to Long Arm, "your people's rightful king, however poorly he rules his kingdom, isn't a party to your agreement with Rose Leaf, Wandering Star, and Morning Sun. But doesn't he decide when and why your people go to war?"

"Don't your people," Wandering Star asked Blue Sky, before the chief warrior had a chance to answer, "sometimes take decisions away from their rulers?"

"My people sometimes do that," Blue Sky replied. "Are your people stopping the war?"

Long Arm didn't hesitate. "More than anything else, our

people need leaders."

"To lead them where?" Blue Sky asked.

"To live in peace with your people," Long Arm replied. "Lightning Spear made an unforgivable mistake. He not only invited Thunder Hunter into the war but also let him take it over. You saw it yourself that day on the plain. Thunder Hunter's warriors killed every tenth of our warriors who'd refused to attack your people—because they knew your warriors would surely kill most of them. Lightning Spear should've known what would happen after he let Thunder Hunter do that."

"Without Thunder Hunter's warriors," Blue Sky said, "Lightning Spear might not have won the battle on the plain."

"Lightning Spear didn't win that battle," Long Arm countered. "Your people killed too many of our warriors. Thunder Hunter lost very few of his. He won the battle on the plain."

"Lightning Spear," Wandering Star added, "left his and the lesser chieftains' tribes to the mercy of Thunder Hunter's warriors. Our people never liked their king. They paid tribute to him—and all they got out of it was the positioning of the tents of his favorites. Now they despise him. Many of his own people want to see him dead."

"We never should've fought the battle on the plain," Long Arm said. "We never should've started this damned war."

No matter how stridently the three individuals speaking together that evening now opposed a meaningless war, they were the same people who'd started it.

"What should Lightning Spear have done?" Blue Sky asked the man whose prisoner he'd become. "Once he had his daughter back? And my people's prince with her because he loved her?"

"He should've listened to you," Long Arm replied. "You offered to let our people hunt in the forest and fish in the river. That's all we ever needed. He could've claimed he'd won the whole valley back for our people. Both parts of it. He didn't have to insist on your people leaving it."

Blue Sky stared at him. "Are you willing to let my people come back to the lower valley?"

"Why not?" Lightning Spear's chief warrior asked.

"And let us peacefully grow our crops," Blue Sky asked, "raise our livestock, and rebuild our houses and barns?"

"Why not?" Long Arm asked once more. "As long as my people can hunt in the forest and fish in the river?"

"Does your agreement with Rose Leaf and Morning Sun include that?"

Long Arm glanced at Wandering Star, who, knowing what was to come, laughed.

"It does," Long Arm replied. "Except that some of my people might want to grow crops and raise livestock themselves."

"The agreement includes that, too," Wandering Star took pleasure in saying.

Long Arm looked at his prisoner again.

"Nobody listened to Wandering Star," he said. "I refused to myself. He said our people have to go out and find what they need to stay alive. Sometimes they don't, and they die. Your people grow what you need and always have it near you. Everybody else said he didn't know what he was talking about. The high tellers said he was the abomination you'd expect to result from Lightning Spear's giving tribute to go with Dancing Song. The gods had sent Wandering Star to us as our punishment for that."

Wandering Star—a being like Blue Sky with hell-gods for parents who'd met his true brother in a gully and, with their first kiss, brought down two kingdoms—laughed again.

"Then Rose Leaf and Morning Sun came to us," Long Arm continued—somewhat under-emphasizing his own role in their journey. "They convinced us Wandering Star was right all along. Our people never needed to go to war with your people. It was all over nothing that mattered—just a meaningless boundary in the mountains."

Blue Sky put his hand on Long Arm's shoulder.

"Since Morning Sun was a party to that agreement with you," he said, "his people who know about it are bound by it. That includes me now."

Wandering Star smiled. That was the way both the hill and valley tellers talked, much to the amusement of their peoples.

"But even if I had a choice in the matter," Blue Sky added, "I'd wish to be a party to your agreement."

133

*****

After bathing in the river and doing what they most needed to do that evening, Wandering Star and Blue Sky sat naked on the riverbank outside their tent. The night sky was clouding over. The wind was from the south, blowing up a storm.

"Many Numbers asked me if I had an agreement with Long Arm," Wandering Star said. "I told him who the parties to it were. He said he'd pass that information on to your father and mother. But I also told him they might want only a few of your people knowing about it yet."

"It's that hill boy running home," Blue Sky said. "You don't want him to find out."

"I promised Many Numbers they'd hear from us," Wandering Star continued. "In the meantime, they might not want to put your life in jeopardy. That would happen if Thunder Hunter found out Rose Leaf, Long Arm, and Lightning Spear's bastard son were traitors plotting with the farmers. All our lives would be in jeopardy. That wouldn't help your people."

Wandering Star turned to Blue Sky, lightning flashing above his head.

"We've got everybody stopped in their tracks," he said, "as long as Thunder Hunter's warriors don't get their hands on you. We've bought some time, and that's what we need most."

The lightning was coming closer.

"I understand," Wandering Star continued, "you, Many Numbers, and Early Harvest were running things in the upper valley."

"Who told you that?"

Wandering Star snickered. "All your people I spoke with told me that."

"That's a bit simplistic," Blue Sky said. "My father listens to Many Numbers and Early Harvest. He listens to his son, too—and a lot of other people."

"Your father is wise," Wandering Star said. "Maybe someday his son will be, too."

"My father wasn't convinced that last battle on the riverfront was either necessary or wise. He told me we weren't taking into consideration what might happen if we lost it. I told him we had no need to consider losing the battle. That was only, I had the nerve to say, for cowards. I've always treated my father badly. He was so gigantic in my mind—the great hero of the last war with the hill people. And yet I've always wanted to outdo him. I'm that insane."

The wind was rising.

"But your people fought the battle anyway," Wandering Star said.

"We forced my father into it. He knew we were going to fight it whether he went along with it or not. He did go along with it, though. He legitimized what the people had gotten themselves swept up in. He also took full responsibility for what could and did happen."

The families of the two dead apprentice tellers were in the gorge when Blue Sky said his goodbyes. He embraced them all—their aunts, uncles, and cousins included.

"Isn't it strange?" Wandering Star asked. "In the stories our peoples will tell, your father will get the credit for winning that battle—and making Thunder Hunter agree to stop the war."

All that afternoon they'd passed the remnants of villages the hill warriors had put to the torch the previous autumn. In most cases only ashes remained. Here and there, though, parts of charred walls were still standing. Whenever Thunder Hunter's warriors passed near one, they demolished it.

Not unlike boys, Blue Sky thought, snuffing out the life of a hapless toad or hare just to amuse themselves. Boys who were angry because they hadn't gotten their way.

"That's how I'd want the stories told," Blue Sky said.

"I would, too," Wandering Star agreed. "Your father wisely let you, Many Numbers, and Early Harvest have your way. That's how he won. That's how he'll be remembered."

*****

Wandering Star found out, with the rain pounding on his tent, what Spring Rain, Noon Breeze, Many Numbers, and all the apprentice tellers knew: Blue Sky woke at least once every night sobbing and, left to himself, couldn't stop.

Whatever had happened to his mind, Blue Sky could tell, the battle on the riverbank had only made worse.

It was like a final wound a warrior knew he'd never survive.

Chapter 8

Late in the afternoon of the third full day of walking down the valley from the upper gorge, Long Arm's men, Wandering Star, and the hostage arrived on the bluff where the valley people's town used to be. New vegetation—a lot of it wheat and barley where the granaries had stood—was already growing among the ashes.

Second Brother took Blue Sky to Morning Sun's tent.

They found the farmers' prince and the children of Long Arm and his brothers engaged in a spear-throwing contest. When Morning Sun's turn came, he deliberately threw his spear so short even the youngest of the children had outdone him. Although his opponents laughed at first, they soon decided they wouldn't allow such a weak effort to count. They insisted he throw his spear again.

The prince looked up just then and saw Blue Sky coming toward them.

"Farmer boy," he said in the valley people's language.

"Farmer boy," some of his opponents repeated, looking at Blue Sky, using the valley people's word for "farmer" together with their own for "boy."

Morning Sun had told them in their language what a "farmer boy" was. He'd also told them such a person, a boyhood friend of his, would arrive when Lightning Spear and the warriors returned.

"He isn't a boy," one of the younger girls protested.

"He's the hostage," an older brother or cousin said, silencing the others.

Wandering Star had told Blue Sky what the children knew: when Lightning Spear and his warriors returned with the farmers' hostage, something bad would happen to Morning Sun, and not even Long Arm could stop it. Thunder Hunter had insisted upon it. The king had agreed to it.

"Even I could do better than that," Blue Sky said to Morning Sun, in the hill people's language. "Your opponents tried their best. Why can't you? Aren't you supposed to be a prince?"

His opponents laughed.

For his reply, Morning Sun simply threw the spear with all his might.

His opponents were duly impressed with the margin of the

farmer prince's victory, some of them venturing to say only Long Arm, the father of some of them and the uncle of the others, could throw a spear that far. And even he might end up losing to the farmers' prince.

First Brother, Second Brother, War Cloud, and True Hunter— all hard-bodied, tall, and practiced—could only hope to come close to them.

When Second Brother informed the opponents they'd finished their games for the day and needed to return to their chores, the older boys were especially reluctant to end their talk with the farmers' prince and hostage.

Morning Sun had told them Blue Sky had occasionally beaten him at spear-throwing.

The boys nevertheless obeyed Second Brother and went back to work. Long Arm had told them the purpose of their labor was nothing less than setting an example for all their people.

Someday, he said, it could save them from their indolent king, the ill-tempered but weak man they were required to wait upon—and the people were incredibly required to obey, as if he were a god.

*****

Blue Sky waited until the boys were out of sight before he looked at Morning Sun again.

They'd both bravely held back their tears.

"I made a terrible mistake," Blue Sky said, blubbering.

Morning Sun shook his head. "What was your mistake?"

"I didn't see the danger," Blue Sky replied. "I was careless. With you. With everybody."

"We were all careless," Morning Sun was quick to add. "We didn't take seriously the people roaming the hills beyond our mountains. They were beneath our contempt. We thought our men who'd most recently come of age only had to intimidate them in the encampments in the mountains. You were the only one who thought differently. You were the only one who guessed the truth."

Those words failed to stop Blue Sky's tears.

138

"I might've thought differently," he said, "but I hardly knew the truth. If I had, I wouldn't have done anything to put you and Rose Leaf in danger."

Morning Sun shook his head again. "What does it matter now?" he asked. "The important thing is our people are safe in the upper valley. You kept our people alive."

"I didn't do that," Blue Sky said, wiping his tears. "I was one warrior among many."

Morning Sun laughed. "That isn't what the hill people say. They tell me my farmer boy fights as if he's crazed. They say he yells at his comrades all the while. And they always do what he tells them to do. They say he's killed way too many of their warriors. Far more than his share."

"We all fight like we're crazed," Blue Sky countered. "Fighting in a war is the most disgusting thing a person can do. People in their right mind can't do it."

"The hill people also tell me," Morning Sun continued, "you single-handedly stopped the battle on sunset pass. They say one of our warriors had gone too far down the slope. And that same man had told Lightning Spear to go to hell."

"In both cases," Blue Sky confirmed, "that warrior was Noon Breeze."

"They say other warriors followed him. You yourself did, to save him from the hill warriors. Then you saw what was happening. You ordered both sides to stop. You gave the order in both languages. They say they'd never seen anything like that before. Both sides obeyed you. They withdrew. The battle was over. There was no more killing that day. Many hill people are grateful to you for that."

"All both sides needed was a moment to see they'd have no advantage if the fighting went on. Not fighting in crevices. Not fighting around blind corners. Not fighting on that damned mountain-side anymore. They could all see quitting was a better idea. I didn't make them quit."

"You merely brought it to their attention quitting was a good idea? Is that what you did?"

Morning Sun ran his hand up and down Blue Sky's left arm.

"The hill people told me you broke it," he said. "Long Arm set it for you. And the mighty farmer-boy warrior screamed and passed

139

out. While two armies watched."

Now that the court was ashes, Blue Sky could see the river from what used to be his people's courtyard. He could follow it with his eyes, like a bird, all the way to the lower gorge.

"I'm glad about one thing," he said. "You didn't have to fight in those battles."

Morning Sun looked at Blue Sky and embraced him.

"Farmer boy," he said, "when we were younger, I would've told you not to cry."

"And I," Blue Sky said, hesitating precariously throughout his response, "would've told you the same thing. But neither of us, no matter what we say, will stop this time."

*****

"My mother?" Morning Sun asked. "How is she?"

They were sitting on a flattened log outside Morning Sun's tent drinking wine, not far from the place where the king, queen, and prince had sat during ceremonies in the courtyard, all of them wearing the river people's linen Rainbow Evening favored.

"She misses you and Rose Leaf," Blue Sky replied. "She lives in a house with Fair Judge. My mother and father are next door."

"She's well?"

"She's well."

Being a farmer boy, Blue Sky had never understood Rainbow Evening's liking for linen. He'd recently allowed himself to think, though, it might've been her answer to Sturdy Limb's brutality, even perhaps to war itself. She'd let Blue Sky know, when he was becoming a man, how much she enjoyed the time she spent with Fair Judge, Spring Rain, and Many Numbers.

She'd asked Spring Rain to spend a year of his life with Blue Sky in his encampment and introduce that son of dreamers to the real world—which Green Field and Gentle Brook, safe in their village with the love of all the people behind them, hadn't acquainted him with.

Morning Sun touched the sleeve of his shirt against Blue Sky's cheek.

"Why are you crying now?" he asked.

"Your mother isn't well," Blue Sky said, taking back his lie. "She refuses to come out of the house she lives in. The only persons she'll talk with are Fair Judge, my parents, Spring Rain, Many Numbers, and me. She says that's because we were the only persons who opposed going to war with the hill people—the only persons who opposed putting your life in jeopardy. She's right about that. Nobody else agreed with us. We failed. No matter how much the people favored us, we were strangely alone. We opposed a war that would surely bring an end to our people's problem with the hill people forever. And it would save you and Rose Leaf. We failed to convince the people it was a mistake. It was the seven of us against everybody else. And look where it brought us, against our will?"

Both of their faces were wet again.

"People say she's losing her mind," Blue Sky said. "But I think we're all losing our minds. Too many people have died. She knows what danger you're in, what Rose Leaf might have to do. Who can blame her if she's lost her mind? I admit I've lost my own."

Morning Sun wiped his eyes and straightened himself up.

"People have to realize," he said, "if I die tomorrow, it's because I'm the prince. I didn't ask to be the prince. But that's just the way it is. They have to accept it. And go on from there."

"I'll sure as hell," Blue Sky declared, despite the cracking of his voice, "try to stop it."

Morning Sun embraced him again.

"Please don't do that," he said. "Save yourself. You, Rose Leaf, Wandering Star, and Long Arm can change things. Let Thunder Hunter have me killed if that's what it takes."

"Lightning Spear told Wandering Star he'll see us," Blue Sky said. "We're going with Rose Leaf and Long Arm. The four of us will beg him to spare your life."

Morning Sun shook his head. "It won't do any good. I've heard what you'll offer him. He'll never accept it. Long Arm says it's hopeless. So does Wandering Star. They know Lightning Spear better than anybody else."

He embraced Blue Sky a third time.

"Thank you anyway for trying," he added.

"If Lightning Spear has you killed tomorrow," Blue Sky said, his hands on Morning Sun's shoulders, his voice no longer quavering, "I promise you we'll make him pay for it. Rose Leaf, Wandering Star, Long Arm, and I. You can be certain I'll be present the moment he dies. I can only hope I'll be the one who kills him."

"Farmer boy," the prince said, "I didn't mean to get you into this."

"You didn't get me into anything. We all got into it the moment we were born."

Morning Sun looked at Blue Sky, a wan smile flickering across his face.

"Maybe that means we can hope to get out of it again," he said, "the moment we die."

*****

"Wandering Star said Long Arm lets you see Rose Leaf," Blue Sky said.

Morning Sun smiled. "Long Arm and his family have taken great risks in handling their prisoners so gently. Lightning Spear would have to come down hard on them if Thunder Hunter's people found out what they're doing. Lightning Spear gave Rose Leaf to Dark Storm. He publicly ordered Long Arm not to let her see me. Don't ever forget how kind Long Arm and his family have been to both Rose Leaf and me. Promise me you won't."

Wandering Star had told Blue Sky that Morning Sun and Rose Leaf saw each other every day, almost since the night they were abducted. It was always in Morning Sun's tent, the inside of which was much more orderly than Blue Sky would've expected it to be. Long Arm's people had given him enough furs for two people to sleep on. The prince had learned how to clean them.

Long Arm and his brothers and their mates made sure nobody else could see where Rose Leaf was going to or coming from. It was usually after dark. She often stayed with Morning Sun the entire night.

Long Arm's family never talked about it. Some of the older children probably suspected the truth, as Blue Sky had regarding his mother and Full Harvest. Children learned it was sometimes best not to speak of certain things they weren't supposed to know.

"She just comes to my tent," Morning Sun said. "She just does it. She's their princess. They do what she wants them to do."

Long Arm's great moment of glory among his people, as well as his deep regret for what he'd done to earn it, had arrived together in his life like twin children.

"Did you know," Blue Sky asked, "Early Harvest was in love with Rose Leaf?"

"That other farmer boy," Morning Sun said, laughing. "My rival. Yes, I knew. He told me he'd promised Rose Leaf he'd go to a lower-valley encampment if she'd come to see him."

"He still tells our people Rose Leaf wasn't wrong for choosing you instead of him. He still insists your being prince didn't have anything to do with it."

Morning Sun took a drink of his wine. "He would say that. Rose Leaf and I were damned glad when we heard you and Wandering Star got him back from the plain alive."

Rose Leaf and Morning Sun had taught Long Arm's family how to make wine. They all drank it, too, despite the prohibition Lightning Spear had laid down during the last war.

"The hill people talk about him, too," Morning Sun said. "They say the tall, left-handed farmer kills a lot of their warriors—although not nearly as many as the regent's son does."

Blue Sky told Morning Sun he and the other farmer boy had shown the people, including their fathers, how adults could ride horses, even when they were running as fast as they could.

Well before Blue Sky was done explaining how that had happened, the prince was wiping his tears again with his sleeve.

*****

Although the warriors loyal to the king and the lesser chieftains still outnumbered Thunder Hunter's, Long Arm's people believed the second most powerful chieftain would win a civil war.

And a civil war was what it would take to keep Morning Sun from dying the next day.

Lightning Spear and the lesser chieftains had lost too many of their warriors. And after the upper-valley debacles the farmers had inflicted upon them, many of those still able to fight had lost any desire to do so again.

And even if Lightning Spear did win such a war, Wandering Star said, the number of warriors slaughtered on both sides would easily surpass the number killed on the plain.

Morning Sun had decided—and he'd gotten Rose Leaf to reluctantly agree with him—they should do nothing to instigate such a war.

"Go ahead and cry," Morning Sun said.

He was looking at Blue Sky through new tears of his own.

"At least I'm drinking wine with you one last time," the prince said.

"We can attempt an escape," Blue Sky said. "Our fathers did. We're not even tied up. We'll take Rose Leaf with us, too. the same as they did. Wandering Star told me he'll go with us. He'll help us all the way, if that's what you and Rose Leaf want. We'll take his mother as well. With a head start and a little luck, we might make it through the forest to the upper valley."

Morning Sun shook his head. "Wandering Star is kind," he allowed. "But don't consider doing that. If we got away with it, Long Arm would go from being a hero to a villain. We'd undo everything he's done—getting Rose Leaf back, capturing the farmer's prince, separating their people's warriors. Thunder Hunter would be free to kill his entire family, the old men, women, and children included. Did Wandering Star tell you that?"

"He said it was something that might happen."

"There's not a chance it wouldn't happen. Lightning Spear would have to let Thunder Hunter's warriors kill them all. And our people would be stuck in the upper valley forever. Fighting battle after battle to keep the hill people out."

Wandering Star had specifically warned Blue Sky about that, too. But the choice wasn't Wandering Star's or Blue Sky's to make. It was Morning Sun's.

"It'll just be something that happened," the prince said. "Everybody will get over it. It'll just be the way things turned out for us."

"I'm supposed to stand there tomorrow and watch you get killed?"

"That's right. You're a brave farmer boy. You can do that."

"Brave?" Blue Sky asked, pointing at his own face. "Do you see these tears?"

"I see them, but they'll go away. They'll dry up. They always do."

The prince extended his arm around Blue Sky as if the farmer boy were the one who was condemned to die the next day.

"Rose Leaf and Long Arm can change everything," he said. "If you and Wandering Star help them. You can change everything for our people and theirs."

Blue Sky was in the position his father was in at the gorge.

"And you surely don't want to find out," Morning Sun said, "Thunder Hunter's warriors killed Long Arm's family and all their children."

As if Blue Sky were an ox in need of some coaxing, the prince was squeezing his neck.

"Promise me one thing," Morning Sun said. "Don't cause any trouble for Long Arm's family."

The prince was laying down the same ultimatum the regent's son had given his father in the upper gorge: take the deal, as unpalatable as it was personally, and save the people.

Second Brother's older children brought the prince hot water for a bath.

As soon as his eyes fell on them, Blue Sky knew he couldn't wish to cause them any harm.

As difficult as it might be for him to do so, he realized he'd have to behave himself for them.

He'd get back, though, at the vicious gods who'd put Morning Sun, Rose Leaf, and him where they were. He'd remove them from their preposterous heaven. He'd henceforth openly declare beings so evil couldn't possibly exist, and everything in this world that happened to humans came about either by chance or through their own, often inept, conniving.

Rose Leaf was coming to Morning Sun's tent that night, perhaps for the last time.

For the people, Blue Sky had agreed to become a hostage.

145

Morning Sun had agreed to die.

*****

Second Brother took Blue Sky to Rose Leaf's tent.

More than three seasons had passed since he'd last seen her.

Her brave attempt at a smile gave way to tears as soon as she saw his.

They and Morning Sun were all within the courtyard of their childhood again.

But the court was gone. The town was gone. The buildings were ashes. Far too many of their people were dead.

Blue Sky and Rose Leaf embraced, neither of them saying a word.

Blue Sky knew the tears would come. Their growing up with Morning Sun the prince had come to this. The gods, assuming they existed, had somehow transmuted that heaven into this hell.

Rose Leaf stepped back and looked at the youth she and he'd believed was her brother.

"I've heard the story the people tell," she said. "My farmer brother blames himself for what happened. I wish you didn't. I wish my hill brother didn't blame himself, either. Neither you nor he nor Morning Sun nor I harmed one person. It's the war that shouldn't have happened. And we didn't make it happen. Lightning Spear, Thunder Hunter, Tall Oak, and Sturdy Limb did."

Blue Sky knew he'd blame himself for what happened until the moment he died.

"What did it matter," Rose Leaf continued, "if the hill people took Morning Sun and me away? I would've survived. I was their king's daughter. Morning Sun might've survived. If Tall Oak and Sturdy Limb had stayed home and defended the valley, what good would it have done Lightning Spear to kill the farmers' prince? Why wouldn't he keep him alive just to see what might happen? To see if he could get something—anything—for him?"

He could've at least gotten the valley people's agreement not to harass or kill the hill people's hunters who ventured too close to the

146

encampments in the mountains.

"Wandering Star told me what happened," Rose Leaf said. "You, our parents, Rainbow Evening, Fair Judge, Many Numbers, and Spring Rain opposed attacking the hill people."

"And nobody else agreed with us."

"Long Arm's people told me my farmer brother almost got himself killed before the battle on the plain. I understand my hill brother had to beg our father for your life."

Not one person Blue Sky had taken leave of in the upper gorge had failed to ask him to let Rose Leaf and Morning Sun know they loved them both and would never forget them.

Long Arm's people said Lightning Spear never complained about the time Blue Sky was taking.

Thunder Hunter, his sons, and their cousins, though, loudly demanded to know why the regent's son thought he could keep their entire army waiting. Was it really necessary for him to speak with and embrace every last person in his damned kingdom?

Lightning Spear knew what he was doing. If the valley people cared for Blue Sky as much as they seemed to, they'd never do anything to cause his death. Lightning Spear's warriors could see for themselves the regent's son was the perfect hostage.

Rose Leaf wept again when Blue Sky told her about Rainbow Evening, who was still wearing linen long after everybody else had put theirs away.

She smiled, though, when he told her Early Harvest and Good Harvest had discovered, as they and the prince had, that Green Field's rule against older children and adults riding the horses made no sense.

Somewhere along the way, Blue Sky assumed, Rose Leaf must've realized she'd have to choose between Morning Sun and Early Harvest. It must've been difficult to turn Early Harvest down.

"Now all our people are riding the horses?" she asked.

"All the time. Every excuse they can invent."

Blue Sky told her the celebrations following the birth of a foal had begun to rival those attending the delivery of a child.

Rose Leaf once again wiped her eyes.

"I can't help it," she said. "I miss our people. Our horses, too."

*****

As soon as his visitors sat down, Lightning Spear surprised Blue Sky by asking him if the hill people were treating him well.

"There's no reason you shouldn't enjoy living with us," the king said. "As long as you stay with Long Arm's people, of course. And make no attempt to escape."

"I won't try to escape," Blue Sky promised.

"The tellers have given me their advice," Lightning Spear continued. "They say I can permit a hostage and an exile to share a tent in my encampment. If that's what you and Wandering Star wish to do."

Only a teller with the learning of a Fair Judge, Many Numbers, Spring Rain, or Wandering Star could say for certain, but Blue Sky suspected neither people had a single story involving a hostage and an exile who wished to share living quarters in a king's encampment or court.

Wandering Star had insisted upon the arrangement as a means to keep Blue Sky safe from Thunder Hunter's warriors. Although Heaven's Voice and the high tellers despised Wandering Star and had made it known they were scandalized by his going with a farmer, Lightning Spear must've tipped them off in advance not to oppose him in this matter.

"That's my wish," Blue Sky affirmed.

"As long as you obey Long Arm," Lightning Spear added. "The tellers say I have to put both of you in his care as if you're children. So Long Arm will now act as your father."

Blue Sky smiled at that. "I'll be happy to obey Long Arm in everything I do."

"As will I," Wandering Star added.

Too bad Noon Breeze and the apprentice tellers weren't present to hear those remarks. They'd already agreed Long Arm was most pleasing to see—and what a fortunate woman his mate was. But the day they were caked with blood and dust in the upper gorge, and he walked among the hill warriors barking orders at them to keep them from killing one another, they whispered their everlasting love for him, their willingness to do anything he might ask them to do.

148

Blue Sky thought Lightning Spear's tent was considerably grander than it had any reason to be. The hill people had contributed far too many hides to a dwelling for one person. Thistle Dew had long since taken to her own tent, which was considerably more modest than the king's.

In it Rose Leaf had introduced Blue Sky and Thistle Dew. The hill people's queen seemed pleased he was her daughter's brother when Rose Leaf lived among the valley people.

Blue Sky was no less pleased Thistle Dew the defiant was Rose Leaf's hill mother.

Blue Sky knew many of the valley people, perhaps a majority of the farmers, had thought the luxury of Tall Oak's court was unjustified. Blue Sky had also come to understand, though, a people might wish to provide abundantly for a good and wise king and his family simply to show their gratitude for what royalty had to go through. But however much the people provided, it would all be a waste if the ruler was neither good nor wise.

"I bear no grudge toward you personally," Lightning Spear said. "Wandering Star told me you opposed your people's attack on our people. As did your father and mother and others close to you. You may see Rose Leaf as often as you wish. I realize you and she were raised as brother and sister. She's convinced me you didn't know the truth of the matter. She also tells me your parents were good to her. I'm grateful to them for that."

Propped up with furs at his back and beneath him, the king sat cross-legged on his side of the low table where he took his meals. His daughter, son, chief warrior, and hostage were sitting in a semicircle across the table from him, on the deep piles of furs provided for the king's visitors.

The entrance flaps at both ends of the tent were open. The red after-sunset sky above the mountains behind Lightning Spear seemed to smolder like a distant dying fire.

The king continued staring at his hostage. "I'm sure you've heard my people say Rose Leaf and Wandering Star are sister and brother. I'm supposedly the father of both of them."

Lightning Spear's notorious refusal to speak publicly of his paternity of Wandering Star amused the hill people. What, they wondered aloud, laughing, was the point of any further secrecy regarding the subject?

"Did you know," Lightning Spear asked, "I favor Wandering Star because he's my son?"

Blue Sky decided he was supposed to laugh at that. He had no trouble doing so.

The favors Lightning Spear's supposed son appreciated the most were the king's orders expelling him from the tellerhood and sending him into exile—to say nothing of his father's later refusal to let War Cloud kill Blue Sky.

The king continued. "That's what the people of my kingdom say about me behind my back. They like to have fun at my expense. I indulge them. I long ago decided a good king pays no attention to that sort of thing. They think I gave part of my tribute to go with Dancing Song."

Blue Sky bestowed upon the king the friendly smile True Hunter had rejected outright.

"Wandering Star tells me you've met his mother," Lightning Spear said.

Lightning Spear glanced at Wandering Star and snickered.

"Little do they know," the king said. "She would've gone with me without the tribute."

He looked at Blue Sky again and laughed.

"At least, that's what she told me," he added.

Blue Sky didn't hesitate. "She led me to believe that, too."

The king, caught unawares by Blue Sky's remark, gave his hostage an appreciative wink.

The king's visitors could see his guards, cousins of Long Arm's, in the twilight. When Lightning Spear met privately in his tent with his subjects, he required his guards to remain a specified distance away. Wandering Star said it was just beyond where a person with even the best ears could hear what the king and his visitors were saying.

"Father," Rose Leaf said, unwilling to dally any longer, "we've come here to beg you to let the farmers' prince live."

Lightning Spear glared at Rose Leaf. He'd known this was coming.

"I can't do that," he said.

"A king," Rose Leaf countered, "can do anything he pleases."

Most of the valley people—Blue Sky's family always included—openly laughed whenever they heard some toady make a remark like that to Tall Oak.

"If you let Morning Sun go back to his people," Rose Leaf continued, "I promise you I'll never try to see him again. I'll gladly become Dark Storm's mate. I'll bear his children. I'll even promise you won't have to order your warriors to hold me down."

"The farmers' prince," Lightning Spear mused, glancing at his hostage. "I do feel sorry for him. Our people all say he's a fine man. I truly regret he has to die."

"He doesn't have to die," Rose Leaf persisted.

"I promised his father," Lightning Spear came back, "his son would die if he attacked us. His father chose to attack us. I promised Thunder Hunter the enemy prince would die at the end of the war. We fought the war to a successful conclusion. So now the time has come for the farmers' prince to die. I keep my word. I'm very sorry. There's no alternative."

Lightning Spear looked at Blue Sky again.

"Wandering Star tells me," he said, "Morning Sun, Rose Leaf, and you were childhood friends. It's a shame he was your prince and not just another boy. It isn't easy being a prince or a king in this world. Nobody knows that better than I do."

"If Morning Sun returns to our people," Blue Sky said, "he'll become their king. If you let him return, he'll also abdicate."

"Abdicate?" Lightning Spear asked. "Why would he do that? Even if he did, what good would that do me—or my people? Wandering Star told me your father is next in line to the kingship after the prince. Wouldn't he just become king instead of regent? Wouldn't everything be the same as it is now?"

"My father would also abdicate," Blue Sky replied. "So would I. So would all our people known to be in the line to the kingship."

Lightning Spear stared at Blue Sky in disbelief.

"Why would your father do such a thing?" he asked. "Why would you and the others?"

"We'd all abdicate," Blue Sky replied, "in your favor."

Lightning Spear couldn't take his eyes off his hostage.

"In my favor?" he asked. "You'd make me your people's king?"

"Our people would accept you as their king," Blue Sky said. "They'd acknowledge your dominion over the entire valley—both valleys."

"You'd be the king," Wandering Star said to his father, "of the lower valley and the upper valley."

"And the farmers?" Lightning Spear asked. "What would become of them?"

"They'd remain where they are," Blue Sky replied. "In the upper valley."

Long Arm had initially doubted the farmers would ever agree to what Blue Sky proposed.

"They'd accept their enemy's king as their own king?" he'd asked.

Rose Leaf and Wandering Star, though, had no such doubts.

The valley people's rejection of Blue Sky's proposal would've condemned Morning Sun to death. Blue Sky couldn't imagine even one of them speaking against it.

"I," Lightning Spear asked, "would rule farmers?"

"Why not?" Wandering Star asked.

"Farmers are evil," Lightning Spear replied. "They do the hell-gods' work."

"Some of our tellers say that," Wandering Star said. "Our gods don't."

"Our gods speak of the people as hunters," Lightning Spear countered. "They never describe them as farmers."

"There was obviously a time," Wandering Star said, "when everybody hunted and nobody farmed. In those days, when the gods still spoke to us, they had no need to speak of farmers. Then somebody somewhere learned how to farm."

"Nobody farmed," Lightning Spear repeated. "The tellers say that's what the gods wanted. That's why nobody farmed."

Long Arm was shaking his head.

He reminded Blue Sky of his own people listening to the tellers debate the wisdom, virtues, and other eccentricities of the gods and

152

goddesses. Anybody could see on the listeners' faces their disappointment in being reminded that, whoever was right, it would have no bearing on the abundance of their harvest or the plenitude of their livestock.

Lightning Spear laughed. "I'd settle disputes among farmers?"

"They could settle their own disputes," Blue Sky said.

"Thunder Hunter's people do," Long Arm interjected.

"Morning Sun or my father would be their chieftain," Blue Sky continued. "You could overrule them if you wished. But how often would you need to or want to?"

"Our people," Long Arm said, "could hunt in the upper valley, too."

"There's a lake where the river begins," Blue Sky said. "Wherever on its shore you stand, you can scarcely see the opposite shore. Some of your fishing people who live with us now have an encampment near it. They tell me the lake is well-stocked with fish. I've eaten their fish with them on numerous occasions. Your people are happy living there. Some of the farmers trade them grain and wine for their fish."

One evening on the way from the upper gorge Long Arm's people had made a meal of fish they'd caught in the river. In the course of the supper, Blue Sky mentioned the lake and the hill people encamped upon its shore.

He immediately faced a barrage of questions. To a person, Long Arm's brothers and cousins wanted to see for themselves what he'd described, leaving Blue Sky to wonder if they doubted such a place existed except in his tortured mind.

"My people's army," Blue Sky said to Lightning Spear, "will also fight on your side."

Lightning Spear stared at Blue Sky.

"Who'll be on the other side?" he asked.

"Thunder Hunter," Long Arm quickly replied.

"We've learned his desertion rate has gone up," Rose Leaf added, surprising her father, who turned his gaze to her. "Especially since the farmers wiped out his encampment at the gorge. He'd be a fool if he tried to fight both your warriors and the farmers at the same time. He'd soon realize he and his sons would all end up dead."

Lightning Spear turned again to Long Arm as if his daughter

hadn't spoken.

"Why," he asked, "would I wish to fight Thunder Hunter?"

"It's quite simple," Rose Leaf replied for Long Arm. "Your people hate him and his warriors."

"The princess," Long Arm replied, "is correct. We always complained about the brutality of the farmers when they killed our hunters who got too close to their guard posts. But what the farmers did was nothing compared to what Thunder Hunter and his warriors have done."

"Our people," Rose Leaf said, "would gladly give the lower valley back to the evil farmers if it meant they'd be rid of Thunder Hunter's warriors."

"You might not know that," Wandering Star said. "Maybe none of your yes-men has told you that, but Rose Leaf is right."

"The best thing for our people," Long Arm said, "is for Thunder Hunter and his warriors to go back to the lands they've always roamed. That's what our people want more than anything."

"They'll go back," Lightning Spear said, "after the farmers' prince is dead. After the blessing ceremony for Rose Leaf and Dark Storm. After she has his child in her body. Then they'll gladly go back to their lands."

"Thunder Hunter's warriors," Long Arm immediately begged to differ, "insist he's made no such promise to you."

"We agreed," Lightning Spear came back. "The warriors—all our warriors—would go home. Why wouldn't his warriors go back to their lands?"

"Why would they?" Wandering Star asked. "They say the war isn't over yet. The farmers are still in the upper valley. As long as they are, they say you've fallen short of your goal. Your kingship will be remembered as a failure. The gods are calling on Thunder Hunter to save your people from you. He'll live for the day when a grandson of his is our king. In the meantime, he and his sons, and not you, will run the kingdom, including in particular the lower-valley part of it."

"He has the brutal warriors to do it," Rose Leaf said, "and you don't."

"He agreed," Lightning Spear repeated, still addressing Long

154

Arm as if his children weren't taking part in the discussion, "the farmers could remain where they are."

"He agreed," Wandering Star countered, "not to attack the farmers as long as your hostage lives. If he dies—if you no longer have a hostage—the farmers have no right to live anywhere. The war resumes. You've gained nothing. His warriors come back from feeding their families. Thunder Hunter pardons their desertions."

"After that," Long Arm said, "you'll do what he tells you to do. Otherwise, you'll risk fighting a civil war with him and losing."

"You let him do," Wandering Star said, "what he did to our warriors on the plain."

"You know," Rose Leaf added, "his warriors killed grandmothers and children merely for speaking their minds, after they saw their sons and fathers killed in the battle."

Lightning Spear turned to his children, who sat together in the middle of his four guests, directly across the table from him.

"Neither of you was brought up to be a king," he said. "The tellers never told you the stories of my father, grandfather, and great-grandfather. And how they fought war after war with the farmers to take back the valley they'd stolen from us."

"The valley the farmers wrongfully expelled our people from," Rose Leaf said. "But now they see the error of their ways. They wish to share it with us. Both parts of it."

"That's an easy way to look at it," Lightning Spear said. "If it were the truth, it would mean all our people's fighting for the last several generations was for nothing."

"That's exactly what it means," Wandering Star quickly agreed.

"Then I myself," Lightning Spear said, looking as intently at Wandering Star as he had Long Arm, "have fought two wars all for nothing."

"That's right," Rose Leaf said. "A lot of people died for no purpose whatsoever."

"That can't possibly be right," Lightning Spear said, reluctantly looking at his daughter.

"There's a way to get yourself out of it," Rose Leaf said. "Just admit it was all foolish and wrong and lead your people in a new direction."

Lightning Spear looked at Blue Sky.

"I decline to accept your people's offer," he said.

The king continued to stare at his hostage.

"Rose Leaf and Wandering Star don't understand what's at stake," he said. "If your people and my people were to live together in peace, your people would dominate mine. Rose Leaf and Wandering Star—and maybe even my chief warrior—don't understand that. You and I do."

"What are you saying?" Blue Sky asked. "Your people would wish to become farmers?"

"Of course," the king replied. "You and I both know it's true. And I can't allow it to happen. The wars are between hunters and farmers. They aren't between brutal people and kind people."

"That's your mistake," Wandering Star said. "Choosing to see it that way."

"I agree with my brother," Rose Leaf said. "Your and the lesser chieftains' people admire the farmers' prince. If you have him killed, they'll see you're as brutal as Thunder Hunter."

"But it won't do you any good," Long Arm said. "You'll still be subservient to him. You'll be a king who killed the farmers' blameless prince just to placate a chieftain."

The sky was dark then. The king's visitors could see the stars over the mountains.

"You made a huge mistake," Long Arm said. "Now you're making it worse."

Behind the visitors the guards started a fire. The flames lit Lightning Spear's face.

"A king makes these decisions," Lightning Spear continued, still staring at Blue Sky, ignoring both his children and chief warrior. "Your prince dies tomorrow morning. I'm sorry."

He turned to Rose Leaf and Wandering Star.

"I can only hope," he said, "I'll stand for something more in our people's stories than kindness."

"There's no chance you'll be remembered for kindness," Wandering Star said.

"Not after all the people," Rose Leaf added, "you've made to

156

suffer early deaths."

Lightning Spear stared at his children and laughed.

"Well put," he said. "Both of you."

He turned to face Rose Leaf eye-to-eye.

"I don't blame you," he said, "for falling in love with Morning Sun, even if he is the farmers' prince. Several times now I've seen him myself. He's undoubtedly a fine young man. Long Arm's family, especially those nasty boys who bring my meals, adore him. They speak highly of him in my presence—as if I'm their prisoner, unable to disagree with them because that would make me look even more foolish in their eyes than I already do."

"I'd have to say," Rose Leaf said, "he's rather like the two fine young men you captured in the last war. And scarcely deserved what you ordered your warriors to do to them."

Lightning Spear, not having expected to hear that kind of remark from his daughter, turned back to Blue Sky again.

"I'm very sorry your prince has to die," he repeated. "Tomorrow will bring me no possible joy. I'll only be glad to see the day come and go—and I'll be done with it forever."

Blue Sky silently promised himself he'd do everything he could to make certain Lightning Spear wouldn't be done with tomorrow until the day Morning Sun's farmer boy, the spawn of hell-gods, killed him.

A single human, Lightning Spear in this case, could order another innocent human, Morning Sun, taken from the arms of his daughter, Rose Leaf, who clearly loved him, and killed.

Blue Sky could only choose to see Lightning Spear dead—or admit the world he lived in was as meaningless as hell itself.

RON FRITSCH

Chapter 9

Long Arm came to Wandering Star and Blue Sky's tent at dawn.

Lightning Spear, who knew his people and those of the lesser chieftains didn't think the execution of the farmers' prince was necessary, had forbidden the women and children from attending.

Thunder Hunter had gone along with the ban but had insisted Lightning Spear command all the men in the kingdom within one day's walk of the place of execution to attend. The order would include nearly their entire army.

Lightning Spear had agreed every man who could reasonably do so should consider it his duty to view the execution of an enemy prince. And the order would apply to—Thunder Hunter had insisted he add—exiles and hostages, even if they were otherwise, legally, children.

"I'll attend Morning Sun's execution," Blue Sky said, opening his eyes, "whether Lightning Spear and Thunder Hunter require my attendance or not."

As hard as it would be to witness the brazenly unjustified killing of a person who'd done no wrong—a person he'd fallen in love with—nothing could excuse Blue Sky's failure to be with Morning Sun when the moment arrived.

Wandering Star sat up on his furs and looked down at Blue Sky.

"Thunder Hunter wants to rub our noses in his cruelty," he sneered. "He wants to make us so afraid of him we'll never oppose him again. We'll be good little boys after we see what he does to your prince."

Long Arm ignored the sarcasm, as he almost always did, and turned to Blue Sky.

"Thunder Hunter would welcome your giving him an excuse to kill you along with your prince. You might want to keep that in mind."

As good little boys did, both Wandering Star and Blue Sky assured Long Arm, their legal guardian, they'd attend the execution.

They even promised him, and through him Rose Leaf and Morning Sun, they'd behave themselves—and do everything else they were expected to do.

*****

The execution didn't take place that morning.

It was late afternoon before the last of the hill people's warriors, a number of whom had been hunting in the forest, straggled into the place agreed upon by Lightning Spear and Thunder Hunter for the execution, Long Arm having suggested it: the bowl where the valley people had staged their wrestling, spear-throwing, and running competitions.

Thunder Hunter, saying no man who called himself a warrior would choose not to see with his own eyes the execution of the farmers' prince, had kept asking Lightning Spear to delay. So long as any warriors could be seen on the paths approaching the bluff, he got his wish.

For Blue Sky this provided the larger part of an extra day to spend with Morning Sun.

All of Long Arm's family, distant cousins included, who'd gotten to know the farmer's prince during the three-quarters of a year he'd lived with them, came by to embrace Morning Sun.

Dancing Song came with Thistle Dew, both of them unable to stop their tears.

Long Arm's children and nieces and nephews came as a group, along with their mothers. The older children and mothers knew what was going to happen, but the younger children had only been told Morning Sun would be leaving that day, never to return or see them again.

All was well as long as the older children kept a brave face, but when, almost simultaneously, they found they could do it no longer and began sobbing, their younger sisters and brothers quickly realized the bad thing that was going to happen to Morning Sun, thanks to Lightning Spear and Thunder Hunter, was as bad as it could be.

Their mothers, themselves in tears, had to take them away.

Like oxen with wooden poles on their shoulders, First Brother and Second Brother brought a large basket of clean hides, supposedly for Morning Sun's guests to sit on.

160

They took the basket into his tent, left it there and waited a long while, doing guard duty and talking with Blue Sky, who'd come close to killing both of them in the upper gorge.

They asked visitors to sit and talk with them and the hostage. Morning Sun was occupied just then with "a personal matter," they explained.

The visitors questioned the hostage at length. How had he done it? How had he killed so many of their warriors?

He truly didn't know, he replied more than once.

The visitors whispered to one another—as Blue Sky read their lips—that's just what you'd expect a hero to say, making no claim for himself.

"I'm not a hero," Blue Sky heard himself loudly insisting, giving the visitors all the proof they needed they were right.

He could even hear their whispers. He had eyes, ears, and strength other humans didn't have.

Then, after new guards arrived, First Brother and Second Brother went to Morning Sun's tent for the basket, now supposedly laden with the prince's old hides.

Both times they carried it, Rose Leaf was hidden inside it.

*****

Eventually, though, the summons came. The king, the chieftains, and all their warriors were waiting. Long Arm was to bring the doomed prince to his execution at spear-point.

Long Arm took the lead, his spear pointed toward the ground.

Morning Sun followed, Blue Sky on one side of him, Wandering Star on the other.

Long Arm's brothers and cousins came after them. They also had their spears pointed at the ground and not, as Thunder Hunter had wished, at the condemned man's back.

They were on the path the court people and tellers used to take going to and coming from the competitions. The valley people would grumble the uphill climb back to the town was so much harder to negotiate than the walk the other way. As if, Blue Sky used to think, their copious drinking during the games had nothing to do with it.

"I'll never forget that day down there," Blue Sky said to

Morning Sun. "The day the people bullied the tellers and got away with it."

Morning Sun, even on the day of his execution playing the innocent, looked at his friend and smiled.

"The people bullied the tellers?" he asked. "When did they do that?"

"The day they forced the tellers to make you and Early Harvest run a second race for the championship. You know what I'm talking about."

"The people forced the tellers to do it? Is that what happened? I thought the tellers decided the first race ended in a dead heat."

"That's what the people decided," Blue Sky said. "You won the first race that day. You didn't win by much, but you did win. The two high tellers at the finish line saw it, too. They were close enough. They saw you won that race. So did I."

"You could see that?"

"Of course I could."

"With your good eyes. The eyes that make you the hero of every battle you fight in."

"But the finish-line officials didn't dare tell the people the truth. Not after what Law Keeper had done. They had to give in to the crowd and make you run the race again."

Morning Sun looked at Blue Sky and smiled again. "You saw I won that race?"

"So did you. You didn't say a word, though. You let the people get away with it."

Morning Sun peered down at the running track at the bottom of the bluff, which was as crowded with hill warriors as it had been with valley people the day they were recalling.

"The people wanted another race," he said.

"And that's what you gave them. And then you tried as damned hard as you could to win it, too."

"Of course I did. If I hadn't, it wouldn't have been fair to that other farmer boy."

Blue Sky was well aware how much his friend the prince longed to be known in their people's stories as the only person who'd

162

won all three coming-of-age competitions. And yet he gave up his victory in the third because the people wanted another race—another reason to drink the king's wine and sing and dance.

"Where are those stupid gods now?" Blue Sky asked. "You've always been a perfect prince. And they can't save you?"

Morning Sun looked at his friend, saw his tears, and took his hand.

Blue Sky was making a spectacle of himself in front of the hill people's warriors, who all knew his falling in love with his people's prince before he fell in love with their people's bastard prince was a part of the story they'd somehow found themselves in.

"When you see those bullies again," Morning Sun whispered in his ear, "be sure to tell them how much I loved them."

*****

The hill people's warriors lining the path stared at Morning Sun in silence. Even Thunder Hunter's men appeared to view the proceeding as a grim necessity and nothing more.

The execution of the farmers' prince wasn't the victory they'd been promised. Wandering Star said all those present that day knew a resumption of the war with the farmers, in some form or the other, lay ahead.

Thunder Hunter's people had never seen Morning Sun. Their chieftain had learned the hill people who met the farmers' prince took a liking to him. As a result, he'd forbidden his own people from going near him, a prohibition Long Arm and his family had welcomed.

Now Thunder Hunter's warriors were crowding against one another for a good view of the man their princess had fallen in love with, a man who was doomed not for anything he'd done but for the rash decision of his father and uncle to blindly attack an army far greater than they could've imagined it would be.

Lightning Spear, Thunder Hunter, the lesser chieftains, their highest-ranking warriors, Heaven's Voice, and the high tellers were assembled at the center of the racetrack infield.

Wandering Star told Morning Sun who they all were. Dark Storm and War Cloud stood near their father. Their closest cousins, Dark Cloud and True Hunter, stood behind them.

Thunder Hunter had chosen Dark Storm, his older son, to kill Morning Sun.

Long Arm, ignoring Lightning Spear, strode directly to Thunder Hunter.

"This is Morning Sun," he said. "The farmers' prince."

The crowd murmured at Long Arm's choosing not to call him the prince of the thieves.

Thunder Hunter stared at Morning Sun. If he had the slightest doubt as to the necessity of killing the innocent youth who stood in front of him, he succeeded in hiding it.

"I beg you personally, one last time," Long Arm said to the mighty chieftain. "I plead with you to release Lightning Spear from his promise to you to kill this man. He's done absolutely nothing to harm our people. Nor, I give you my guarantee, will he ever. My family will hold him prisoner for the rest of his life, if you wish. Killing him is needless, senseless, and cruel."

The warriors repeated Long Arm's words to their farthest ranks.

"His father attacked us," Thunder Hunter said. "Even after our king warned him an attack would bring the certain death of his son, their prince, this man."

"His father didn't attack us," Long Arm said. "He and his army blundered into our land. We had them surrounded. We attacked them. We could've sent them home. It would've saved the lives of countless numbers of our comrades, who would still be with us today. So would our people who've starved to death in the absence of the dead warriors. This man had nothing to do with any of that."

"You've come under the spell of Wandering Star," Thunder Hunter said. "The spell of that bastard traitor."

"I've come under the spell of our people," Long Arm countered.

The warriors murmured.

"That's the same thing," Thunder Hunter said. "A proper leader doesn't follow the people. He leads them. He decides what's best for them."

He turned to Dark Storm.

"Kill the prince of the thieves," he ordered his son. "That's what's best for our people. That's what our king has decided must be done. Kill him."

Long Arm turned to Lightning Spear.

The king, staring at Morning Sun, remained silent.

Long Arm motioned for Wandering Star and Blue Sky to step aside.

Blue Sky's feet, though, failed to move. He couldn't remove his arms from Morning Sun.

First Brother and Second Brother handed their spears to their cousins, and each grabbed one of Blue Sky's arms, attempting to pry him away from Morning Sun.

Blue Sky couldn't fight them—not because he was their prisoner, but because they were his comrades. He nevertheless clung to Morning Sun as long as he could.

Eventually, though, the brothers prevailed. Blue Sky could resist them no longer.

Long Arm put his arm around Morning Sun's shoulders and positioned him so that the mountains to the north and west were behind him as he faced Thunder Hunter and Dark Storm.

Long Arm asked the nearest warriors to stand back and form a circle. He'd correctly guessed that the innermost ranks around the circle would consist of the chieftains and their highest-ranking, and therefore oldest, warriors—most of them still feeling the pain of injuries inflicted upon them in the previous war with the thieves.

The only youthful warrior in the front line was Dark Storm.

He stepped forward.

"He's yours," Long Arm said.

Those were the words the doomed person's guard always said to the executioner in both peoples' executions. They were supposed to be the last words the prisoner heard before he felt the spear piercing his gut.

Long Arm released Morning Sun.

"I beg your forgiveness for abducting you and Rose Leaf," he said, stepping away from his prisoner. "You never did anything to deserve it. I'll carry my unbearable guilt to my grave."

As the hill warriors repeated Long Arm's remarks, the late-afternoon sun was in Dark Storm's eyes.

He moved forward anyway, his spear raised.

Morning Sun moved forward himself, leaping.

Long Arm and his brothers had closely observed Dark Storm fighting in battles. They could tell something was wrong with his vision. Either War Cloud or True Hunter—sometimes both of them together—often had to come to his aid.

The afternoon of the execution he couldn't see the farmers' prince until it was too late.

Morning Sun grabbed his spear out of his hands, turned it on his would-be executioner with the same motion, and plunged it deep into his belly, laying him flat on his back on the ground.

As if on cue, the king, the chieftains, their highest-ranking warriors, the first teller, and his high tellers screamed.

The ordinary warriors, though, collectively drew their breaths. They hadn't expected what they were seeing: Morning Sun jumping on Dark Storm, one foot on his chest, the other on his groin, yanking out the spear.

"Kill him!" Thunder Hunter turned to his warriors and bellowed, taking his eyes off Morning Sun. "Kill him!"

Morning Sun, having pulled the spear out of Dark Storm's belly, swung it as delightfully as many of those in attendance had ever seen a spear wielded.

Thunder Hunter reached to protect his throat too late, just as the apprentice tellers had.

He fell in the direction his older son's spear had flown, his own blood spurting ahead of his body onto the ground.

War Cloud was the first of Thunder Hunter's warriors to approach Morning Sun, who had too little time to take aim at his belly or throat but sank Dark Storm's spear into his thigh anyway.

True Hunter came next, this time before Morning Sun had a chance to retrieve the spear.

True Hunter thrust his spear into Morning Sun's belly, forcing him to fall backward. True Hunter stood on Morning Sun as Morning Sun had stood on Dark Storm, retrieved his spear, and drove it down again into his abdomen, just below his ribs.

"Enough!" Lightning Spear screamed. "Enough killing for one

166

day!"

Thunder Hunter's warriors looked to War Cloud for instructions.

But he, lying on the ground next to his father and brother, gave them none.

Long Arm and his brothers and cousins having already raised their spears, Lightning Spear's warriors and those of the lesser chieftains raised theirs, crowding closer.

"Farmer," Lightning Spear yelled to his hostage, "bury your prince."

As Blue Sky approached Morning Sun, True Hunter pulled his spear out of his belly and turned to the hostage.

"Your prince was brave," he said.

In the tumult, nobody else could hear him.

He looked down at Morning Sun. "Too bad," he added, "he's a farmer and has to die."

He looked at Blue Sky again.

"As you," he chose to add, "and all your warriors will, before this war is over."

Morning Sun was attempting to sit up.

Blue Sky knelt down and gently placed his arms around the prince, holding him.

"Farmer boy," Morning Sun whispered in the valley people's language, "tell Rose Leaf I love her."

"I'll gladly tell her that," Blue Sky promised.

Morning Sun, blood pooling in his mouth, made a valiant attempt to smile.

"I got my wish," he said.

"Your wish?" Blue Sky asked.

"Green Field is our people's king now, and you're the damned prince."

He pressed his hands to his wounds, clenching his teeth.

True Hunter was kneeling next to Blue Sky.

"Does your prince want to get it over with?" he asked.

Morning Sun, his blood pumping from his mouth, could no longer speak.

He nodded his head, though, in answer to the question.

"Lay him down," True Hunter said to Blue Sky.

Blue Sky laid him on the ground softly, as if he were a wounded calf or lamb.

Wandering Star had to lift Blue Sky off the prince.

True Hunter stood back, precisely swung his spear, and with one stroke slit Morning Sun's throat.

Blue Sky fell to his knees again and took Morning Sun in his arms, paying no attention to the blood spraying from his third and final wound.

"I'm sorry you're farmers," True Hunter said. "He was brave."

Blue Sky could feel Morning Sun's body giving up, falling into its final sleep.

"No," Blue Sky whispered instead of shouting, keeping his promise not to give Thunder Hunter's warriors any excuse to kill him, "no, no, no, no. . . ."

And soon lost track of how many times he repeated that vile, hateful word.

Morning Sun was looking at him, just as the two apprentice tellers had, knowing all hope was lost. And yet he was still amazed, as Blue Sky was, at what he'd done.

Then Blue Sky could tell Morning Sun's eyes no longer saw him. The prince and his "farmer boy" friend were beyond the finish line, their games together behind them.

*****

Blue Sky and the hill people buried Morning Sun that evening.

Wandering Star and Blue Sky carried him on a litter to the valley people's graveyard on the bluff. Long Arm and his brothers helped them dig a grave for him next to his cousin Valley Defender's.

Morning Sun had practiced for his execution time after time with Long Arm and his brothers. Morning Sun had insisted upon it. He most wanted to kill Thunder Hunter, but they'd never imagined he could do it with one blow and take down War Cloud as well. They'd assumed War Cloud, not True Hunter, would be the one who killed the prince.

But War Cloud, unlike True Hunter, they told Blue Sky,

168

wouldn't have put Morning Sun out of his misery as soon as Morning Sun and Blue Sky gave their consent.

As Blue Sky, Wandering Star, Long Arm, First Brother, and Second Brother dug, a surprising number of Lightning Spear's people gathered around them.

Hearing them whisper "Rose Leaf," Blue Sky looked up. She was coming down the path from where the courtyard used to be. Thistle Dew and Dancing Song were on either side of her.

The hill people were making way for them.

She was, Blue Sky reminded himself, their princess.

Some of the younger hill tellers had asked Rose Leaf and Blue Sky if they could conduct a funeral ceremony for Morning Sun. It would have to be sung in the hill people's language.

Wandering Star told Blue Sky that most of the tellers present, not unlike Evening Shadow and Night Whisper, had learned the valley people's language well enough to sing their ceremony songs, but they could scarcely admit it.

Only Long Arm's family felt confident enough to do that. They justified it by saying they'd learned the farmers' tongue in order to care for Morning Sun, Rose Leaf, and Blue Sky. Even though all three of those individuals spoke the hill people's language and didn't require care, each of them gladly doing as much of the day-to-day encampment work as anybody else did—and certainly a great deal more than the king, the chieftains, their chief warriors, the first teller, the high tellers, their cronies, and their kept men deigned to do.

Thunder Hunter's warriors had taken their former chieftain's body over the bridge headed toward the eastern forest. They couldn't bury Thunder Hunter in soil desecrated by farming.

Speaking on behalf of his brother Dark Storm, their new chieftain, War Cloud had expressly invited all the hill people's warriors to attend his father's funeral.

He didn't omit that Dark Storm would hardly consider their attending a funeral for an enemy prince an adequate excuse for not honoring his late father with their presence at his.

Heaven's Voice and the high tellers officiated at Thunder Hunter's funeral. Lightning Spear and the lesser chieftains were first-row guests, but a great many of their warriors had obviously chosen to attend the funeral for the enemy prince in the graveyard on the bluff instead.

When Rose Leaf reached the grave, she looked down at Morning Sun. Blue Sky had closed his eyes and washed off his blood. Long Arm's family had covered his wounds with hides. An observer who didn't know he'd been killed might've thought he was merely sound asleep.

The day before, Rose Leaf had told Blue Sky she was fully expecting to see Morning Sun dead, even mutilated. But she'd also agreed with what he'd said to her as well as Blue Sky: they'd be true to him by taking the next steps forward with Wandering Star and Long Arm.

A young teller sang the goddess of love's part. Blue Sky imagined him and Spring Rain singing it together, each of them effortlessly switching back and forth from one language to the other as Wandering Star and Blue Sky did whenever they spoke together—like confident lovers giving and taking pleasure in equal portions, having no need to worry if one gave or received more or less than the other.

When it came time for the god of war's part, Dancing Song stepped forward.

Wandering Star stared at his mother. Even he hadn't expected this.

Hill women often sang ceremony songs privately, as the valley people's women did. Since the hill women weren't allowed to be tellers, though, they never sang a solo part in a public ceremony. And it would be highly unusual even for one of the valley people's women tellers to sing the war god's part in public.

Dancing Song, however, held nothing back. At times it seemed she intended using her woman's voice to mock the god. And this being the funeral of a beloved enemy prince at what was supposed to be the end of the most senseless war ever fought, why not?

At other times, and especially when the god blessed a dead warrior for slaying the foe and saving the lives of the people by giving up his own, it was as clear as it needed to be: Dancing Song was expressing the gratitude of many of her people to Morning Sun for killing Thunder Hunter.

The war god's part hadn't previously made as much sense to

Blue Sky.

Perhaps his own intense desire for revenge had something to do with that.

*****

Long after they'd covered Morning Sun, long after the people had left, long after the evening twilight had vanished, Rose Leaf and Blue Sky remained at the grave site.

One day in their youth when Morning Sun, Rose Leaf, and Blue Sky were in the forest with the horses, and the prince was riding Green Field's stallion as fast as he could get him to go, a deer, perhaps spooked by a wolf, leapt into the clearing, causing the horse to swerve to avoid it.

Morning Sun, screaming, fell to the ground.

When Rose Leaf and Blue Sky reached him, he lay quite still with his eyes closed.

Rose Leaf and Blue Sky quickly got off their horses.

"Is he dead?" Rose Leaf asked, her voice trembling.

"I don't really care if he is," Blue Sky, accustomed to Morning Sun's play-acting, replied.

Rose Leaf knelt down, caressing Morning Sun's face with her hands.

"Well, I do," she said.

Blue Sky could see the prince was breathing normally. He could see the regular pulse in his neck.

Morning Sun suddenly smiled.

"I'm alive," he announced, opening his eyes and laughing.

Rose Leaf, quickly removing her hands from his face, stood up.

"Damn you," she said, wiping away her tears. "Don't you ever do that to me again."

RON FRITSCH

Chapter 10

Dark Storm's warriors brought their wounded chieftain to Rose Leaf's tent the next day.

Despite Rose Leaf's angry protestations, Lightning Spear and the hill people's first teller, Heaven's Voice, said she had no choice but to obey the gods' law requiring a witness to acts intended to result in the procreation of a descendant of a king.

Rose Leaf could get away with making her heated remarks. She was the princess.

She was aiming her remarks well. The hill women all knew she opposed forcing them into marriages with men whose children they didn't wish to bear. She was their princess.

The witnesses were almost always brothers of either the man or the woman. If both had brothers, the higher-ranking of the man or woman chose among them. Lightning Spear's witness with Thistle Dew was his younger brother, who was killed in the older brother's first war.

From the days when the valley people's kings and first tellers still required witnesses, there were stories of a certain few of their princes and princesses who for some reason chose the other person's brother. The telling of such tales frequently led to speculation that the witness so chosen might've been especially pleasing to the eye—and even that more than two people in some cases might've participated in the acts leading to procreation.

War Cloud insisted he, as the only brother of either Dark Storm or Rose Leaf, would be the witness. Rose Leaf, claiming both higher rank than Dark Storm and the existence and presence of two brothers, Wandering Star and Blue Sky, vehemently insisted she'd choose.

Long Arm took the matter to Lightning Spear, who took it to Heaven's Voice.

The king and first teller summoned Rose Leaf and War Cloud to make their arguments outside the king's tent so that anybody who wished could hear them.

No hill person doubted what would happen. A huge crowd quickly gathered.

War Cloud, whose injury kept him from walking without the assistance of his cousins, Dark Cloud under one arm, True Hunter under the other, asked the king if he could sit in the chair his warriors had thought to bring for him.

Lightning Spear generously replied that anybody who wished to sit down could do so.

He ordinarily required supplicants and on-lookers to remain standing while he held court. Only he had "seating privilege," as the hill people called it, in the same chair he sat in on the battlefield.

Lightning Spear had told Wandering Star he made his people "stand up" because he was afraid that otherwise they'd never "shut up."

But the king obviously didn't care how long this particular argument took. He, Heaven's Voice, Rose Leaf, and War Cloud went back and forth all morning.

War Cloud had the better argument by far: he was simply the only brother of either Rose Leaf or Dark Storm. To claim that Rose Leaf had a brother was nonsense—no such person existed. Lightning Spear and Thistle Dew had one child, the princess the thieves had abducted and given the name Rose Leaf, and that was that.

The crowd grew quite still when Rose Leaf began her argument concerning Wandering Star. Knowing she'd have the crowd's full attention, she proceeded to do what no hill person had done before: she publicly stated, in the presence of Lightning Spear, that he'd gone with Dancing Song outside his union with Thistle Dew. She didn't mention the tribute, seeming almost to imply that Dancing Song's participation in the affair was predicated on her affection for the man as well as the physical pleasure he brought her. In any event, their activities together clearly resulted in Dancing Song's impregnation and Wandering Star's birth.

Lightning Spear tried his best to remain stony-faced during this part of the argument. But it was all too evident he was pleased with Rose Leaf's version of the story the on-lookers had heard countless times before, only with emphasis on the alleged tribute.

In his rebuttal, War Cloud first waxed sarcastic.

Accusing such a chaste king as Lightning Spear of going with a whore, he argued, was like saying the sun rose in the west or winter followed spring. And hearing the king's own daughter give voice to the charge was even more shocking than the accusation itself.

The crowd enjoyed those remarks.

Then War Cloud invoked a legal principle the valley people laughed at whenever it made its appearance in their ancestors' stories.

Rose Leaf herself, War Cloud continued, surely hadn't seen the king and Dancing Song going together. The tellers all said Rose Leaf was several years younger than Wandering Star.

Who, War Cloud asked, was prepared to provide testimony that Lightning Spear and Dancing Song had gone together at the requisite time to procreate the perfidious exile in question?

War Cloud—True Hunter at his side, whispering in his ear—knew Dancing Song could've done it, but he and True Hunter also knew the law didn't permit either her or Lightning Spear to provide the testimony.

Surprisingly, Heaven's Voice interrogated Rose Leaf closely on her childhood with the farmer thieves.

And he often chose to stare at Blue Sky during his questions as well as Rose Leaf's answers. Several times he looked Blue Sky up and down and gave him a knowing smile when their eyes met, as if the farmer hostage might actually be available for what he evidently had in mind.

The most powerful part of Rose Leaf's argument was in her summation, hinting more than once she'd submit to Dark Storm without being forced only if her father permitted her, the princess, to choose one of her brothers.

After deliberating privately with Lightning Spear and the high tellers for most of the afternoon, Heaven's Voice rendered his decision.

The first point to clarify, he said, was that only two brothers were in contention, War Cloud and the prince of the thieves.

The whore's son, Heaven's Voice adamantly stated, glaring at the person in question, wasn't a brother of Rose Leaf's in any sense of the word.

Wandering Star and Dancing Song looked at one another and openly laughed. The older boys in Long Arm's family felt free to laugh themselves at that pointless lie. As did their people.

Across the space in front of the king, the warriors on War Cloud's side stood unsmiling. It wasn't absolutely clear a bastard son

175

of a king couldn't become his heir, and the mere possibility of Wandering Star's ascendancy to the kingship was no laughing matter to them.

He and his hostage friend had somehow engineered the death of their chieftain and the severe wounding of his eldest son. And Long Arm and Lightning Spear were letting them get away with the murder and maiming.

The first teller, though, was more favorably disposed to Rose Leaf's claim that Blue Sky was her brother. Without doubt, she and he, through no fault on their part, had been raised as siblings, and having spent their entire childhoods together, she always viewed him as her brother.

Heaven's Voice further reported he'd consulted with a number of the older and wiser of the hill tellers. Not one of them could recall a story where a hill prince or princess hadn't been allowed to choose such a "brother" as a witness.

The first teller didn't say whether he or any of the "older and wiser" tellers had wondered if such a highly unusual question had previously arisen.

Lightning Spear had obviously let the first teller know he wished to give in to his daughter. She was the princess, after all. What would the people think, short-sighted as they were, hearing he'd permitted Dark Storm to go with his daughter against her will while his warriors held her down?

The oldest and wisest tellers closed ranks behind Heaven's Voice and agreed that even a thief could be a witness—and even if the brother-and-sister relationship between the thief and the princess was based on fakery from the moment it began in the valley people's forest, a few days after the abduction of the princess.

"To our princess," Heaven's Voice concluded, "he seemed a brother. So be it."

Those were the ten words Long Arm had told the first teller he might wish to say.

Lightning Spear accepted the decision. Rose Leaf, he said, could therefore choose between War Cloud and Blue Sky for her witness.

"I choose my brother," she quickly said.

Long Arm just as abruptly turned and led the princess and Blue Sky past War Cloud and his warriors.

"Make way," Long Arm said. "The king has spoken. Make way."

The warriors stepped aside, shaking their heads, falling silent. They were to believe the prince of the ungodly farmer-thieves, and a ruthless enemy warrior as well, was the brother of their princess, negating the obviously valid claim of War Cloud that he was the only legitimate brother of either the man or the woman? And the oldest and wisest tellers had gone along with it.

As Blue Sky drew near, True Hunter looked him in the eye.

"Our king and our first teller," True Hunter spat, loudly enough for those two individuals to hear him, "must be attempting to amuse us. Did I hear them say our princess can choose for her witness a damned thief who is no relation to her whatsoever?"

"I suppose," Blue Sky said, facing him, "you were looking forward to holding her down—and watching Dark Storm go with her against her will."

Wandering Star had said War Cloud and True Hunter would've done the holding down.

Long Arm turned around and placed himself between True Hunter and Blue Sky.

To be sure, though, neither True Hunter nor any of the other cousins of Dark Storm and War Cloud had menaced Blue Sky. They appeared instead to be as shocked by his outburst, making its way to the farthest reaches of the crowd, as he was.

Taking no chances, First Brother and Second Brother each once again grabbed one of Blue Sky's arms and led him away, following closely behind Rose Leaf and Wandering Star and only a step ahead of Long Arm. They had Blue Sky surrounded by five people nobody would dare attack.

"The farmer thief," True Hunter bellowed at the top of his voice so that everybody present, including the king, could hear him, "thinks we're stupid and corrupt!"

*****

177

Heaven's Voice and the high tellers conducted a blessing ceremony that evening in front of Rose Leaf's tent, with the king and queen in attendance.

When Heaven's Voice, the high tellers, and their acolytes offered Thistle Dew their greetings, she ignored them, staring at Rose Leaf, letting them know she was present only because she was the queen and had to attend such a ceremony in order not to cause unnecessary trouble for her daughter.

Lightning Spear accommodated her by shooing away the tellers with his hand.

Dancing Song had several times found Thistle Dew watching Morning Sun from a distance. The queen especially enjoyed seeing him engaged in some contest or other with the younger members of Long Arm's family.

One day Long Arm took Morning Sun to Thistle Dew's tent and introduced him to the woman who'd given birth to Rose Leaf.

She was said to have been rather shy in his presence at first. After that, though, she went to his tent on her own on numerous occasions, her visits not being prohibited by the terms of his confinement.

Rose Leaf and Dark Storm sat on hides and furs, he with another high pile of furs behind him to prop him up. More hides and furs covered his wound. He frequently took a drink of the pod tea Long Arm had given him. Drool from it often appeared at both corners of his mouth. But he was coherent enough to know what was happening.

He wiped his sleeve against his mouth from time to time to keep himself presentable.

Thistle Dew wept all the way through the blessing ceremony.

So did Blue Sky. So did many others present that day, thinking what might've been.

Rose Leaf, though, sat throughout the proceeding with a regal bearing, as if her face and posture were stone.

*****

The next morning Long Arm and his men took Blue Sky to testify before the king. Only the witness could provide evidence. It wasn't possible to hear from the woman. The gods had long ago decreed women couldn't attend such a proceeding. Nor could the man be heard. His story regarding such a matter might too easily deviate from the strict truth.

Heaven's Voice put the usual questions to Blue Sky. In response, the hostage swore to all the gods, whom he invited to strike him dead if he failed to tell anything but the truth, Dark Storm had indeed performed the deed expected of him on the night of his blessing ceremony. He also swore that, as performed, there was no reason on Dark Storm's part why the undertaking couldn't produce an heir. Blue Sky further swore the act revealed Rose Leaf to have been a virgin.

Statements as vague as those weren't good enough for War Cloud. He insisted on hearing details, standing next to Heaven's Voice, leaning on True Hunter, giving the first teller one question after the other to put to the thief. Many concerned the moment when his brother's body lost its tension, and where exactly his fluid could've gone. Many others concerned Rose Leaf's maiden blood. Where was it? How much of it was there? In what sort of light had the witness seen it?

War Cloud kept saying he only wanted to make certain nobody could later claim his brother hadn't fathered the next heir to the kingship.

And Lightning Spear was letting him do it.

"Just ask his questions," the king told Heaven's Voice.

"Of course," the first teller simpered. "I'll ask anything War Cloud wants me to ask."

The king turned to Blue Sky. "I know my daughter seems to you to be your sister. But just keep telling them the truth, difficult as it might be. That's all you need to do."

The person who'd allowed the killing of Morning Sun was acting like an understanding parent instructing a child whose obedience was beyond question.

Some of the questions and answers, especially those concerning the shape and size of Dark Storm's male organ when fully erect, provoked the tellers standing behind the king into smirking—as if War Cloud, Heaven's Voice, and Blue Sky had rehearsed a dialogue whose only purpose was to amuse.

When War Cloud and his warriors glared at them, the tellers couldn't help but openly laugh and cause the crowd, especially the older boys, to follow their lead.

All through the proceeding, Heaven's Voice stared at the witness's loincloth.

If Blue Sky hadn't promised Rose Leaf, Long Arm, and Wandering Star he wouldn't create another uproar, the first teller's presumptuous leer might've tempted him to bounce his fist off the old man's face—and without giving him the benefit of any warning either.

*****

It was true Rose Leaf had agreed to go with Dark Storm, and Blue Sky had agreed to witness her doing so. It was also true neither of them had any intent to keep those promises.

Long Arm had given them spears. His brothers had concealed them under hides in Rose Leaf's tent. If Dark Storm had actually tried to go with her, Rose Leaf and Blue Sky would've killed him.

The hostage was prepared to argue Dark Storm had attacked him, angered by his own inability to perform, and Blue Sky had killed him in self-defense. Blue Sky was prepared to lacerate his own body to prove Dark Storm had struck first. The conspirators would be gambling that Lightning Spear wouldn't fail to side with his daughter again.

Morning Sun, though, had played his part as well as it could've been played. He'd severely injured Dark Storm without finishing him off, choosing to slit Thunder Hunter's throat and wound War Cloud instead.

As it turned out, Rose Leaf and Blue Sky never had to fear for a moment they'd have to kill Dark Storm and answer for his death. The man was in such intense pain, and so needful of pod tea to alleviate it, he couldn't possibly do what he'd promised the first teller and the king he could and would do.

Alone with him in the tent, Rose Leaf and Blue Sky quickly took pity on him. They gave him all the pod tea and water he wanted

180

to drink. When he felt cold, they covered him with as many furs and hides as he wished. When he was too hot, they took his coverings off and sprinkled water on him.

Long Arm and his brothers brought them wine, which Dark Storm hadn't previously tasted. Rose Leaf and Blue Sky got him drunk, sometimes enough for him to fall asleep for a while.

Rose Leaf and Blue Sky took turns sleeping themselves and sitting up next to Dark Storm. He couldn't perform his excretory needs on his own.

His condition steadily worsened, as Valley Defender's had returning from the plain. But Rose Leaf and Blue Sky kept him clean and propped him up outside the tent when his people came to see him. Dark Storm cooperated, making every effort to conceal his pain and assuring War Cloud he was rapidly improving and would soon be hunting with him and their cousins again.

Two more mornings Blue Sky went to the king and testified Dark Storm had once again done what he was supposed to do. When Heaven's Voice finished his perfunctory questioning those days, War Cloud remained silent. He stood next to Heaven's Voice glaring at Blue Sky. True Hunter also chose to remain silent. The tellers found no cause for laughter.

Deep under hides and furs in a cold phase, late in the afternoon of the fourth day after Morning Sun had wounded him, Dark Storm died.

The conspirators had hoped for Dark Storm's early death, but when it came, it brought them no joy. They'd killed a man in his youth, who'd suffered his fatal blow only one day before his blessing ceremony with his people's princess. It's true he'd offered to kill Morning Sun and, before the battle on the plain, Blue Sky.

And no doubt Dark Storm would've killed them if he'd gotten the proper chance to do it. But what else, under the circumstances, being Thunder Hunter's oldest child, was he supposed to have done? It wasn't possible for him to stand mute in the face of his younger brother's swagger.

Having concealed his flawed eyesight for as long as he could, he was only the latest of the many victims in a meaningless war nobody could accuse him of starting or wishing to continue.

*****

War Cloud buried his brother in the eastern forest next to his father. Held up again by Dark Cloud and True Hunter during his funeral oration, he soon got to the point, fixing his eyes on Lightning Spear.

"My father and my brother," he said, "gave their lives in the cause the gods have always told our people to fight: to take this valley back from the thieves who stole it from us."

Lightning Spear stared back at him, daring him to go on.

"Both parts of it!" War Cloud bellowed. "The entire valley!"

Lightning Spear visibly stiffened.

"Not just this so-called lower valley," War Cloud sneered.

He grabbed True Hunter's spear and pointed it in the direction of the upper valley.

"That part of it, too!" War Cloud declared. "The whole valley!"

"Your father," Lightning Spear yelled back at him across his father's and brother's graves, the latter still uncovered, "agreed the gods wanted our people to have the valley I've won for them. He agreed we can hold the thieves prisoners in their upper valley. That's what your father and all the other chieftains agreed the gods have told us."

The lesser chieftains, standing behind Lightning Spear, nodded in agreement.

"He never told me he'd made any such agreement," War Cloud came back, glaring at the king and the lesser chieftains, "with you or with anybody else."

War Cloud was probably telling the truth. Long Arm and Wandering Star had advised Lightning Spear he should summon Thunder Hunter's sons to his tent the day he and the chieftains made their agreement. Lightning Spear had rejected their advice on the ground that his needing to include a living chieftain's sons in any matter concerning the kingdom would make him appear to be weak.

War Cloud looked down at his brother's body and his father's grave.

"I promise you both, and I promise the gods," he said, lifting

182

his eyes toward heaven, "the war will go on. It'll go on until the valley belongs to our people again. The whole valley."

He turned his angry gaze on the hostage.

Blue Sky's family and their neighbors used to come to this part of the forest for firewood.

"And every last thief is dead," War Cloud added.

True Hunter, Blue Sky recalled, hadn't promised to kill any women, old men, or children.

War Cloud turned to Rose Leaf.

"And this is my promise to you," he continued. "If my brother hasn't already implanted our next king in your body, I'll do it myself."

He turned to Blue Sky again.

"With your thief brother," he sneered again, "as the witness."

On this point he again had the hill people's law on his side. In the case of the death of a man who'd entered into a union with a woman, any brother of his who didn't have a mate could claim the dead brother's rights to the widow.

War Cloud, though, would have to wait for the full moon after the next one to do it. Rose Leaf was required to mourn her dead partner throughout one full-moon period, and during the mourning neither the dead partner's brother-in-waiting nor anybody else could touch her body.

"And I've no doubt whatsoever," War Cloud said to Blue Sky, "you'll enjoy watching me do it."

If War Cloud were with a willing partner who wasn't a person Blue Sky had always thought was his sister, the regent's son who'd become a hostage might've agreed he would've enjoyed watching War Cloud do it.

*****

Leaving the funeral, Blue Sky overheard one of the lesser chieftains attempt to convince Lightning Spear what they'd heard was only a young man's "hot-headed funeral talk."

"He's just lost his father and brother," the chieftain said. "I'd be angry myself."

"He doesn't have enough warriors," Long Arm drily and maybe more usefully remarked. "Not enough to do what he promised us he'd do."

"And our people's other warriors," Wandering Star said, "don't wish to help him."

"Nor would their princess," Rose Leaf added, "want them to."

When Green Field and Tall Oak abducted the infant Rose Leaf, they had no reason to know the extent of the problem they created for the hill people. Except for his missing daughter and bastard son, Lightning Spear had no close blood relatives, and the hill tellers couldn't definitively state who was next in line to the kingship. Many of the tellers in the tribes of Lightning Spear and the lesser chieftains would privately concede Thunder Hunter had the best claim, but at least two of the lesser chieftains had arguable claims of their own.

If Rose Leaf were dead or still held a prisoner by the farmers, and if Lightning Spear died without any other legitimate descendant, the result might very well have been a bloody civil war.

All the hill people knew that. It wasn't surprising only the horror of the battle on the plain could stop the celebration after Long Arm had found Rose Leaf and brought her home.

The agreement regarding Rose Leaf's union with Dark Storm therefore yielded undreamed-of advantages for both Lightning Spear and Thunder Hunter. Lightning Spear won the might to finally chase the farmers from the valley and become the most glorious king his people had ever known. Thunder Hunter gained for one of his heirs an unobstructed path to the kingship.

Lightning Spear could have the glory. Thunder Hunter, the leader of the fiercest warriors in the kingdom and the father of the father of the next king, would have the power.

The lesser chieftains remained silent, as did Lightning Spear, staring at Rose Leaf.

Their people's future would come out of her lithe body. And in certain of their stories—which were, of course, the same as the valley people's stories—a boy king's mother, sometimes for good and sometimes for ill, had exercised the full power of a king.

And the gods had let it happen.

*****

As they neared the bluff, Wandering Star separated himself from Blue Sky to approach several of the younger hill tellers and exchange greetings—and hurriedly whispered bits of information, as if they were sarcastic jibes that couldn't be told out loud to those returning from a funeral.

Heaven's Voice soon sidled up to Blue Sky.

"I hope," he said, "our people are taking good care of you."

"They are," Blue Sky replied, staring at the path ahead, refusing to look at the first teller.

"I can't find it in my heart," Heaven's Voice said, "to consider you an enemy."

"It hardly matters what's in your heart," Blue Sky replied. "I'm a farmer, a thief, and a hostage. I can't imagine how I'm not your enemy."

Heaven's Voice laughed at that. He was keeping to the dark side of the path, lest he be seen speaking with the hostage.

"Such a fine-looking young man as you," he whispered, "could never be my enemy."

Heaven's Voice and Green Field were approximately the same age. But for quite a few years now, this man hadn't seen fit to hunt, gather berries and grapes, dig for roots, cut firewood, haul water, or cook food. He didn't have to worry he'd somehow get injured or killed in a battle. None of the hill people's warriors with any sense would've wanted to fight by his side.

Even Law Keeper occasionally worked in the fields with the other tellers, although he could've legitimately claimed the affairs of the kingdom took too much of his time to permit it.

Heaven's Voice, on the other hand, took little interest in his people's disputes. He let his high tellers handle them all. They only needed to inform him of situations in which persons pleading their cases had left themselves open to mockery or ridicule. He greatly enjoyed any story lending itself to cynical laughter.

"You might wish to save your compliments," Blue Sky said to him, "for fine-looking young men stupid enough to think they matter."

The hill people's first teller laughed again.

"Those young men don't interest me," he whispered. "You do."

As quickly as he'd appeared at Blue Sky's side, he was on his way again, no doubt not wanting to be seen engaging in anything more than the usual pleasantries with the farmer hostage.

*****

After Blue Sky had learned the hill people's language, Wandering Star told Blue Sky a story about Heaven's Voice. It was his response to Blue Sky's story concerning Spring Rain and Law Keeper.

The day Wandering Star became an apprentice teller, he noticed Heaven's Voice gazing at him. At the time, though, Heaven's Voice was sharing his tent with another young teller.

The high tellers had blessed their union in a public ceremony. In the proceeding, Heaven's Voice and his lover promised life-long fidelity to one another, just as Spring Rain and Many Numbers had once chosen to do—and had done successfully until Blue Sky came along.

By the end of Wandering Star's apprenticeship, noisy arguments between Heaven's Voice and his partner, some in public, raised questions as to whether their union would continue. When Wandering Star became a teller, the young teller was no longer sleeping in the first teller's tent.

Heaven's Voice turned his attention to Wandering Star, who wasted no tact informing him he had no wish to go with a person as disgusting to him as the hill people's current first teller was.

Even when he was still an apprentice teller, Wandering Star had often loudly mocked his elders.

The people within earshot always fell silent, not wanting to miss a word the king's bastard son might say, whatever the subject.

He expressed some of his opinions so bluntly and disrespectfully his listeners, whether they otherwise might've agreed with him or not, couldn't resist cheering him on, since the high tellers and their associates he scorned were persons they despised.

Heaven's Voice already had all the evidence he needed to ask Lightning Spear to expel Wandering Star from the tellerhood and send him into exile. And after Wandering Star rejected him without a modicum of mercy, the first teller also had a good reason for doing so:

revenge.

When Blue Sky remarked to Wandering Star on what he saw as a coincidence, their peoples both having first tellers who weren't above using their power to gain access to young tellers, the bastard son laughed at his farmer lover as if he were a hopeless dolt.

"That's exactly why people want to be a first teller, a high teller, or at least a friend of a first teller or high teller," Wandering Star said. "So they can have their pick of the young tellers. That's the way it is with my people. And that's the way it must've been with your people, too. Only now, you farmers—or some of you at least—have gotten so superior you're turning up your noses at anything smelling like that."

He looked at Blue Sky and laughed again.

"Too bad," he saw fit to add, "I wasn't born a farmer."

Chapter 11

A messenger came the next morning. War Cloud wished to pay a visit to the princess.

Rose Leaf sent the messenger back to War Cloud with her reply: she'd be pleased to see him outside her tent after Long Arm and his party—which included his brothers, their cousins, their older boys, and the exile and hostage who lived with them—returned from their day's hunt in the forest.

The hostage, being so new to hunting, wasn't much help yet, although he did luckily surprise one elderly waterfowl on a pond with the only arrow he shot that day. The bird and the deer and the other waterfowl the party had killed were ready for roasting over the main fire when Long Arm sent for the brother-in-waiting.

War Cloud, hobbling on his bad leg as best he could, showed up with his highest-ranking warriors, insisting, the closer he approached the princess, he didn't need any help from his cousins.

Rose Leaf stood expressionless at the entrance to her tent.

Long Arm and his brothers stood on one side of her, the hostage and the exile on the other.

Not surprisingly, a large crowd, some of them drinking Long Arm's wine, had gathered.

War Cloud, paying no attention to anybody else, not even Long Arm, stopped at a point the distance of two grown men lying end to end in front of Rose Leaf.

"Your father, our king, Lightning Spear, promised you to my father' sons," he said. "After our mourning for my brother is over, I've come to inform you, I'll take you for my mate."

Rose Leaf chose not to reply, merely giving him, as Blue Sky had seen her give Morning Sun, Early Harvest, and Valley Defender, a look indicating she appreciated their physical appearance but was far more interested in hearing what they had to say.

"The gods require it," War Cloud continued. "Either my brother or I will be the father of our people's next king. Neither you nor I have a choice in the matter."

Rose Leaf's valley admirers never would've made those presumptuous remarks.

The tellers present murmured. Even those most favorably disposed to Thunder Hunter's tribe would've had a difficult time explaining how the gods specifically required that Dark Storm or War Cloud be the father of the hill people's next king.

Other chieftains had sons who'd survived their people's battles with the farmers and given voice to their willingness—eagerness, even—to impregnate Rose Leaf.

Several, Blue Sky had discovered, were pleasing to look upon and speak with. He would've been happy to see Rose Leaf choose any of them.

"I'd only hope," War Cloud continued, "you can see for yourself how pleasurable it will be for you to go with me—without being held down."

Many in the crowd audibly gasped. Not even Wandering Star had anticipated War Cloud would make such a crass remark to Rose Leaf in public.

A glance at War Cloud's loincloth right then told those who could see it either his desire for Rose Leaf was genuine, or he simply hadn't gone with anybody since Morning Sun attacked him.

War Cloud was blatantly ignoring the hill people's mourning law. Not even a brother-in-waiting was allowed to speak so shamelessly to a dead man's mate.

On the other hand, he and everybody else present knew neither he nor Rose Leaf was mourning Dark Storm.

Despite his injury, War Cloud was clearly enjoying the sudden turn of events, first his father's death, and then his brother's, which elevated him to the very top of his tribe. In that position he was second only to the king himself in power and influence in the kingdom.

As for Rose Leaf, she and Blue Sky had just spent three days in her tent shedding far too many tears. Caring for Dark Storm was the only thing that took their minds off Morning Sun. That was their mourning period, and it had to be over, whether they wanted it to be or not.

They'd mourn the loss of Morning Sun for the rest of their lives. But they had other business to attend to now. Its successful conclusion was the only way they could ever give meaning to his loss—to say nothing of the loss of the many other persons who'd died as a result of the events the three of them had set in motion.

Many Numbers once estimated the total of those persons, both valley people and hill people, was at least ten times ten times ten times ten times five.

Even Blue Sky was reluctant to imagine horror so immense. It could only mean that if gods ruled the human world, they were hell-gods.

"The advantages for you are obvious," War Cloud brazenly continued, glancing down at his own loincloth. "There's no reason why you and I shouldn't both take pleasure in what we must do together."

If his intent was to shock into stunned silence the many on-lookers, he fully succeeded.

War Cloud was the kind of man who went with women but would also let tellers take care of him whenever the need arose.

Since he was Thunder Hunter's son, a number of the hill tellers were more than happy to accommodate him, often bragging to the other tellers about their latest encounters with him.

Sadly, Heaven's Voice, his older high-teller friends, and their hangers-on, no matter their status in the first teller's hierarchy, didn't qualify.

War Cloud would only let the most attractive younger tellers please him.

"True Hunter is one of them," Wandering Star had informed Blue Sky. "He's usually, I understand, War Cloud's first choice."

Could anybody in their right mind, Blue Sky wondered, blame War Cloud for that?

Rose Leaf surveyed War Cloud intently, letting her eyes linger in the area of his loins.

"I wholeheartedly agree," she said.

Not even Blue Sky had imagined Rose Leaf would so boldly play with War Cloud.

She knew, as well as War Cloud did, every person in the kingdom would soon hear their conversation repeated and debate its meaning and implications endlessly.

"But all your many obvious advantages," Rose Leaf continued, looking War Cloud in the eye, "don't settle the matter between you and me."

It was rather sad, Blue Sky thought, to see War Cloud's lovely grin disappear.

"I understand," Rose Leaf said, "you wish to dishonor your father's agreement with my father. Our fathers agreed the war with the farmers had come to its end. But now you wish to restart it. You say our people have got to fight on into the upper valley, send many more of our warriors to early graves, and let their children, mates, and parents starve."

"My father made no such agreement with your father," War Cloud countered.

"He did," Rose Leaf came back. "They had an agreement. All the chieftains confirm it. Everybody knows they did. You're the only one who denies it. Don't insist on it to me any further. Don't make a bigger fool of yourself than you already have."

War Cloud remained silent.

"I'm telling you this," Rose Leaf continued. "No man who dishonors his father's agreements with my father will enter into a union with me. If you dishonor your father's agreement regarding the upper valley, I'll dishonor my father's agreement regarding me."

War Cloud glanced at the hostage. "Our princess takes the side of the farmers."

"I'm on the side of both of our peoples," Rose Leaf said. "I'm against the war you insist on resuming. I'm against any more senseless killing, whether the victims are farmers or our people."

"The war must go on," War Cloud insisted.

He pointed his spear toward the upper valley.

"Thieves live at that end of our valley," he said.

"Then understand this," Rose Leaf said. "You can't continue the war and mate with me. You'll do the one or the other. You'll never do both. The choice is yours."

She had War Cloud where she'd had Morning Sun and Early Harvest in their late boyhood and early manhood: obsessively desiring her and desperate to know if they could please her.

And War Cloud's victory mating with Rose Leaf, a princess the farmers had raised as one of their own, would endure forever in the stories their people would tell.

But War Cloud wished to kill humans as much as he enjoyed, due to his position and appearance, having them satisfy him. If he'd been in the encampment below the upper gorge, he would've been one of the few warriors who actually did the killing, laughing in the rain of blood, even if it was his own people's blood.

"You can tell your father this," he said. "He'll live to regret the day he breaks his promise to my father regarding you."

Long Arm, his timing as precise as Spring Rain's in song, raised his spear.

"That's treason," he said.

With his brothers and cousins, who also had their spears raised, he approached War Cloud.

"Kill the traitor!" someone among the older sons and nephews of the brothers and cousins yelled.

"Kill the traitor!" the crowd quickly agreed. "Kill the traitor! Kill the traitor!"

War Cloud's party were greatly outnumbered. Long Arm's warriors had them surrounded, too. War Cloud could see, if fighting began, he and all his warriors with him would be killed.

And if fighting began, Blue Sky, who wasn't allowed to carry a spear unless he was with a hunting party, found himself wanting, more than anything else, to be in the middle of it.

He had his eye on the spear an old teller standing near him carried. Surprisingly, the shaft looked almost as sturdy, and the point almost as sharp, as his own people's spears.

Taking the spear from the teller would be the easy part.

Blue Sky would also have to get to War Cloud before Long Arm or one of his brothers did.

But Blue Sky was certain he could beat his competitors even if he had to grab somebody else's spear to do it. If he got to War Cloud first, his comrades would have to protect his flanks and let him go in for the kill. They could kill War Cloud's cousins instead. There would be glory enough for them all to share. Wandering Star, too, after he grabbed another old teller's spear.

Blue Sky, though, wanted to be the one who killed War Cloud. Driving a spear deep into the man's guts would've given him so much pleasure it frightened him to imagine it.

193

But he also knew if fighting began and War Cloud and his warriors were killed, a bloody civil war would begin. Blue Sky and his allies couldn't let that happen. Not yet.

The old teller would keep his spear and never suspect Blue Sky had coveted it.

"You'll take your warriors now and leave," Long Arm said to War Cloud in a voice every on-looker heard.

Long Arm motioned with his spear to those of his warriors who were standing behind War Cloud and his men.

"Make a path for them," he ordered. "When they move between you, don't touch them. Don't say anything, either. I'll personally punish any of you who defy me."

Long Arm's warriors stepped back, creating the passageway their chief warrior demanded.

Long Arm motioned with his spear to War Cloud.

"Move your men through," he ordered. "I give you my word you'll all go unharmed."

War Cloud and his warriors complied.

Fortunately for the conspirators as well as for Long Arm and his men, no fighting, however much Blue Sky had wanted it, came.

Unfortunately for War Cloud, though, he'd given Rose Leaf and Long Arm the opportunity to face him down in front of Long Arm's warriors.

And everybody in the hill people's kingdom would soon know they did it.

*****

Deer Tracker, his aunt, and every other hill person who'd made it to the upper valley had told the same story. After Lightning Spear agreed with Thunder Hunter to keep the army together during the winter following their two disastrous attempts to invade the upper valley, Thunder Hunter's warriors who'd stayed behind in the lower valley soon took it upon themselves to keep people in the other tribes from coming into the valley to hunt.

They did so by occupying the same encampment areas to

which the valley people had sent their new men of age. Because Thunder Hunter's warriors lacked knowledge of the terrain they were guarding, they didn't do the job as well as the farmers had.

That was why Wandering Star, who had acquired detailed knowledge of the mountain passes where the farmers had located their encampments, could send a constant stream of refugees to the upper gorge.

Lightning Spear had never issued an order providing for this state of affairs. But when any of the lesser chieftains or his own people complained to him about it, he put them off.

"What was I to do?" he asked, staring at his hostage on the other side of his table again. "Thunder Hunter had his warriors in the valley. I didn't have any of mine there. Neither did the lesser chieftains. What good would it have done for me to issue an order? Thunder Hunter's warriors would've ignored it—and made me, the king, look like a fool."

Lightning Spear had invited Rose Leaf, Long Arm, Wandering Star, and Blue Sky to join him in his tent for what he called "a friendly evening discussion." It was the second time he'd done so since the botched execution that resulted in the deaths of the executioner and the executioner's father in addition to the condemned person.

Blue Sky had discovered why Long Arm's people were freely drinking the wine they'd made. In the privacy of his tent, Lightning Spear drank it himself.

Wandering Star had taken a jug of it with him to one of his meetings with his father, who soon developed a thirst for it.

"But don't tell my people," Lightning Spear, laughing, had told Blue Sky the first time the hostage saw Long Arm fill the king's cup with wine. "I certainly wouldn't want them to think their king is some kind of hypocrite."

When the lesser chieftains had complained that Thunder Hunter's warriors weren't letting their people hunt or fish in the valley, Lightning Spear told them to wait until spring.

"We'll all go back to the valley," he said. "Our people will hunt wherever they please."

That wasn't, though, the way things turned out.

After the battle on the riverbank, the hill people's army came back to the valley, but Thunder Hunter's warriors, now War Cloud's,

195

were telling the other warriors they could hunt only in the vicinity of the encampment on the bluff.

Skirmishes had broken out. In the last three days, warriors and non-warriors on both sides had been killed.

Lightning Spear had more need of his wine than usual during that evening's "friendly conversation."

Rose Leaf, Long Arm, and Wandering Star told him his and the lesser chieftains' people had suffered enough—enough from the war, and enough from Thunder Hunter and War Cloud's warriors. They were starving because their warriors hadn't come back to them in the autumn, and because Thunder Hunter's warriors had kept them out of the valley. Some of them had become so desperate they'd gone to beg for food and shelter from the farmers.

Lightning Spear had assumed that after the ceremony for Dark Storm and Rose Leaf, Thunder Hunter would return with his warriors to their usual hunting grounds, leaving only enough warriors behind to guard Dark Storm and man the encampment at the upper gorge.

Thunder Hunter, though, had never unambiguously stated he'd do that, and Long Arm and Wandering Star were certain he wouldn't—not until the farmers had been chased out of the upper valley. And then he'd insist on splitting the whole valley between his tribe and the tribes of Lightning Spear and the lesser chieftains.

Lightning Spear's people were now hearing from War Cloud's warriors that they planned to remain in the valley. Some of their families had already arrived to be near them.

There was no reason for them to leave the valley. Lightning Spear and the lesser chieftains couldn't force them out. And War Cloud couldn't hope to restart the war with the farmers in the upper valley anytime soon if his warriors returned to the lands they customarily roamed.

Rose Leaf, Long Arm, and Wandering Star agreed that Lightning Spear, having no means short of a civil war to make War Cloud's warriors obey, shouldn't order them to leave the valley.

"The trick," Wandering Star said, "is to get as much out of War Cloud as you can without making him fight back."

"Seeing where the line is," Long Arm said. "Knowing how far

you can go."

"That's right," Lightning Spear said. "That's what a wise king has to do."

"And he has to know the people to ask," Rose Leaf said. "To find that out."

Lightning Spear, appearing offended, glared at his daughter and bastard son.

"I believe I've done that," he insisted, glancing at Long Arm. "I asked the commander of my warriors to my tent, and here he is, advising me what to do."

Once again, Long Arm didn't hesitate: "Do what Rose Leaf and Wandering Star think you should do. Split the valley with War Cloud at the river. We and the lesser chieftains take the west side. War Cloud takes the east. We'll have no more quarrels about where the boundary is. You can at least get that."

"We can fish the river from our side," Wandering Star said. "And they from theirs."

Lightning Spear turned to Rose Leaf.

"Split it at the river," she said. "War Cloud isn't stupid. He can't fight a war with the farmers on his own. He doesn't have enough warriors to do that. He'll get more out of the deal than he deserves. He can see that. He has to appease our people and those of the lesser chieftains."

Lightning Spear looked at his hostage. "I assume you agree I should split the valley."

"I wouldn't presume to advise you," Blue Sky said. "I'm only your guest here."

The hill people's king laughed again. "My honored guest," he added.

The farmer who was superior to the hill people, Blue Sky imagined the hill people's king meant, as farmers—to him—were.

"Did you know," Lightning Spear asked Blue Sky, "Wandering Star told me how to fight the war with your people? He had it all figured out. And after Long Arm brought Rose Leaf back to me, all I had to do was what Wandering Star had told me I should do."

Blue Sky was certain Lightning Spear was also pleased it was his son who'd seduced the person the hill people referred to as "the farmers' new prince"—even though he wasn't—and set the tale in motion.

Lightning Spear belched.

"The other tellers never brought me advice like that," he said. "They were too busy begging me to expel my son from the tellerhood and send him into exile."

Rose Leaf and Blue Sky had shown the women and girls in Long Arm's family where the farmers' tellers had grown their onions. With his supper that evening, the king had gotten his special request: raw onions. He enjoyed eating them the way the farmers did: dipped in salt.

In his case, it was the salt the panicked farmers had left behind, the salt the fires Lightning Spear himself had ordered had failed to destroy.

The king looked at his son. "I never should've listened to them," he said. "That was the worst mistake I ever made. It was even worse than starting that other war with the farmers."

He took another sip of his wine and turned to Blue Sky, waving his cup in his direction.

"Did you know," he asked, "my people say Heaven's Voice insisted I banish my son because Wandering Star wouldn't go with him? At first, I simply didn't believe it. I couldn't imagine anybody, and certainly not the man I'd appointed first teller, would have the nerve to demand that of my son."

Blue Sky had once asked Wandering Star why he hadn't told his father Heaven's Voice was merely getting back at him.

"What sort of simpleton are you?" Wandering Star had asked in turn. "Can't you see? I wanted to be expelled from the tellerhood. I wanted to be exiled. The high tellers were doing just what I wanted them to do. What better way to let the people know what I thought of their king and first teller and all their toadies?"

"Someday," Lightning Spear continued, "I'll dismiss that wretched man. Then I'll appoint a first teller who knows what he's doing. I have just the person in mind, too."

*****

Later that evening, First Brother and Second Brother went to see War Cloud in his encampment in the eastern forest. They went alone. They readily gave up their weapons to War Cloud's guards.

What they did was undoubtedly courageous. But they were also Long Arm's brothers. Few of War Cloud's people wished to harm them. None was foolish enough to attempt to do so.

The brothers spoke with the new chieftain privately in his tent, setting forth the terms of Lightning Spear's proposal.

War Cloud neither agreed nor disagreed with anything they said. He mostly posed questions, some Long Arm's brothers could answer, others—one of which concerned the procedure for determining the middle of the river—they could only defer to the king.

"To the king?" War Cloud asked them. "Or to the four people he spends evenings with in his tent?"

War Cloud's question confirmed he somehow knew Lightning Spear listened to his daughter who'd lived her life with the farmers and openly favored them, his bastard son who'd become so fond of the farmers he'd taken one of them for his lover, his chief warrior who appeared to be taking the side of of the king's children, and the farmer himself who once thought he was Rose Leaf's brother and was now Wandering Star's lover as well as Lightning Spear's hostage.

Toward the end of the discussion, War Cloud told the brothers designating the river as a temporary boundary might be just what all their people needed.

"This is my answer to Lightning Spear," he said. "I wish to end our people's feuding over hunting rights."

He knew as well as Rose Leaf and the other conspirators did that the warriors claiming allegiance to Lightning Spear and the lesser chieftains, however much they resented many of their leaders and tellers—including their king and first teller—still outnumbered his own.

"He should damned well consider half the lower valley a victory," Rose Leaf said, when Long Arm's brothers returned with his answer. "It isn't, though, the victory he seeks with the hill people's princess. I promise you he'll never win that one. He'll never come inside me."

Lightning Spear not being present in Rose Leaf's tent to hear that remark, Wandering Star and Blue Sky looked at one another

199

laughing, taking pleasure in knowing their sister was in charge.

Long Arm and his brothers, who'd agreed Rose Leaf was the highest ranking member of the conspiracy they'd embarked upon, were no less pleased.

*****

During the summer solstice ceremony the next morning, Lightning Spear issued his edict dividing the lower valley at the river.

That same day, the grateful families of the warriors from Lightning Spear's and the lesser chieftains' tribes began spreading themselves out on the western side of the valley, most of them preferring the forested mountain slopes to the flat land the valley people had farmed near the river.

When they were expected to, they publicly praised Lightning Spear for securing half of the lower valley for them, but they also knew it wouldn't have happened if Rose Leaf, Long Arm, and Wandering Star hadn't insisted upon it. The three of them got their thanks privately.

Certain of Wandering Star's teller allies had volunteered to go into the western forest with the people. Their ostensible purpose was to perform their usual duties wherever the people chose to encamp.

"Do show the people how much we care for them," Heaven's Voice instructed the tellers. "Always seem to be as kind to them as you can be—given the rules you must follow."

Blue Sky and Wandering Star were present when the first teller spoke to the volunteer tellers.

"Just make sure," Heaven's Voice continued, "they keep in mind from now on the full-moon days when we expect their tribute. Pound it into their empty heads we don't want to hear any more of their excuses for their empty hands."

Wandering Star's renegade friends stared at the first teller, struggling not to let their contempt for him show. They wouldn't ask anything of the people they'd be living among.

After Lightning Spear and Thunder Hunter began their war with the farmers, and sent their own people into starvation, the tribute to the hill tellers fell to a trickle and by mid-winter, like a brook freezing over, came to a stop. Many of the hill people got away with that simply by keeping themselves at a distance from the army. Lightning Spear and Thunder Hunter didn't dare send warriors after them—warriors who might very well decide not to return.

Nor could the king and the lesser chieftains order warriors to punish their people who were encamped nearby, those people being the families of other warriors who'd surely come to their defense.

The hill tellers who were still able-bodied were providing food, hides, and firewood for themselves and as many persons in the families of their siblings and cousins as they could reach.

Wandering Star's allies among them, together with Long Arm's family—who Rose Leaf publicly encouraged—were also providing for the first teller, the high tellers, and the other tellers who lived with them.

The provisions weren't as bountiful as those worthies expected the people to pay for their tribute. But they were enough at least to keep them from suffering undue hunger or cold.

"When the time comes," Wandering Star said, "they'll dance to the music we play."

He could get away with saying that when he was drinking with Blue Sky, Long Arm, and the brothers late into the night.

"Or," First Brother said, chortling in the face of his older brother's moonlit frown, his younger brother's admiring smile, and the drunken hostage's laughter, "they might not be dancing at all."

*****

The real but clandestine purpose of Wandering Star's most trustworthy teller conspirators was to establish a line of communication with the farmers in the upper valley.

Mostly younger men, all able-bodied, they were to pitch their tents at carefully chosen intervals in the western forest, all the way from Lightning Spear's encampment on the bluff to sunset pass in the upper-valley mountains. When a communication came from either end, one of the two tellers at any location would immediately, even in the middle of the night, memorize the latest news and leave for the next location without stopping along the way to eat, drink, or sleep.

Wandering Star figured it would ordinarily take even a speedy person seven days to travel from the bluff to the pass. But eliminating any pauses for sleeping, eating, and drinking, as well as any need for the messenger to carry food, water, or sleeping hides and furs on his back—which was what his innovation did—could reduce the days required to three.

The conspirators knew the time would come when they'd need to communicate that fast. The time to see if they could do it was at hand.

Wandering Star's scheme included a means for letting Blue Sky's people know a communication was on its way. Teller allies near the gorge, but out of sight of War Cloud's warriors in their encampment, would light a fire shortly after sunset at a location on a slope so steep none of the hill people would choose it for even a single night's encampment.

Wandering Star had disclosed the location to Many Numbers and Spring Rain the day he came to get the hostage in the gorge. Blue Sky saw the three of them out of the corner of his eye, as he embraced his father, mother, Noon Breeze, and the apprentice tellers one last time. Spring Rain was still in tears, but for some reason they were staring at a location in the western forest beyond the gorge as if they'd never seen it before.

Similarly, Blue Sky's people were to signal when they had a message on its way to sunset pass. There was a certain place on the cliff-top where they were to light an evening fire.

Wandering Star instructed the two tellers who shared the final lap to the top of sunset pass to deliver their message only to Green Field, Gentle Brook, Many Numbers, Fair Judge, Full Harvest, Early Harvest, Good Harvest, Spring Rain, Noon Breeze, Evening Shadow, or Night Whisper, singly or in whatever combination those individuals greeted them.

Certain information couldn't be shared with all the people in the upper valley. Secrets had to be kept.

The first message the conspirators sent was that Morning Sun had been executed, but not without his taking Thunder Hunter and Dark Storm down with him.

The conspirators anticipated Green Field would want all the people to know that.

They'd only need to make certain Rainbow Evening learned properly—which was no doubt from and in the presence of Fair Judge, Gentle Brook, Green Field, Spring Rain, and Many Numbers.

Full Harvest and Early Harvest would be among the first of a long line of people waiting at Rainbow Evening's door to console her. In the days that followed, the seven of them would remain at her side, greeting and speaking at length with the people coming to pay their respects. The visitors might very well include every person in the kingdom, even the lame and sickly.

Blue Sky's former housemates and the upper-valley cousins would feed them all, some of them, Noon Breeze's family in particular, having traveled a great distance.

The valley people and the hill people living with them would mourn the death of the prince at the same time they celebrated his killing the hated Thunder Hunter and his older son.

"How did Morning Sun do it?" the people would be certain to ask.

"It was a blessing from the gods," some would no doubt reply. "They intervened. For him. For us."

Many Numbers and the other ten conspirators at their end of the line, even Spring Rain, would've had a difficult time resisting the urge to deny it was any kind of good luck or blessing from the gods.

They would've learned from Wandering Star's last messenger, sitting at a fire on sunset pass drinking wine with them, Morning Sun had practiced long and hard. He knew what he was doing. He had people helping him. They told him what they'd learned about Dark Storm's flawed vision. They'd carefully thought out all aspects of the execution beforehand. They'd imagined everything that could go wrong—and right.

If the afternoon had been cloudy, they were prepared to beg Lightning Spear to wait until the next morning, to accommodate all the warriors who might still be headed for the bluff. Lightning Spear probably would've gone along with their request—just to show who, ultimately, was in charge of his kingdom, if for no other reason.

They'd carefully arranged Blue Sky's apparently shameless clinging to the prince at the last moment so that Morning Sun would end up where Long Arm had decided he should be, to secure the maximum benefit of his executioner's visual incapacity.

The news in the remainder of the message, though, had to be kept a strict secret.

If it wasn't, all the conspirators would die.

There was a child growing in Rose Leaf's body.

The child's father was Morning Sun.

*****

Heaven's Voice was making certain his path and Blue Sky's often crossed. If anybody was nearby, his greetings were always cordial but brief.

Blue Sky invariably ignored the first teller, acting as if he neither heard nor saw him.

One afternoon the first teller followed him, at a distance, when he went alone into the woods on the bluff-top. Those were the woods where the orphan boys had first gone together.

Since Blue Sky was collecting firewood, he told Heaven's Voice, as soon as the man made his presence known, he was busy and didn't wish to be interrupted in his work.

Unlike others, he said, who didn't concern themselves with the day-to-day needs of the people they lived with. Not even the people who protected them.

Blue Sky might as well have been speaking to the tree behind the first teller.

Heaven's Voice stayed right where he was, telling Blue Sky how pleasing he was to look upon, and how proud the farmers must've been to have him for their prince. He was even more appealing than the one whose execution was still the chief topic of conversation among the people—whose simple minds couldn't seem to get enough of that sort of thing.

Their own king's bastard son, Heaven's Voice saw fit to add, didn't even come close to being as attractive as Blue Sky was.

Moving on from those helpful preliminary comments, the hill people's first teller insisted he could give Blue Sky "far greater

204

pleasure" than he'd ever gotten from Wandering Star.

The first teller's view of pleasure and his own were so divergent Blue Sky could only respond with brief laughter.

"The only person that man will ever love," Heaven's Voice let Blue Sky know, "is himself."

The first teller had apparently failed to note Wandering Star's tears the day on the plain when he begged his father not to let War Cloud kill Blue Sky.

On the other hand, Blue Sky could see how a very fine-looking young man who'd rudely rejected the advances of a high official appointed by his father, and then gratuitously and publicly called into question the official's learning—and getting away with it only because he was the king's know-it-all bastard son—deserved that high official's everlasting contempt.

Heaven's Voice was admirably blunt. He wanted to go with the enemy prince. He'd never, in fact, wished for anything more.

"It'll have to be at night," he said. "Nobody else can know about it."

Like the valley people's former first teller, he'd been considered attractive in his youth.

"Going with an enemy prince is treason," he added. "The punishment for it is death."

Nothing Blue Sky said could convince Heaven's Voice to leave him alone. Blue Sky told him to quit wasting his time. He said he could more readily imagine going with his own mother than the hill people's first teller. He even went on to say if he ever became so desperate as to go with a creature whose being alive was its only appeal, he was quite certain he could find an animal in the forest he'd be more satisfied with than the man who brazenly called himself Heaven's Voice, knowing his voice spoke for him alone.

"I'd love to be the animal you chose," Heaven's Voice quickly responded. "I'm curious, though. What would you do after you had your way with it? Would you kill it?"

*****

Wandering Star's line of communication worked. Messages came from the upper valley.

Green Field had refused to let the tellers conduct the usual ceremony celebrating the ascension of a new king. He said the people shouldn't refer to him as king, Gentle Brook as queen, or Blue Sky as prince. He insisted they continue to call them the regent, the regent's mate, and the regent's son.

He said their people should do that out of respect for Morning Sun, Rainbow Evening, and Tall Oak. When their people lived in the entire valley again, they could resume having kings and queens and princes and princesses. That would be the proper time for a celebration.

Green Field couldn't reveal the true reason for his refusal to be known as a king: whoever presently ruled the kingdom did so only as a regent until the child in Rose Leaf's body, being Morning Sun's child as well as hers, survived its birth and infancy, grew to adulthood, became the valley people's king or queen, and began ruling on his or her own.

To the people who didn't know the truth, Green Field's refusal to hold a ceremony was simply a result of his and Gentle Brook's rather different way of looking at things.

Green Field, Gentle Brook, as well as their children, Rose Leaf and Blue Sky, liked to insist nobody was better than anybody else— when even a fool could see that wasn't the case.

But Green Field, Gentle Brook, and their son, now Lightning Spear's hostage, could've asked the people to call them anything they wished, and the people would've gone along with it. They'd saved their kingdom and its people from annihilation.

Chapter 12

Heaven's Voice followed Blue Sky into the woods a second time.

If they met in the woods at night, Heaven's Voice promised, he'd do whatever Blue Sky asked him to do. It would be entirely one-sided, as it was with War Cloud and the tellers who went with him. He certainly wouldn't expect Blue Sky, the greatest warrior anybody had ever laid eyes on, to do anything for him.

"You were so magnificent in those battles for the upper valley," he said, "I couldn't take my eyes off you."

While Blue Sky and his comrades killed younger tellers Heaven's Voice had gone with, the first teller, from the safety of his position as close to the king as he could get, hadn't been able to take his eyes off the crazed enemy warrior, covered with blood, who did far too much of the killing.

And what this man told his people supposedly came from the gods themselves.

*****

The only hill people going to the upper valley then were family members of the hill people already there. Those still out-running War Cloud's warriors at the gorge were the ablest and most confident. But many of the hill people were taking the long route around the mountains to sunset pass, where nobody attempted to stop them— where the guards gave them food and water the moment they arrived, as well as an escort to the valley floor so they wouldn't get lost in the forest.

Wandering Star thought there were three reasons why more hill people weren't going to the upper valley. First, it was summer, and game and other food were plentiful. Second, they had the west side of the lower valley to hunt in. Third, and most important, if they were free to go live with the farmers whenever they chose, they had no present need to go. They could decide to do it later.

*****

Wandering Star's tent was as close to the edge of the bluff as he and Blue Sky could put it, where they could keep an eye on War Cloud's people. They were sitting outside it with a newly arrived messenger, facing the moon rising over the eastern mountains.

Along with the news that mattered, Noon Breeze wanted Blue Sky to know he was free to stay away from his people as long as he wished. Nobody, he said, not even Spring Rain, missed him.

Spring Rain, though, insisted everybody, including Noon Breeze, greatly missed the regent's son and couldn't wait for him to return.

Wandering Star teased: "Your two comrades can't seem to agree on a crucial point."

"They shouldn't be wasting the messengers' time with nonsense like that," Blue Sky said.

"That's what Many Numbers told the first messenger," the last messenger in that particular line of messengers said, laughing. "We decided to pass the messages along anyway. We thought you might like to hear what your friends are saying about you."

Wandering Star looked at Blue Sky and laughed himself.

"So which of your friends is telling the truth?" he asked.

"Neither of them," Blue Sky replied. "I'm sure Spring Rain misses me. I miss him. I miss them all. I imagine some of them fear you savage hill people will end up killing Green Field and Gentle Brook's son. But it doesn't matter. I've got work to do here. I started a war. I sent a lot of people to early deaths. I'm sure a lot of other people miss them more than anybody misses me."

Wandering Star, no longer laughing, shook his head. "You and I and a number of other people started that war. All of us are responsible for sending a lot of people to early graves."

Looking down at the river, they could see War Cloud's men at his end of the bridge and Long Arm's at the end below the bluff.

Lightning Spear had refrained from ordering his warriors to destroy the bridge the farmers had built. Rose Leaf and Wandering Star had prompted him to get Heaven's Voice and the high tellers to agree that it must've been some naturally assembled obstruction in the river that also provided a convenient means to cross it. There was

208

therefore no need to destroy it.

Lightning Spear had accordingly decreed that the bridge was a natural agglomeration of flotsam and debris in the stream. But Long Arm's people, Rose Leaf, Wandering Star, and Blue Sky were making the repairs to it the valley people formerly had to make every year after the flood waters of spring did their damage. Rose Leaf and Blue Sky showed them how to figure out what was missing and lock a similar log or boulder in its place.

In another two days the moon would be full. The official mourning period for Dark Storm would end.

*****

Blue Sky couldn't accuse Heaven's Voice of a total lack of candor.

"True Hunter wouldn't consider doing anything for me," the hill people's first teller said, having followed the farmers' prince into the woods once again. "But when he goes with War Cloud, he's totally different. He told me that himself. Then he's all loving, giving, and kind. War Cloud deserves that sort of treatment, True Hunter tells me, and I don't."

"And I can easily see why he thinks that," Blue Sky said.

Heaven's Voice laughed.

Wandering Star had already told Blue Sky that True Hunter went with Heaven's Voice as well as War Cloud.

"He's a spy," Heaven's Voice said. "That's the only reason he goes with me. Everything I tell him, he repeats to War Cloud. No wonder he's that man's favorite. But what difference does it make? I never tell True Hunter the truth anyway. And he's quite pleasing to see with his clothes off. It's a good deal for me. I don't discourage his visits."

Blue Sky knew that, despite the first teller's overall candor, the most important of those remarks was false.

Wandering Star only had to explain it once: True Hunter wouldn't continue going with Heaven's Voice if all he got out of the unpleasantness were useless lies.

The spy ensconced in Lightning Spear's encampment was his first teller.

*****

When Long Arm, Wandering Star, and Blue Sky entered Lightning Spear's tent, Rose Leaf was already there. The king had sent for the three of them at her request.

After they arrived, she informed her father she was carrying Dark Storm's child.

Lightning Spear rose and embraced Rose Leaf.

Blue Sky had never seen him do that before.

Lightning Spear wanted Rose Leaf to know how grateful he was for what she'd done for the kingdom.

"I understand his injury festered horribly," he said. "The tellers said he must've been in terrible pain at the end. Going with him must have been very unpleasant for you."

"I knew how much you wished to have a grandchild," his daughter replied.

Lightning Spear embraced her again.

"I don't want anything to happen to the child," Rose Leaf added. "That's why I've decided it'll be best for both the child and our kingdom if I don't go with War Cloud until after the child is born."

Lightning Spear released Rose Leaf and stared at her.

"War Cloud will insist," he said. "He'll order his warriors to hold you down."

"If that's what you wish," Rose Leaf said. "But I promise you I'll fight them. The people will hear my screams. My screams on behalf of my child, your grandchild."

Lightning Spear turned to Long Arm. "Can't your people do it?" he asked. "Gently?"

"Absolutely not," Long Arm replied. "We've discussed this matter more than once. None of us will ever take part in any attempt to force Rose Leaf to go with War Cloud. We'll disobey your direct order to do so. You'll have to declare every last one of us a traitor and order us all, mates and children included, killed."

"And who'll obey your order to kill Long Arm's family?" Rose Leaf asked her father. "Try to do it—and see what happens. Our people will destroy themselves in a civil war. Our people will cease to exist. The farmers will never have to fear us again."

"And nobody will remember," Wandering Star added, "your great victory on the plain."

Lightning Spear, having resumed his usual seat, looked across his table at Blue Sky.

"I suppose you agree with my daughter, son, and chief warrior," he said.

"I'm your guest," Blue Sky replied. "I wouldn't presume to tell you how to rule your kingdom."

For some reason, Lightning Spear thought that was funny.

*****

That same night, Long Arm's family and Wandering Star's teller allies took the news out to the people: Lightning Spear would make an important announcement in the morning concerning the princess.

It was obvious the king welcomed the huge crowds his daughter, son, chief warrior, and hostage were able to draw to events involving them. In the stories his people and the valley people told, kings often came down hard on princes, princesses, and chief warriors whose popularity rivaled their own. But this king didn't seem to mind. He acted as if the attention bestowed upon those he'd created in the present story was also his.

And perhaps, more than he knew, it was.

He let his daughter, son, chief warrior, and hostage know how much he regretted not being present during War Cloud's presumptuous visit with Rose Leaf. He couldn't understand why no one had told him it was going to happen, so he could've been there to see it himself.

He agreed it was important to keep War Cloud in his place.

"We need only one thing from him," the king sneered. "What he's got between his legs."

The king's daughter, son, chief warrior, and hostage, though, had agreed that was precisely what they didn't need from War Cloud, no matter how desirable it otherwise might've seemed to three of them.

Shadows were short and pointing almost due north, and the

noon meal was ready to be eaten, before Lightning Spear chose to emerge from his tent to make his announcement.

Long Arm's family had kept the king informed that morning as to the numbers of his people they could see still trudging up the bluff. They readily agreed with him it would be a shame if those people were denied the opportunity to be present when their king announced he'd soon have a grandchild, an heir.

For too long, Lightning Spear's story was an incongruous mixture of farce and tragedy. He sired a bastard son with a whore because the queen disliked going with him. He impetuously started an unwinnable war with the farmers. He quickly lost his manhood in that war. He got drunk on the farmers' wine and let two captive enemy warriors, one of them a prince, escape and abduct his and the queen's only child, the princess the queen loved.

All that, he whispered to his hostage the morning of his announcement, now meant nothing.

Dark Storm's child, he told the crowd when the moment to do so arrived, was in Rose Leaf's body.

The people in the crowd knew they were supposed to cheer the joyful news, but they chose to remain silent instead.

Thistle Dew and Dancing Song stood on either side of Rose Leaf. Blue Sky assumed they both knew the truth concerning the child's paternity. As Lightning Spear spoke, they looked at one another smiling. Blue Sky doubted they would've done so if they'd believed what the king had said was true.

War Cloud, who'd come to Lightning Spear's tent with his most trusted warriors for the announcement, gave no indication the news pleased him. After all, he wasn't the child's father.

He did state, though, that he, as the child's soon-to-be stepfather—and, he added, glancing at Wandering Star and Blue Sky, only true uncle—would be responsible for the child's upbringing.

Lightning Spear scowled. "That would perhaps be true," he said, "if the child's maternal grandfather weren't your king."

War Cloud glared at the king but chose to remain silent for the time being.

"Since this is Rose Leaf's first pregnancy," Lightning Spear

212

continued, "she's asked that her union with you be delayed until after the child is born."

"I'll never agree to that," War Cloud quickly replied. "The blessing ceremony takes place as soon as the mourning for my brother ends. That's the law in this kingdom."

"I've decided, on this occasion, to change the law," Lightning Spear said.

War Cloud's warriors murmured.

"I'm the king," Lightning Spear said. "I agree with Rose Leaf. It'll be best for the unborn child."

War Cloud's anger was as obvious as the approach of thunderstorms that hot and humid summer afternoon.

"You're breaking your promise to my father," he dared to say.

"I'm not breaking my promise," Lightning Spear countered. "I'm only delaying to you what I promised to him. Under the circumstances, the delay is reasonable."

"You promised your daughter to my brother and then to me," War Cloud argued. "It's my decision to go with her even if I'm in her body with my brother's child."

"In this case, it's my decision," Lightning Spear said, as visibly angered then as War Cloud was. "And I've decided I won't have you bouncing up and down on my first grandchild."

Dancing Song and Wandering Star, glancing at one another, laughed out loud at that—letting loose, like an ice dam in the river breaking in the spring, a flood of guffaws from their and the lesser chieftains' peoples.

Lightning Spear, realizing he'd made, under the circumstances, an amusing remark, laughed himself.

Many of the older boys and girls repeated, with glee, as if they were still children learning to speak, the king's "bouncing up and down" remark.

Nobody had forgotten War Cloud's preposterous visit to Rose Leaf's tent, or Long Arm's sending him on his way.

The warriors behind War Cloud, though, once again proved their discipline. Despite the raucous laughter of the crowd, they remained as grim-faced as their leader.

Blue Sky could only admire them.

In similar circumstances, nothing—no rule, no mere leader, not even his revered father Green Field—could've induced a hint of War Cloud's warriors' sobriety from Blue Sky's former housemates and the upper-valley cousins.

War Cloud might've gracefully contented himself with the offerings of his favorite tellers for the next three-quarters of a year. He chose instead to respond to the insult in kind.

"Any grandchild of yours," he said to Lightning Spear, "should be honored I'm the one doing the bouncing up and down."

He achieved, though, an effect quite unlike any he might've hoped for.

The crowd, having already been given license, roared. Many once again loudly repeated the four words War Cloud had somehow assumed he could throw back at the king and not seem, since the comic act in question would be his own, a fool.

War Cloud, though, acted as if he heard nothing, certainly not laughter, in response to his remark.

Blue Sky couldn't say for sure—and neither could Wandering Star, he reported later—whether War Cloud truly heard nothing laughable in what he'd said, or knew he'd blundered but would be damned rather than let it show.

His warriors once again maintained their discipline.

Too bad, Blue Sky thought, Many Numbers wasn't there to see them. No wonder Lightning Spear's people were afraid of them.

The laughter died.

War Cloud wasn't ready to give up.

"Even the king can't order what the gods forbid," he declared. "The surviving son takes the promised woman at the end of the mourning for his brother. The mourning for my brother ends tomorrow. I go with Rose Leaf tomorrow or you, Lightning Spear, will face retribution from the gods."

"I beg to differ," Lightning Spear said, speaking as forcefully as War Cloud had. "Our first teller has assured me there's precedent for what Rose Leaf has asked me to do."

War Cloud turned angrily to Heaven's Voice.

The tellers among War Cloud's warriors, True Hunter included, shook their heads.

"There's no precedent for that," War Cloud shouted.

Heaven's Voice stood silent.

"Tell us, old man," War Cloud yelled. "What's your precedent?"

"Tell him," Lightning Spear ordered his first teller.

Heaven's Voice began as he always did, making one statement after the other nobody questioned. The gods were meant to be obeyed. So was the king.

The people began whispering to one another.

"Get to the point, old man," War Cloud bellowed. "What's the precedent?"

The people were just as eager to hear it as War Cloud was.

"What's the precedent?" some of them, several lesser chieftains included, asked.

Heaven's Voice raised his hand to silence the crowd.

There was a story, he said, in which a princess pregnant with her first-born child had declined to go with her partner until after their child was born. It was true, he admitted, the story didn't say the gods had condoned her decision. On the other hand, they hadn't punished her. She got away with it. Her kind father the king granted her request out of the goodness of his heart. The gods hadn't seen fit to punish him, either.

"There's no such story!" War Cloud shouted. "You're a damned liar! You're making it up!"

"I've consulted with the high tellers," Lightning Spear said. "They all tell me there is such a story."

The high tellers, all of whom owed their positions to Heaven's Voice, nodded their heads in agreement.

"There's no such story!" War Cloud screamed at them.

"They're making it up," True Hunter agreed, his contempt for the first teller and his high tellers obvious.

Wandering Star had told Blue Sky all the hill people knew War Cloud preferred being taken care of by True Hunter. In War Cloud's position, Blue Sky would've made the same choice.

"They're making it up," True Hunter's teller comrades among War Cloud's warriors agreed, waving their hands dismissively in the direction of Heaven's Voice and the high tellers.

"You're all a bunch of liars," War Cloud said to the high

tellers, sneering.

In the matter at hand, he was once again correct, as the crowd, snickering, guessed.

Rose Leaf had invented the story. Lightning Spear had passed it on to the first teller, who'd repeated it to the hostage. Blue Sky had to pretend he didn't already know where it came from.

"You lie whenever it suits your purposes," War Cloud continued, yelling at Heaven's Voice and the high tellers.

He spun on his heel and glared at Lightning Spear.

"And yours!" he bellowed.

Wandering Star had convinced Blue Sky his people's first teller and high tellers were as adept as the valley people's tellers were at making up, embellishing, or interpreting a story whenever circumstances required. Wandering Star thought the farmers' tellers usually did it for what they thought was the good of all the people, even if they were wrong sometimes—as when they gave Tall Oak and Sturdy Limb the go-ahead to attack the hill people on the plain.

Heaven's Voice and his high tellers, though, made up stories for the benefit of the king and the people close to the king such as the lesser chieftains and themselves.

They asked more and more in the way of tribute from the people because fewer and fewer of them wished to provide for themselves. The king used to be the only person in the kingdom who had no duty to hunt. The tellers had found a way to include themselves, and others of their and the king's choosing, in the royal exemption.

The people knew War Cloud was telling the truth.

Long Arm's people said the same things among themselves—although in a milder tone of voice than War Cloud had chosen. After Long Arm, his brothers, and cousins had captured Rose Leaf and Morning Sun, and Lightning Spear had made him his chief warrior, his people could've lived off the people's tribute. The family of his predecessor had done so. Long Arm, though, wouldn't allow it. He insisted they'd fend for themselves as they always had.

Warriors grown lazy from the lack of hunting, Long Arm told Blue Sky, were warriors no longer. His family, like the most successful of the farming families, had no fear of work. During the previous winter, in fact, the generosity of Long Arm's family was the only thing that had kept many hill people alive to see spring again.

Thunder Hunter's family and tellers had also refused to take the tribute Lightning Spear had offered them. The people knew this, too. Many of Wandering Star's present allies had rejoiced when they learned Thunder Hunter's warriors would be joining them in the battle on the plain against the farmers. Some of them had even hoped the honest and hard-working Thunder Hunter and his warriors would overthrow the deceitful and indolent Lightning Spear.

That was before they saw what happened on the plain.

"It used to be," War Cloud continued, "we did what the gods told us to do whether we liked it or not. Now the people in charge of this kingdom do whatever they please. Then they have the gall to tell the rest of us that's what the gods told them to do."

Rose Leaf and Long Arm were the two persons present that morning who could've told War Cloud to go no further, who could've made him and his warriors leave.

They chose instead to let War Cloud continue.

"If this isn't evil," War Cloud asked, "what is?"

"Are you saying," Lightning Spear inquired, "your king is doing evil deeds?"

War Cloud looked as if he couldn't believe the opening the king had handed him.

"That's exactly what I'm saying," he replied. "I'm also saying the people agree with me."

To be sure, nobody had chosen to disagree with him, no matter how easy it should've been simply to open one's mouth in defense of one's king.

Then War Cloud, having won the crowd over, immediately threw away his advantage as if it were a bare bone good only for tossing into a garbage pit.

"The gods have always told us to kill the farmers in the valley, to kill every last one of them," he raved on. "They told us to do it no matter how many of our own people might die in battle. Nobody can change what the gods told us. It'll always be true: the gods want to see the farmers dead. They sent us here to accomplish that purpose. We can't care how many of us die doing it. We can only kill and kill until there's not one of them left to kill!"

Many of the on-lookers had been present at the first three of the four battles in the current war with the thieves. Many of them had watched the farmers butcher their sons, fathers, brothers, and mates. Most of them wanted to see no more battles like those fought in their lifetimes.

The conspirators working for a new kingdom well knew they'd need to fight on two fronts, the first against Lightning Spear's corruption, the second against Thunder Hunter's—and now War Cloud's—brutality.

War Cloud pointed his spear at Wandering Star and Blue Sky.

"And you, our king, listen to those people!" he continued. "The one a traitor from a whore's body, the other a demon the hell-gods sent to lead the thieves!"

Dancing Song looked at Wandering Star and Blue Sky, slowly shaking her head and biting her lower lip as if she were saddened to discover their true identities.

When Wandering Star and Blue Sky saw what she was doing and openly laughed, War Cloud assumed they were laughing at him.

"You and the princess will turn our people into farmers!" War Cloud screamed at them. "That's what you both want more than anything!"

War Cloud might've been yelling about evil farmers, hell-gods, and traitors. But what Blue Sky heard was that he wanted Rose Leaf, and he wanted her then—and not after she'd grown big with his brother's child, given birth to it, and become a mother.

In any event, Lightning Spear had remained remarkably unimpressed throughout War Cloud's tirade.

"The persons," he said, "you refer to as the sons of whores and hell-gods will never turn our people into farmers. I have no fear they can ever succeed in doing that."

"The gods forbid it," Heaven's Voice hastened to add.

War Cloud held his spear in front of the first teller's face.

"The gods!" he scoffed. "What would you know about the gods? Who are you to know what the gods say? You think the king can deny me his daughter? You think the gods will allow it? I'll show you, old man, what the gods have to say about that."

Heaven's Voice turned to Lightning Spear as a frightened boy would his father.

Long Arm motioned to his warriors with his spear.

"Make a passageway for War Cloud and his warriors," he ordered once again.

"Go back to your people," Lightning Spear said to War Cloud. "When Rose Leaf delivers her child, I'll send for you. I promise you, you can have her then."

War Cloud and his warriors left, but not before he shook his spear in the first teller's face one last time.

"Old man," he said, "you're what's wrong with this kingdom. You'll be the first to go when I take over. I promise you that."

*****

When Blue Sky first briefly outlined for Rose Leaf, Long Arm, and Wandering Star what he proposed to do next, they quickly and unanimously told him he'd never get away with it.

They were eating their noon meal outside Rose Leaf's tent.

The more they thought about it, the more they insisted he'd get himself killed. He'd put himself in a position where Lightning Spear would have to order his execution.

He asked them if they'd first: remain silent for a while. Second: enjoy their roasted waterfowl, raw onions, and bread moistened with drippings from the roast. And third: let him walk them through his scheme step by step.

He shouldn't have expected them to keep their mouths shut except to take their next bite of their food. Despite their midday hunger, they had far too many questions for that. But, as Many Numbers would've wished, Blue Sky was grateful they asked the right questions.

After they heard him out and had no more questions, Wandering Star set down his empty bowl, wiped his hand across his mouth, and looked fondly at his farmer friend.

"Do it," he said.

"Do it," Long Arm agreed.

Rose Leaf, though, looked at him and shook her head. "You

were always such a gentle boy. No other children have ever had a better family, village, and kingdom to grow up in than we had. I never could've imagined you doing what you're proposing to do now."

"That's what was wrong with us," Blue Sky said.

Rose Leaf wiped her mouth with a sprig of mint.

She being the princess, her agreement was necessary for everything the conspirators did.

She took Blue Sky's hand, the one he used to kill enemy warriors.

"Do it," she said.

"Do it," Morning Sun had said to Blue Sky the summer day the farmer boy first climbed on the back of Green Field's stallion.

"Do it," Blue Sky had said to Rose Leaf and Morning Sun the autumn day they told him they'd decided to defy their parents, become mates, and have children together.

"Do it," Blue Sky had said to himself the spring day he wished to let the hill man with the sinewy body in the gully know he'd like to be his friend.

*****

When Heaven's Voice once again found Blue Sky in the woods, and they were alone, he complained that Lightning Spear had put the entire burden on him.

"He sat there and mumbled," he said. "And I had to tell some story nobody had heard before. I had to make a fool of myself. I had to put up with War Cloud's insults and threats. And that finicky Rose Leaf. Lightning Spear deserves to have her for a daughter. He probably wishes you farmers still had her. She should be damned glad Dark Storm is dead, and now she's got War Cloud to look forward to. But she isn't the least bit grateful. If I were Lightning Spear, I'd order War Cloud's warriors to hold her down. True Hunter and Dark Cloud could do it. I'd let her scream all she wanted. If Long Arm's people didn't wish to hear her screaming, I'd tell them to go into the forest and get some work done."

It didn't seem to matter to Heaven's Voice that Rose Leaf and

Blue Sky had been raised as siblings, and a brother might have an entirely different view of what ought to be done.

Blue Sky agreed to meet the hill people's first teller in the woods that night.

*****

Heaven's Voice proved not to be the fantasizing coward Blue Sky had expected him to be. At the agreed-upon place in the woods and position of the stars in the sky, he presented himself.

"If you were to kill me tonight," he said to the king's hostage, laughing, "they'd all think one of War Cloud's men did it. Nobody would suspect the first teller and the enemy prince were in the woods together. You'd get away with it. Nobody would ever know you did it."

Heaven's Voice mocked death as he had everything else in his life.

Blue Sky was thankful the man wasted no further time on idle conversation but got down on his knees as he'd promised he would, pressing his lips to Blue Sky's loincloth.

When Heaven's Voice reached up to undo Blue Sky's belt, the young man who used to be a "gentle boy" grabbed the older man's hands, pushing him backward onto the ground. Blue Sky landed on him with his knees pinning the first teller's hands against his shoulders.

Despite his obvious discomfort, Heaven's Voice didn't seem at all displeased.

"Is this what you do with Wandering Star?" he asked.

Blue Sky wrapped his hands around the man's neck.

"I'll let you wonder about that," Blue Sky replied, "forever."

Blue Sky squeezed.

Realizing too late the hostage wasn't playing some silly apprentice teller's game with him, Heaven's Voice attempted to scream but couldn't get a whisper past his assailant's hands.

Heaven's Voice was too weak, Blue Sky too strong.

Blue Sky squeezed even harder, denying his victim any breath whatsoever.

In Blue Sky's mind, he was fighting a battle again. And it was intensely pleasurable.

Heaven's Voice tried to squirm out from under him the way the hill boy in the mud below the upper gorge did.

Blue Sky dug his knees even deeper into the first teller's scrawny shoulders.

He held the old man's bird-like neck in his hands, wringing it.

Heaven's Voice would never see or touch True Hunter's naked body again.

The light of the full moon was like campfire reflecting off the eyes of a lover doing for Blue Sky what he wanted done.

In warrior training, the instructors told the boys becoming men to keep their grip on their opponent's neck long past his last breath, to be certain he was dead. His losing consciousness was no reason to stop.

This adversary's struggle, such as it was, had reached its end.

His boyhood lessons well in mind, though, Blue Sky stared at the man's face in the moonlight for a long time after that, his hands still tight around his neck.

It's true Blue Sky detested him and wanted to see him dead.

Heaven's Voice, along with several of his high tellers and their current companions following his lead, had openly laughed when Long Arm's brothers had to pry Blue Sky away from Morning Sun before his execution.

Heaven's Voice was later heard to say Blue Sky had clung to his boyhood friend in a bid for sympathy from the common hill people, many of them gullible enough to believe his tears were genuine.

All the hostage really wanted, Heaven's Voice claimed, was to go with the prince, and knew then, thanks to Lightning Spear and Thunder Hunter, he never would.

But hatred for Heaven's Voice, however much the man had earned it, was hardly a sufficient reason to kill him. In order to justify that, Blue Sky had to believe he was doing something beneficial for both the hill people and his own. If he didn't also make that happen, he was fully cognizant, despite the state of his mind, he would've erred grievously, and the gods could rightly do with him as they pleased.

222

For all the killing Blue Sky had accomplished, he'd scarcely be surprised if they'd wish to punish him as harshly as they did the meddling god whose crime gave humans fire. They'd make him suffer the pain of death for eternity.

However that might turn out, Blue Sky knew he'd inevitably see, countless times again, his victim's face as he died, and the hideous drool at the corners of his mouth—in the horrific dream that woke him every night of his life.

*****

Blue Sky dragged the first teller's body to the nearest path and left it there.

Long Arm's people discovered it shortly after dawn.

The chief warrior informed the king the first teller had been found dead in the woods. And bruises on his neck indicated the cause of his death was strangulation.

*****

The high tellers prevailed upon Lightning Spear to summon all the tellers, those with War Cloud's people not excepted, to the king's encampment on the bluff.

When all the tellers were present, the younger and still able-bodied tellers living with the high tellers and their friends surrounded True Hunter at spear-point, confiscated his weapons, and led him to the king's tent, where another throng had gathered.

Two of the high tellers had seen True Hunter speaking with Heaven's Voice the previous evening. The high tellers therefore assumed that Heaven's Voice, heedless of War Cloud's threat, must've agreed to meet True Hunter in the woods later that night.

"It's obvious True Hunter murdered Heaven's Voice," one of the high tellers told Lightning Spear. "It's just as obvious War Cloud sent him to do it."

The high tellers and their associates, as well as the lesser chieftains and their chief warriors—all those who presumed they had the right to live off the people's tribute—murmured their agreement.

"Killing a first teller is treason," another high teller said. "The

223

punishment is death."

"Order us to do it," yet another pleaded. "We'll do it right here and now."

He must've meant that one of their younger, more able-bodied acolytes would do it, although Blue Sky suspected it would take several of them, maybe even as many as ten, to get the job done. And still, more than one of them, not unlike Thunder Hunter and Dark Storm, would end up dead along with the condemned man.

True Hunter supposedly had a good reason for wanting to meet Heaven's Voice in the woods.

The first teller would've confirmed the bogus story he'd told War Cloud came from the king's tent. The news would've been strong evidence that the king's daughter, chief warrior, son, and hostage were conspiring to take over the kingdom.

True Hunter turned to Lightning Spear.

"These lackeys have never served you well," he said, motioning with his hand toward the high tellers. "You should be ashamed of yourself for letting them live off the people. All the people get in return from them is their lies."

Rose Leaf looked at Long Arm and Wandering Star, who'd made the same points numerous times in their conversations with Lightning Spear in his notorious tent.

"And now you've heard another one," True Hunter added.

The king looked at his daughter, chief warrior, son, and hostage.

"I didn't go with Heaven's Voice last night," True Hunter continued. "He told me he had somebody else lined up. I didn't kill him. War Cloud didn't send me to kill him, either."

"And he calls us liars," one of the high tellers said. "Nobody else went with Heaven's Voice last night. He didn't have anybody else lined up. He would've told us if he did."

True Hunter guffawed. "Did that pathetic man tell you he was meeting me last night? You would've been the first to find that out, and you know it. He liked to brag too much not to have told you he was going with me. I'm even more desirable to you than War Cloud. We all know that."

The high tellers looked at one another and chose not to reply.

Most of the spectators, though, laughed, enjoying True Hunter's audacity—and seeing no need for solemnity in a proceeding precipitated by the murder of their first teller.

True Hunter turned to Lightning Spear.

"Don't misunderstand me," he said. "I believe Heaven's Voice deserved to die. He thought he was better than the people. So do his henchmen, these fools standing here demanding that you order me executed for a murder I didn't commit, however much I'd like to brag I did."

Rose Leaf stared at Long Arm, Wandering Star, and Blue Sky. They hadn't anticipated this turn of events.

True Hunter motioned toward the high tellers again.

"I'd like to see them dead, too," he said. "So would the people they demand tribute from."

"You're damned right!" somebody in the crowd yelled. "Damned right!" others agreed.

True Hunter looked at Lightning Spear and laughed.

"You can put me to death," he said, "but it won't do you or the kingdom any good at all."

The conspirators had inadvertently caught True Hunter in their scheme. Blue Sky could only assume they had one defense: they hadn't considered it. They hadn't imagined, although perhaps they should've, who the high tellers would most likely accuse.

Humans, the farmers liked to say, couldn't know which storm, before it came, would merely settle the dust in their fields—and which would blow down their houses, granaries, and barns and destroy their hopes and dreams.

Blue Sky couldn't imagine a king ordering the execution of a person simply because he'd been seen talking with the murder victim. Tall Oak never would've done such a thing.

Rose Leaf turned to Lightning Spear.

"It's full-moon day," she said. "I ask you to put off until tomorrow this man's trial. I think you need to consider the matter further."

The high tellers looked at one another again, shaking their heads.

True Hunter stared at Rose Leaf.

"The princess is right," Long Arm added. "The evidence against this man is flimsy."

True Hunter shifted his gaze from Long Arm to Wandering Star and then to Blue Sky. He clearly hadn't expected the king's daughter and chief warrior to plead his case for him.

His surprise revealed an innocence Blue Sky hadn't expected to see.

Even if True Hunter was guilty of murdering Heaven's Voice, Lightning Spear's execution of the hill people's finest warrior, a beloved hero to all of them, for killing a man the people despised, would've made no sense at all.

Lightning Spear got up from his chair.

"We've had enough killing," he said. "There'll be no execution today. Give the prisoner to Long Arm."

He turned to the high tellers.

"You'll hear from me on this matter tomorrow," he said, retreating into his tent.

*****

Long Arm's taking of the prisoner consisted of asking him to spend the rest of the day enjoying the full-moon festivities with the chief warrior's family.

All Long Arm required was that True Hunter not try to escape. If he did, his people would have to impose fatal blows, however much they didn't wish to do that to him.

Long Arm would himself deliver the finishing and benevolent swipe of his prisoner's throat with his spear. It was as simple as that.

*****

The high tellers shook their heads again.

How festive could a full-moon day be if it included a funeral for their murdered first teller, who was the sole basis for their good fortune in this world?

To be fair, Blue Sky often heard Heaven's Voice, the high

226

tellers, and their associates laughing when they got together. They enjoyed life in much the same way Noon Breeze and the apprentice tellers did. Those around the hill people's first teller would no doubt miss the good company of the man Blue Sky had killed.

Blue Sky loathed their selfishness and disdain for their people who weren't clever enough to avoid working.

He nevertheless regretted he'd disrupted the lives of the high tellers and their associates—no matter how much he knew it had to be done, and he had to be the person to do it.

Chapter 13

True Hunter spent most of the day helping the women and children in Long Arm's family.

Blue Sky was surprised to see a person considered his brutish tribe's finest hunter, warrior, and executioner doing the work of women and children.

But Wandering Star said True Hunter was known for that.

The older boys, Blue Sky noticed, were especially pleased to have True Hunter for a guest.

He heard one of them arguing True Hunter wasn't to blame for what Thunder Hunter and War Cloud had done. He wasn't a chieftain or king who decided a person had to be killed or a war fought. He merely did, quite well, what he was told to do.

That boy, called Aim Far, was Second Brother's oldest son.

Despite their excitement over True Hunter's presence, the boys chose to accompany Wandering Star and Blue Sky into the woods with sledges, loading them down and pulling them back to the encampment with more than enough fallen branches and limbs to keep the feast fires burning all night.

Wandering Star saw fit to tell the boys the farmers would have wheels instead of runners under their sledges, and they'd also have their oxen instead of humans pulling them.

"And horses," Blue Sky hastened to add. "Our horses do that, too."

"I thought only gods have horses," Aim Far said. "Are the farmers gods?"

Second Brother had told his son that Wandering Star and Blue Sky were their friends, and he could trust them. But Aim Far's father had also warned him against following their example in mocking the gods. Whenever they did, he shouldn't pay them any attention.

Blue Sky had noticed Aim Far nevertheless listened.

Upon sighting True Hunter in the encampment again, the boys began a loud argument.

Blue Sky soon learned what the quarrel was all about and why Wandering Star was so amused.

It concerned a hypothetical duel to the death between the farmers' finest warrior and their own, and how it would end.

Some of the disputants were insisting True Hunter would win. Others were just as loudly contending the farmers' new prince, now Lightning Spear's hostage, would.

True Hunter, having left the women and girls to help unload the firewood, found the boys' discussion as amusing as Wandering Star did.

Aim Far spoke up, dismissing the first view of the matter as flatly as he did the second. He insisted True Hunter and Blue Sky would undoubtedly both end up dead.

"Neither of them would consider dying without taking the other down with him," he said.

True Hunter looked at Blue Sky and laughed.

"It'll require more than this farmer to take me down," he assured the boys.

"Let's sneak them some spears," Aim Far said to his companions.

The older boys, making a huge pile of the firewood, snickered.

True Hunter liked the idea. "Bring both of us the strongest, sharpest spears you can lay your hands on," he said to the boys. "I'll show you how to kill a farmer, even if he's the best warrior those thieves have got. You'll get to see his guts spilled out on the ground where farmer guts belong. You'll get to watch him die. Right now. Right here. You'll get to see just how superior to us these god-like farmers really are."

Aim Far chose to respond to that. "Some of us saw a lot of dead farmers at the battle on the plain," he said. "With their guts hanging out, too. They didn't look much like gods then. Or even humans who were supposed to be superior to us."

True Hunter stared at Aim Far, whose contorted face made it clear he hadn't finished what he intended to say.

"We saw a lot of our own dead warriors, too," he continued. "We dragged them off the battlefield and laid them in their graves. It was horrific work, and it went on and on the whole damned day."

True Hunter had watched the farmers kill friends of his, Wandering Star told Blue Sky, men he'd gone with because he considered them his equals, and not because they were an old teller

230

willing to give him one-sided gratification along with secrets, too.

True Hunter wisely chose not to respond to the boy's remarks.

Some of the younger children who were nearby, overhearing what Aim Far and True Hunter had said about the spears, hadn't realized their remarks were in jest.

One young girl ran to her mother with the frightening news: the older boys were going to give spears to True Hunter and the hostage.

"True Hunter gave them his word," she said. "He promised them he'll kill that nice farmer prince who lives with Wandering Star. He'll pull his innards out and slit his throat. That's what they say he did to the other farmer prince. Can't the men stop True Hunter from doing it again?"

For Blue Sky one of the saddest things after the battle on the plain was overhearing his people's children speculating about what must've happened to their brothers, fathers, cousins, uncles, and neighbors who'd never returned from it.

"Picked to the bone," he heard more than one child say.

First Brother and Second Brother soon came running.

The job of piling the wood having been accomplished, First Brother sternly ordered all the children to go help their mothers and sisters prepare for the feast and "leave the prisoners alone."

*****

After the children and their fathers left them, True Hunter, Wandering Star, and Blue Sky stood looking at one another.

True Hunter spoke first. "I don't know what you, Rose Leaf, and Long Arm think you'll get out of this. I never asked you to save my life. And I'll never feel I owe you anything for doing it."

"What are you talking about?" Wandering Star asked. "We had nothing to do with saving your life. Rose Leaf and Long Arm weren't convinced you killed Heaven's Voice. The king listened to his daughter the princess and his chief warrior. That should be no surprise. They're supposed to advise him. You'll have to ask them why they think you're innocent."

True Hunter glared at Wandering Star.

"Don't toy with me," he said. "You're all in it together. Rose Leaf, Long Arm, you, and this farmer hostage. The four of you."

231

He looked at Blue Sky and laughed.

"You should've let them kill me," he said.

"Even if you didn't kill Heaven's Voice?" Blue Sky asked.

"What difference does that make?"

Wandering Star attempted a response to that. "A king or chieftain is supposed to punish people for wrong-doing, not just for being the people they are."

"That sounds good," True Hunter offered. "But it isn't what kings and chieftains do."

He turned to Blue Sky again.

"What do you want from me?" he asked.

"Not a damned thing," Blue Sky replied.

Wandering Star looked at Blue Sky and laughed.

"True Hunter expects you to tell him you want to go with him," he said.

True Hunter, who was still looking at Blue Sky, snickered. "I've assumed all along he does," he said.

It was a reasonable assumption, too. Many times he'd caught Blue Sky staring at him.

"Doesn't everybody?" Blue Sky asked.

True Hunter enjoyed that.

"But you're out of luck," he said. "Unlike your friend here, I don't go with farmers."

"Is that the only reason," Blue Sky heard himself asking, "I'm out of luck?"

True Hunter looked him up and down. It wasn't the first time he'd done that. After all, Blue Sky was considered the fiercest warrior the farmers had.

"That's it," True Hunter replied. "I don't dirty myself with farmers. I kill them every chance I get. That was the first thing I learned as a child. Our people don't go with thieves. We kill them. Unlike the king's bastard son, I think that's all I need to know."

"I do want something from you," Blue Sky said.

"And what might that be?" True Hunter sneered.

"First, I want you to understand I don't think you're stupid or corrupt. In fact, I think you're exceptionally honest and intelligent.

And second, I hope you stay that way."

True Hunter stared at Blue Sky. "That's all you want from me?"

"That's it," Blue Sky replied.

*****

The hill people held a funeral for Heaven's Voice that afternoon.

In the meantime, the high tellers had agreed to recommend to Lightning Spear that he appoint one of their own to be the new first teller. Their funeral orations accordingly included quite a few more references to the supposed virtues of their candidate than to those of the deceased.

Lightning Spear soon made no attempt to conceal his weariness with the proceedings. Each speaker was making certain not to omit any point the previous orators had made, apparently assuming any deviation might be perceived as a difference of opinion.

If that sort of thing had ever happened among Blue Sky's people, the on-lookers would've quickly interjected sarcastic remarks. If that didn't work, they'd yell at the speaker, even a chief warrior or a first teller, demanding he say something new or sit down and shut up.

When the funeral was finally over, Lightning Spear summoned Rose Leaf, Long Arm, Wandering Star, and Blue Sky to his tent.

"What a horrible day this was," he complained, taking his cup from Long Arm. "I'd hoped we'd attend a joyous blessing ceremony for Rose Leaf, with a feast afterward. Instead, we had to sit through a funeral for that man I was foolish enough to appoint first teller. I thought they'd never be done. I should've stopped them. I don't know why I didn't."

Lightning Spear looked at Wandering Star.

"Did True Hunter kill Heaven's Voice?" he asked.

"He didn't," Wandering Star replied.

"How do you know that?" Lightning Spear persisted.

"He would've admitted it," Wandering Star answered. "He would've thrown it in your face. War Cloud would've ordered him to confess if he got caught. He would've wanted the people to know he'd ordered Heaven's Voice killed. Of course, True Hunter would've denied War Cloud had anything to do with it, but nobody would've believed that part of his confession."

"And I would've ordered him executed," Lightning Spear said. "Right then and there."

"True Hunter would've played his part in that," Wandering Star agreed.

Lightning Spear had another question for his bastard son.

"If True Hunter didn't kill Heaven's Voice," he asked, "who did?"

"Somebody who hated the man," Wandering Star replied. "And saw a good chance to do it after War Cloud had threatened him. Everybody would assume War Cloud was behind it."

Lightning Spear stared at Wandering Star. "Did you kill him?" he asked.

"No," Wandering Star replied. "A lot of people despised your first teller. It could've been any one of them."

Lightning Spear wasn't done with Wandering Star.

"You could've agreed to meet him in the woods," he said, "just to kill him."

"No," Wandering Star countered, shaking his head. "He would've told the high tellers."

"Bragging about going with the king's son?" Lightning Spear asked.

"At long last," Wandering Star replied.

Lightning Spear smirked at his son by Dancing Song.

"Why don't I order True Hunter's execution anyway?" he asked. "Whether he did it or not? I'll have him killed tomorrow morning and be done with it. He's got a damned nasty mouth, telling me in front of all those people it's my fault the people hate the high tellers."

"True Hunter didn't kill Heaven's Voice," Rose Leaf said. "Wandering Star has made that clear. You can't execute a man for a murder he didn't commit."

Lightning Spear looked at Rose Leaf and smiled.

"My dear sweet daughter," he said.

He smiled again. Wandering Star had told Blue Sky the king

234

was openly pleased when, at his first meeting with Rose Leaf, he discovered for himself how attractive his daughter had become.

"Is that a rule you learned from the farmers?" Lightning Spear inquired.

"Yes, it is," she replied. "But it would be prudent for any king to adhere to it."

Lightning Spear turned to Blue Sky. "Did you know, when she returned to us, the first thing she requested was that we continue calling her 'Rose Leaf'?"

Lightning Spear had to know his hostage would've heard that story already, but Blue Sky could hardly blame him for wanting to tell his hostage his version of it anyway.

"She got her own mother to side with her," Lightning Spear said. "Wandering Star's mother also weighed in on the subject, of course. And the women in Long Arm's family were soon coming here insisting I should let her keep her farmer name. It had nothing to do with farming, they said. Our people use that name, you know. And it does fit the princess, I must say."

He glanced at Rose Leaf and smiled again.

"Of course, I gave in and let Rose Leaf keep the only name she'd ever known," he said. "She told me your father and mother gave her that name. They chose well."

An evening breeze passed through Lightning Spear's tent.

"You believe that, too?" Lightning Spear asked Blue Sky. "I can't execute a man for a murder he didn't commit?"

"You can, but I don't think you should," Blue Sky replied.

"You see, that goes to the heart of the matter," the king said. "I must say, from what you, Wandering Star, and Rose Leaf tell me, your people are hopelessly impractical."

Long Arm vigorously shook his head. "In the upper gorge and on sunset pass, we had many more warriors than they did. Yet nobody could count the number of our warriors they killed. And they lost no warriors of their own. I'd hardly call the people who did that impractical."

Lightning Spear had stared at the wine in his cup all through those remarks.

"An execution," he began again, "has never required guilt of a crime on the part of the person executed. I agree it's usually nice for a king to know the person he's ordered killed is guilty of something, but the king can still execute any person he pleases."

He held out his cup, as he'd taken to do, sweeping it across his field of vision from one of his visitors to the other, meeting their eyes over it, as if something had gone wrong with his mind.

"How can a king," he wanted to know, "rule a kingdom without being able to do that?"

Rose Leaf was quick to reply. "I'm quite certain it can be done."

Lightning Spear turned to her, a wan smile on his face this time.

"My dear sweet daughter," he said. "All joking aside, please listen to me. A king has to be able to act, and act now. He can't be listening to speeches and arguments. He has to act."

Except, apparently, when he was listening to his daughter, chief warrior, bastard son, and hostage.

"A king I once knew and greatly respected did that," Rose Leaf said. "He refused to listen to speeches and arguments. He and his brother decided to act instead. They marched their people's army onto a plain to teach their hated enemy a lesson. They led their warriors into a trap instead. They found themselves vastly outnumbered and surrounded. Almost all of them died that day. I hear the plain was as crimson as a sunset. I hear vultures and wolves came and ate their flesh. You can still see their bones bleaching on that plain. I've seen them myself."

Lightning Spear's view of the battle on the plain was surprisingly different.

"The same king and his brother," he said, "somehow inspired their warriors to stand and fight that entire day. They forced the enemy warriors to kill them one by one. They forced the enemy king to force his own warriors to keep fighting. They forced him to order a number of his own warriors slaughtered as an example. They killed so many of the enemy king's warriors his army couldn't finish them off. They fled to the safety of their upper valley. I hear they live there in peace and happiness even now. Do you know who told me that? The person you thought was your brother. I assume he was telling me the truth."

236

Lightning Spear drank from his cup. His remarks were the kind he'd freely make to these visitors in his tent but to no one and nowhere else. Other people had to tell him he'd finished the matter with the farmers and had found nothing but success in his second glorious war with them.

Lightning Spear looked over his cup at Long Arm and Wandering Star.

"I should've let the tellers execute True Hunter this morning," he said. "The people might've despised Heaven's Voice, but I can't let War Cloud's tribe get away with killing him."

Wandering Star shook his head. "Do you intend to punish War Cloud himself?"

"Our people," Rose Leaf interjected, "don't want to see True Hunter executed even if he did murder Heaven's Voice. They love him. They think he was the one War Cloud sent to do it. They think he was putting himself at risk of execution for War Cloud. War Cloud's the one your people want you to kill. Are you ready to do it?"

"I agree with that," Long Arm said.

Lightning Spear stared at Long Arm. "War Cloud is my ally. I don't care whether he killed Heaven's Voice or not. In fact, I'm glad Heaven's Voice is dead, no matter who did it. But while I'm king, War Cloud's warriors and mine will never fight against one another."

"They will," Rose Leaf countered. "You're wrong. He wants to rule the kingdom. He wants to resume the war with the farmers. Your people and the lesser chieftains' people don't want him ruling their kingdom. They don't want him resuming the war with the farmers. The battle between War Cloud and your people will come."

"There's no way to avoid it," Wandering Star added.

"What you've got to do," Long Arm said, "is to choose the proper time and place for it."

Lightning Spear changed the subject. "I believe True Hunter killed Heaven's Voice. I agree War Cloud probably told him to admit it if we caught him, but True Hunter got scared instead. Got scared and denied he killed Heaven's Voice."

"There's an easy way to find out if that's correct," Wandering Star said.

"What way is that?" Lightning Spear asked.

"Send True Hunter back to War Cloud," Wandering Star

replied. "If your theory is correct, War Cloud will kill him. If War Cloud doesn't kill him, you'll know True Hunter didn't kill Heaven's Voice."

Lightning Spear was suddenly smiling again.

"If he killed Heaven's Voice but was too scared to take the blame, he dies," he said. "If he didn't kill him, he lives."

"The people," Wandering Star said, "will think he killed Heaven's Voice in any event, and they'll be grateful."

Lightning Spear looked at Blue Sky and laughed.

"But we'll know True Hunter and War Cloud didn't do it," he said.

"You can tell the people this," Wandering Star said. "You don't believe War Cloud would dare kill a first teller or order him killed. You can point out that True Hunter denied he did it, and nobody ever said he wasn't an honest man. You can say you aren't required to, but in this case you wish to be certain you execute the person who really committed the murder. You can say that's what a good king does. You can say he causes no harm to any of his people except to protect them."

"They'll like that," Rose Leaf affirmed.

"And they'll still think," Lightning Spear said, "War Cloud ordered the murder and True Hunter did it."

"But you'll be giving True Hunter the benefit of the doubt," Long Arm said. "The people will like that. They admire him. They don't want to see him executed."

"And you won't have to explain why you let War Cloud go free," Wandering Star said.

"Please send True Hunter home," Rose Leaf said.

"I'll send him home," Lightning Spear agreed. "Tomorrow morning. Worry no further."

He looked at Blue Sky and laughed.

"You know, I don't care if he killed Heaven's Voice anyway," he said. "That man's murder is clearly a benefit to me and my kingdom, whoever committed it. They say he was strangled. Somebody did it with his bare hands. I wish I'd been there. I would've enjoyed seeing it."

*****

By dawn a multitude had converged on the bluff above the river where the valley people's town used to stand. Word had gotten out, again from Long Arm's family and Wandering Star's teller allies, that something of great importance to the people would happen that day.

Despite Lightning Spear's having declared a period of mourning for Heaven's Voice extending to the next full moon, the atmosphere was festive, even so early in the morning. Hunting in the lower-valley forest had produced an abundance of game. Many of the families were pitching tents and preparing feasts.

War Cloud had let it be known none of his people would attend unless they wished to die.

If Lightning Spear were to order True Hunter killed in the presence of their tribe's warriors, Long Arm quickly decided, they might feel obliged to come to his assistance, perhaps starting the civil war both sides had so far attempted to avoid.

The high tellers came as a group to Lightning Spear's tent, their candidate for first teller in the lead. They seemed surprised so many of the common people were in attendance.

"Entice them with a bloody execution," Blue Sky heard one say, "and they'll show up."

Another sighed. "All that game for them to feast on, and they still have the nerve to say they can't make their tribute."

"Don't forget the one thing they always do best," a third said. "Lying to the tellers."

"Oh, well," the first said. "I can't really blame them for not wanting to miss True Hunter's execution. He's almost as pleasing to look upon as the farmers' prince he killed."

Perhaps believing, as Blue Sky suspected, that last remark was intended for the ears of the hostage, Wandering Star whispered a warning to him to keep his mouth shut.

"They'll be singing another kind of song," he promised, "before this day is done."

Lightning Spear remained in his tent most of that morning. The lesser chieftains who gained entry to it came out with the story that the

239

king once again wished to give as many of his people as possible a chance to attend the day's proceedings.

And once again it was almost noon when Lightning Spear emerged. He chose to remain standing.

Speaking loudly and clearly, he set forth at length the grounds for suspecting that True Hunter might've murdered Heaven's Voice. Since, however, the suspicion depended upon War Cloud's having ordered True Hunter to commit the deed, the king had to view it with skepticism. War Cloud was, despite his public and comedic temper tantrums, Lightning Spear's ally, friend, and loyal subject.

The high tellers looked at one another and shook their heads in disbelief.

Lightning Spear next explained, again at length, it wasn't necessary for him to believe that True Hunter was actually guilty of the crime of murder. A king was free, even at his whim, to order any subject executed. In this case, True Hunter's execution would serve the purpose of sending a warning to War Cloud, who had, after all, rashly and openly threatened Heaven's Voice. It would also satisfy those among his people who honestly believed True Hunter had murdered Heaven's Voice at War Cloud's behest.

The high tellers were now solemnly nodding their heads in agreement as if they'd never doubted the king would ultimately side with them.

On the other hand, Lightning Spear said, bringing the high tellers back to the real world, a good king never sent the least of his subjects to their death without finding it absolutely necessary for the good of the people. A wise king could therefore choose to be as compassionate as he could be cruel. In this case, where True Hunter had steadfastly denied committing the crime, and all the people considered him to be an honest person, Lightning Spear would grant True Hunter the benefit of the doubt and let him live.

"We expected justice from Lightning Spear?" Blue Sky heard one of the high tellers whisper.

"Better to expect blood from a blade of grass," another high teller remarked.

True Hunter stared at Rose Leaf, Long Arm, Wandering Star,

240

and Blue Sky. He knew they'd saved his life, but he looked as if he still couldn't figure out why.

Yesterday at court he must've assumed, as Morning Sun had on the day of his execution, he'd soon be dead—not for anything he'd done, but only for being who he was.

Now the great warrior was wiping tears from his eyes for all the boys to see.

*****

Lightning Spear ordered True Hunter to remain at court long enough to hear his next announcement. Lightning Spear trusted that True Hunter would report its substance to War Cloud's people.

The king, however magnanimous he'd appeared to be in ruling in True Hunter's favor, couldn't resist the opportunity to balance the account with a bit of malice.

"I note none of your kinsmen is here with us today," he mocked his prisoner. "I can only assume they didn't care what I did with you. They might take interest, though, in what I do with the kingdom they share with us."

True Hunter, knowing why none of his tribe was present, remained silent.

Lightning Spear turned to the high tellers.

"You and the recently departed first teller," he said, spitting out his words, "advised me our people's army could never defeat the farmers' army."

This was what the ordinary hill people, standing motionless, silent, and sweating in the noonday summer sun in what used to be the farmers' courtyard, had come for. The sparing of True Hunter was good news, even if he was War Cloud's cousin, but it was only a preliminary to this.

"The farmers were too strong," Lightning Spear bellowed. "That's what you and the first teller told me. And we were too weak. That was your craven advice."

The high tellers looked at one another.

They'd come to court the day before only asking the king to punish the man who'd unquestionably murdered their friend and benefactor, who was the first teller no less.

241

Now the king had set the insolent killer free and was leveling accusations at them.

"All we could do was to avoid another war with the high-and-mighty farmers," Lightning Spear continued. "We were no match for them. That's exactly what you all told me."

The high tellers' only defense to the charge would be to agree with War Cloud that Lightning Spear hadn't yet won his war with the farmers.

They instead remained silent, glancing at one another, shaking their heads.

They'd had good reasons for their opposition to a new war with the farmers.

They enjoyed life, Heaven's Voice had admitted to Wandering Star in the woods one afternoon, and they didn't want it interrupted by another of their "crazy king's damned wars."

"One of the young tellers came to me," Lightning Spear raved on. "He told me our people were far stronger than the first teller and you said we were."

The hill people were well aware of that part of the story by then, but it still must've sounded new coming from the king himself in open court where everybody could hear it.

It was also where their interests and the king's came together.

"He told me my army could defeat the farmers," Lightning Spear boomed to the farthest reaches of the crowd, ignoring the high tellers now. "He even laid out for me, step by step, specifically how we could do it."

But he wasn't finished with the high tellers yet. He turned in their direction again, even waving his spear at them.

"And how did you and the first teller's respond to that young teller?" he asked, dramatically raising his voice. "You and the first teller insisted I expel him as a teller and send him into exile from our people! That's what you and the first teller did!"

True Hunter looked from the four main conspirators to the high tellers and back again, openly sneering. Now he understood what the conspirators had done.

"And it happened just as the young teller had told me it

242

would," Lightning Spear continued. "The farmers attacked us. And just as he'd predicted, we joined together and greatly outnumbered and defeated them and took back our valley from them."

Lightning Spear, enjoying the moment, knowing he had the crowd with him, paused.

True Hunter bravely chose that moment to resume his argument with the king, who, if he'd dared, could've reversed his decision not to have him executed.

"But Wandering Star also tried to stop your more recent war with the farmers," True Hunter shouted. "Do you remember that, old man? Do you remember him begging you to spare the thieves?"

Lightning Spear looked at True Hunter and laughed.

"Of course Wandering Star tried to stop it," he shouted, again to as many of his people as could possibly hear him. "He tried to stop it after we'd already won it and had the farmers' army in our grasp. That's what he did."

Lightning Spear was more prepared for True Hunter's question than Blue Sky had imagined he'd be.

But it was the moment Lightning Spear was waiting for, knowing what he'd say would shock every person who heard it.

"And the war could've been stopped then," he continued.

If it had been stopped then, the people facing the king wouldn't be mourning the loss of many children, parents, and lovers.

"And the war," Lightning Spear dared to say, "should've been stopped then."

In his conversations with the conspirators in his tent, Lightning Spear had so often voiced this version of the events leading to the war that he'd proved he'd come to believe it was true.

Now it was time for him to share it with his people.

"The farmers' king," he continued, "could've sent Wandering Star and his friend, their prince's cousin, to me with a message. Their king and his brother could've done that rather than attacking us without warning. They could've offered to remove their people to the place where they are now."

The crowd gave Lightning Spear the stunned silence he'd hoped for.

"I would've agreed to that," he insisted, letting his tears fall without restraint, knowing that's what it would take to get the job done. "Your sons and your fathers and your lovers could be with us this day, standing next to you here."

Blue Sky had to admit Lightning Spear was clever. Who could possibly say he wouldn't have agreed to something that had never entered anybody's mind at the time?

"We didn't need to fight that war," the king said, choosing to look at his hostage, Blue Sky. "Neither your people nor our people should've fought that war. Neither side should've lost a single person. All those warriors of yours we killed and all those warriors of ours your people killed—they all could've been saved."

True Hunter didn't dare point out to the people that such an outcome—which brought back to life, however momentarily, their many dead—was never possible.

He and they remained silent.

So did Rose Leaf, Long Arm, Wandering Star, and Blue Sky.

Long Arm and Wandering Star had scoffed at the notion that Lightning Spear and Thunder Hunter would've allowed the farmers to keep the upper valley.

And that assumed Wandering Star and Blue Sky could've convinced Tall Oak and Sturdy Limb and all the valley people that the size of the hill people's army required their exodus to the upper valley. Which would've been no small achievement.

On the other hand, Long Arm and Wandering Star saw no reason to express an opinion in public on the matter, no reason not to let their people believe the king's view was the proper one.

Nor did Rose Leaf or Blue Sky have any reason to disagree with what was really only a matter of what-might-have-been.

Blue Sky, Rose Leaf, and Morning Sun had lied to their parents every time they rode the horses after Green Field had told them not to. Their parents had likewise lied to them every day they let them believe Rose Leaf was Green Field and Gentle Brook's daughter.

None of the conspirators saw any reason for the hill people not to believe an agreement with the farmers had always been possible and would've prevented the killing and starvation of a great number of their people.

"Therefore," Lightning Spear announced, almost as an

afterthought, "I hereby revoke Wandering Star's exile. I hereby also restore him as a teller."

What came next was what Lightning Spear had decided his kingdom needed, he'd told the conspirators one night in his tent, more than anything else.

It was unquestionably what he needed just to show what he could get away with.

It was also what the hill people had come for, and why they were prepared to sing, dance, drink, and feast the remainder of that day.

"The gods have spoken to me," Lightning Spear announced, shamelessly. "They've told me our people's new first teller should be Wandering Star."

As if he admired what the conspirators had done, True Hunter stared at Rose Leaf, Long Arm, Wandering Star, and Blue Sky and remained silent.

The crowd, though, roared its approval. They'd gotten what they'd come for.

Chapter 14

Lightning Spear had insisted he wasn't joking when he told his daughter, son, chief warrior, and hostage that Wandering Star should be the kingdom's first teller.

Wandering Star had also insisted he wasn't joking when he told the king and his co-conspirators he'd never accept such a position.

He said the high tellers and the younger men who lived with them were a bunch of status-obsessed layabouts. Why would he wish to have the title of first among them?

Besides, he said, he and his farmer companion enjoyed mocking the gods. A first teller couldn't go around doing that.

"Oh, who cares?" Lightning Spear came back, laughing. "The current first teller and his high tellers don't believe in the gods any more than you and the farmers' prince do."

"They just won't admit it," Long Arm agreed, making no attempt to conceal his contempt for the hypocrisy of the first teller and his high tellers. "They couldn't believe in the gods and expect to get away with what they do—which is brazenly living off the people."

Lightning Spear looked at Long Arm and laughed. He knew that comment could apply, and was perhaps meant to apply, to himself and his cronies as well.

Long Arm rarely spoke of the gods, but many in his family believed they existed and needed to be obeyed. They repeated the same thing Thunder Hunter's people, now War Cloud's, said: they believed in the "old gods," the gods their people used to look up to, before the present-day troubles began.

Blue Sky had noticed, though, he couldn't extract any useful information from them when he questioned precisely how and why those troubles had begun.

Second Brother had once told him the gods could've ordered humans not to raise their own animals and plants, but he agreed with Wandering Star they'd never laid down any such prohibition. And that was a powerful reason for believing farming was permissible, and killing farmers—to say nothing of getting killed by them—was pointless.

It also explained why he and his family had no use for Heaven's Voice and the high tellers.

"It's all a joke to them," he'd told Blue Sky. "They laugh at the same gods they say require your people to be our people's enemy forever and ever. A requirement leading to one bloody war after the other. And one generation after the other maimed and ruined. And yet they laugh."

Long Arm, who rarely laughed at anything, had turned to Wandering Star and Blue Sky during one of their discussions in the king's tent.

"At least you're honest about it," he said in that monotone his sons and nephews liked to imitate for their amusement. "But I agree with you on one thing. No god will come down from heaven to save us. We have to save ourselves or perish. I can only assume that's how the gods must want it."

He looked at his three fellow conspirators as if the king weren't present.

"The gods didn't abduct the farmers' prince and our princess," he said. "Humans did. I was there and saw them do it. I was their leader. I did it. And I'll live with the guilt it brought me for the rest of my life."

No boy or apprentice teller in either the hill people's kingdom or the valley people's admired Long Arm more than Blue Sky and Wandering Star did, whether he believed in the gods or not. He could almost magically separate warriors ready to kill one another. Maybe he was a god come to the human world in disguise.

He'd have to deny it, of course.

The king couldn't compel his people to accept his bastard son as their rightful prince. If he did that, War Cloud would start a civil war. Thunder Hunter had made it clear his tribe would fight to the last person to keep it from happening. Lightning Spear could, though, appoint his son the first teller, and that's what the conspirators' discussions with him were about.

At one point, Lightning Spear turned to his hostage.

"At the battle on the plain," he said, "the people came to tell me what Wandering Star and you were doing—making that pod tea for the wounded warriors. They told me some people were even saying Wandering Star should be our people's king instead of me."

Lightning Spear looked at Wandering Star and laughed again.

"Of course," he continued, "I had to assume those people meant you should be king only if I got myself killed in the battle. Otherwise, what they were saying would sound, to my ears, a bit too much like treason."

The king, still laughing, turned to Blue Sky once more.

"And then I found out," he said, "those were the pods the tellers were complaining about when they told me I had to send Wandering Star into exile. They told me the gods forbade our people from using them to relieve pain. Can you believe that? Even our wounded warriors couldn't use them? Wandering Star told me the gods must've put them on earth for some reason. He said it was up to me whether our people could use them. The same as it's entirely my decision whether our people can drink this lovely beverage you farmers make."

He looked down at the wine in his cup and smiled.

"Once again, of course," he added, "Wandering Star was right and his adversaries wrong."

He asked Wandering Star to explain to him what the tellers should do, since nobody liked what they were doing then.

Wandering Star was only too glad to oblige him, itemizing one point after the other, each of which they argued at length and with no little vitriol, causing Rose Leaf and Long Arm to repeatedly ask both of them to get to their point. Blue Sky would've gladly added his voice to their pleas if he hadn't been the guest of one of the disputants and the companion of the other.

The argument, in any event, seemed excessively hypothetical, given the king's blunt admission that he didn't know how to get rid of Heaven's Voice without causing a grievous upheaval in his kingdom, perhaps even leading to the untimely usurpation of his authority.

The unanticipated slaying of Heaven's Voice, though, changed all that.

On the same day Lightning Spear appointed Wandering Star first teller, the king announced the most important reform he and his son had eventually agreed to: the people would no longer pay tribute to the tellers.

Henceforth the tellers would support themselves, as they used to do.

Despite the loss of so many able-bodied men in the battles on the plain, in the upper gorge, and at sunset pass, the inability of most of the people to give anything to the tellers didn't mean a family's obligation to pay tribute for that period of time was forgiven. It was only delayed.

The people often said the high tellers and their associates were good at two things only: keeping precise track of which families owed what, and not letting the laggards forget either their debts or the extent to which they continued to accumulate.

Wandering Star had insisted that the younger and able-bodied tellers should continue to provide for the older tellers who were no longer capable of fending for themselves, even if their own sloth had put them in that position. Their provisions, though, didn't need to be anywhere nearly as abundant as Heaven's Voice, the high tellers, and their friends had previously demanded.

The younger and able-bodied tellers, Wandering Star said, should provide only enough to keep the beneficiaries in the same comfort their benefactors would want for elderly and incapacitated members of their own families.

And the younger and able-bodied tellers were overwhelmingly in favor of such an arrangement. They'd much rather spend their time hunting and gathering than dunning the people for tribute they didn't have and had little hope of coming up with—and making enemies of them.

Heaven's Voice and the high tellers couldn't understand this, but Wandering Star could.

One of the most important duties of the hill people's tellers was to settle disputes among the people, the same as it was for the valley people's tellers. It surely wasn't easy performing such a function if they were at the same time demanding tribute from the disputants, who might rationally begin to wonder if the generosity of their response could influence the tellers' decisions.

So Lightning Spear and Wandering Star had agreed: the tellers would fend for themselves.

The order abolishing teller tribute specifically wiped out all the people's previous debts for it as well as any future obligation on their part to pay it.

There was another part of the deal Wandering Star had made with his father: all the king's people would be free to make, trade, and drink the "lovely beverage" the farmers and the king himself had become so fond of.

*****

True Hunter paused when he got to Wandering Star and Blue Sky.

He was leaving with First Brother and Second Brother to rejoin his tribe east of the river. The brothers were acting as his guards. Long Arm was afraid the tellers who stood to lose the most from the death of Heaven's Voice would seek revenge by attacking True Hunter.

Wandering Star found Long Arm's caution amusing. He estimated it would take at least two times ten of the ablest of the tellers in question to mount the attack. And he wouldn't have been surprised if half of them suffered fatal wounds before True Hunter did.

"Those men are lazy and corrupt," the new first teller opined. "But they're not stupid. They saw True Hunter killing farmers on the plain."

Noon Breeze had seen him kill Solemn Promise and a number of Morning Sun's other town companions who were considered to be among the farmers' fittest and most skillful warriors.

True Hunter spoke in a voice so low that only Wandering Star and Blue Sky could hear him.

"I give you credit for abolishing teller tribute," he said. "It's shameful for tellers to live off the people."

Wandering Star kept his voice just as low.

"Maybe someday," he said, "you'll realize you and we don't have to be enemies."

True Hunter looked at Blue Sky. "We'll always be enemies. You have a farmer for a companion. You share your tent with him."

"He enjoys doing that, too," Blue Sky said, not without smirking. "And I hope whatever else you do with the remainder of your life, you'll enjoy it as much as my companion does."

True Hunter was still looking the king's hostage in the eye.

"I know who saved my life," he said. "I also know those four

251

people will live to regret they did it."

Blue Sky looked at True Hunter without blinking. "If I were one of the people you speak of, I can assure you I wouldn't worry for a moment about your poorly considered threat."

True Hunter chose not to respond.

"Those four people," Blue Sky continued, "might instead wish to have as their friend and ally the person making the threat. And you might wish never to forget that."

*****

A group of high tellers and their entourage came by Wandering Star's tent that afternoon.

"I'm glad to see you," Wandering Star said. "I didn't think you'd have the courage to pay us a visit."

"We'll need courage," one teller said, "facing certain starvation, thanks to you."

Wandering Star laughed. "We able-bodied tellers will never let you starve. We'll want you around. Don't worry about that. We need you to hold up to the people as examples."

"Examples?" another high teller asked.

"Of how not to be tellers," Wandering Star replied.

The high tellers and their friends laughed.

"It's good to know our new first teller has a sense of humor," a third high teller said, looking at Blue Sky. "But, of course, we always knew he did. He tells people he got expelled as a teller because he wouldn't go with Heaven's Voice. He'd have you believe his arrogance as the king's not-so-secret son had nothing to do with it. Isn't that a joke? Why would he tell people such a thing if he didn't want them to laugh?"

"Poor Heaven's Voice," a fourth high teller added. "He couldn't resist Lightning Spear's bastard son. He even resorted to threats to get him to go with him."

"We all know how desirable Wandering Star is," a fifth high teller said. "Even the farmers' prince, the one who kills our warriors at will, wants to share his tent. Can you imagine that?"

"None of us has gone with a farmer," a sixth said. "Let alone one of their princes."

After becoming a hostage, Blue Sky was surprised to learn how many hill people had it in the back of their minds—although they'd never admit it—that farmers were somehow superior to them.

Blue Sky supposed, being a farmer, he could've taken it as a compliment. It wasn't, though, an idea helpful to what the farmers and their allies among the hill people wanted to do.

By then it was apparent to them the hill people and the valley people—the hunters and the farmers—were the same people. At some point in the past they'd split, and all the looking up and looking down ever since had been a grievous mistake.

The hill people taught their children that farming was unnatural and evil. The valley people had learned at their parents' knees that a life of hunting and gathering was backward and brutal. And all that instruction justified their killing one another every chance they got.

The first high teller to speak took another turn. "And now the king's son has gotten his father to make him first teller. If somebody else tried to use their influence with the king that way, the bastard prince would be the first to object. Loudly, too. Everybody would hear him screaming: 'Oh, the favoritism! Oh, the corruption!'"

"I didn't ask to be appointed first teller," Wandering Star said. "I can assure you it was my father's idea."

Wandering Star had convinced Blue Sky the able-bodied tellers would take care of these old men. Blue Sky felt sorry for them anyway. They knew Wandering Star would very quickly demote them all, leaving them with no say-so over any of the other tellers. None of their present associates would need to pretend they were friends any longer.

That would no doubt hold true especially for their younger companions, many of whom already seemed forlorn.

Some of them, though, chose to smile at Wandering Star and Blue Sky—who might not only guarantee them a safe passage to old age but also prove a pleasure to go with.

But it was difficult for Blue Sky to feel much sympathy for them.

They'd chosen to go with a high teller, knowing the companionship would last for only a year or two at most. But they did what they did hoping to become one of the few of those young tellers who got to remain close to the first teller and the high tellers all their lives, sooner or later maybe even becoming high tellers themselves. They knew what kind of "human waste pit," as Wandering Star called it, they were getting themselves into. And they did it anyway.

It was also true the high tellers picked out their young friends when they were still apprentice tellers.

Blue Sky had seen for himself how impressionable most of his people's apprentice tellers were. One could reasonably argue that Noon Breeze used his friendships with the regent's son and his people's chief warrior, as well as the most beautiful man in the kingdom, to enhance himself in the eyes of the apprentice tellers and create more opportunities than he might otherwise have had.

Blue Sky would have to admit he'd done the same thing himself. He did try to warn his partners they'd never gain anything from going with him other than the momentary pleasure he would give them. He did still go with several of the apprentice tellers, and afterwards he sometimes overheard them bragging to their comrades about having gone with the regent's son.

Like Early Harvest and Good Harvest with the young women without male partners, Blue Sky never considered simply ignoring their physical appeal and turning the apprentice tellers down.

Despite all his many disclaimers, Blue Sky was nevertheless taking advantage of the apprentice tellers, as they were of him.

In their people's stories, he was born to be the son of the great and wise regent who took over the kingdom after Tall Oak's calamitous blunder on the plain. Blue Sky knew he'd be less than honest if he said being the regent's son was a burden and nothing else.

He agreed Wandering Star should replace all the current high tellers with honest and hard-working tellers the people respected. It did seem somewhat cruel, though, to so suddenly and completely destroy the lives of the high tellers and their companions.

They were only human, and humans, Blue Sky would be the very last human to deny, sometimes made grievous mistakes.

*****

254

On the bluff where the farmers had built their court and town, the hill people who'd come to celebrate, along with the tellers who still had their respect, began singing and dancing, quietly and slowly at first, but, as the afternoon progressed, with a great deal more abandon.

After all, Long Arm's people were serving them the farmers' wine the princess and the farmers' former prince, the one who killed Thunder Hunter and Dark Storm, had taught them to make.

Although the king was no doubt glad to see his people so pleased by what he'd done, he soon took to his tent with the lesser chieftains and their closest followers.

A crowd the size of the one that day on the bluff, choosing its own course like a flood or fire—who could say what it might do?

The evening became far more pleasant for the king and his guests, though, when Rose Leaf, Long Arm, and Wandering Star, jugs of wine in hand, went to them and said they'd asked the crowd not to go near the king's tent.

The people in that crowd, they all knew by then, would do whatever their princess, chief warrior, and newly appointed first teller asked them to do or not do. Even if that included not inflicting intoxicated retribution upon their now helpless rulers for some past injustice they'd suffered and would never forget.

*****

In the evening, with the festivities ending, the new first teller and the king's hostage joined their teller allies in the woods.

The place chosen for their moonlit entanglements was the glade where, two nights prior to that, a heinous villain had lured the old first teller to his death.

Despite knowing who that premeditated killer was, his hill-teller allies sought him out.

*****

In the days that followed, Blue Sky often noticed Lightning Spear staring at him.

When the next full-moon day arrived, the king chose to join

Long Arm's family in their festivities.

He brought with him none of his usual entourage of lesser chieftains and their chief warriors. He knew they wouldn't be welcome.

By then, he was openly drinking, and enjoying, the farmer's "lovely beverage."

He was still at a distance when Blue Sky noticed him approaching.

Blue Sky raised his cup to the hill people's king, who drew close enough to whisper but still make himself heard above the noise of the crowd.

"I hear True Hunter is still alive," the king said to his hostage.

"I've heard that myself," Blue Sky said.

"Wandering Star and Long Arm tell me that means he didn't kill Heaven's Voice."

"They've both told me the same thing."

Lightning Spear smiled at Blue Sky. The pleasure he was taking in their conversation was obvious.

"I've been wondering who actually killed Heaven's Voice," he said. "If neither True Hunter nor Wandering Star murdered the man, I've considered who might've had what it took to do it. Maybe, I've thought, it was somebody who knew he could get away with it."

The younger members of Long Arm's family were playing the same spear-throwing game Blue Sky had found them playing with Morning Sun, the day a child said Blue Sky was no longer a boy.

Lightning Spear was only getting started.

"Heaven's Voice," he said, "didn't let his teller friends know he was meeting someone that evening. The person must've been somebody he couldn't tell them about."

The king was daring his hostage to look away.

Blue Sky, though, chose not to.

Lightning Spear continued. "That person knew Heaven's Voice couldn't tell anybody he was going with him in the woods. The person also knew he could never be accused. He'd figured out he could kill my people's first teller and get away with it. Nobody, not even the king, could name him. If the king did, he'd have to order the execution of his hostage, and the king could never do that. The farmers would resume the war."

At that point, Lightning Spear had his arms around Blue Sky's shoulders as if they were lovers.

The king's pleasure in telling the story was as intense as Blue Sky's had been in living it.

"I can't tell you," the king said, "how much I admire the person who did that."

He closed what little gap remained between them and embraced his hostage.

"Excellent," he whispered in Blue Sky's ear. "Excellent."

He stepped back from his hostage again, looking him up and down.

"Of course," Blue Sky said, "the person you're speaking of would never wish to admit he did such a thing. Infringing upon your hospitality—killing your people's first teller. He could never tell anybody he did that. He'd have to take the secret to his grave."

"Of course," Lightning Spear agreed, laughing, his one hand still on Blue Sky's shoulder. "He couldn't actually tell anybody he did it. No decent person would expect him to."

The hill people's king put his cup to his lips but lowered it again without drinking from it.

"Though I would want that man to know one thing," he said.

"What would that be?" Blue Sky asked.

"How much I appreciate what he did."

Blue Sky laughed. "And I'm quite certain he'd be pleased to hear that."

"Wandering Star probably convinced him," the king said, "what grief I would've come to if I'd tried to remove Heaven's Voice from his position—and replace him with my bastard son."

"Wandering Star even convinced me of that."

Lightning Spear laughed again.

"They say the killing was carried out quite efficiently," he said. "A quiet bloodless strangling in the woods. Not a sound to be heard. Not a drop of blood to wash off. Poor old Heaven's Voice couldn't have put up much of a struggle. Of course, the killer knew beforehand he couldn't and wouldn't."

Lightning Spear looked Blue Sky up and down again.

"I'd have to say that was excellent," the king said. "Flawless, in fact."

Several young teller allies had come by and were playing their instruments and singing for the children.

Long Arm's family's other guests that evening—Thistle Dew, Dancing Song, Rose Leaf, and Wandering Star—had joined the children, the better to hear the music.

"I must say," Lightning Spear remarked, suddenly, "I've never strangled a person, but I've often wondered what it would feel like to kill a person that way."

He looked at Blue Sky and smiled.

"The person who killed Heaven's Voice could tell me," he said. "Maybe I'll be lucky enough to speak with him about it someday. I'll have a lot of questions for him. Specifics. Details."

The person who'd killed Heaven's Voice imagined wrestling the king to the ground and showing him right then and there what a fatal strangulation felt like for the both of them.

It would've given the children in Long Arm's family, distant cousins included, something to talk about for the rest of their lives: the feast day the farmers' hostage prince throttled their king while they stood watching, horrified but not unhappy.

But the killer, still calling himself "Blue Sky," couldn't do that.

Rose Leaf hadn't yet given birth to her and Morning Sun's child.

The other guests and Long Arm's family, children included, were dancing, their shadows in the light of the setting summer sun absurdly elongated across the valley people's old courtyard. They seemed the size gods might be if they ever chose to visit the human world again.

Blue Sky set the king's cup and his own on a flattened log.

They joined the dance as partners.

The children, poking one another, looked at them and laughed.

It wasn't often they saw a farmer prince dancing with a hill king—and certainly not a king their parents despised even as they provided for and protected him.

Whenever the former farmer prince saw the children, he

greeted them by saying their names. So did the new farmer prince. So did their own princess and the king's bastard son.

Those high people knew who the children's mothers and fathers were, who their brothers and sisters were, who their aunts, uncles, and cousins were.

When the king saw them, though, he hadn't any idea who they were. He recognized the sullen boys who brought him his food, water, bath, clean clothes, and firewood, but he never spoke with them, much less thanked them for their service.

He was a king the children, being children, liked nothing better than making fun of, sometimes openly.

As the king and his hostage danced, the shadow of each person on the top of the bluff that late in the day, even the smallest child's, was so long it was like the story those humans found themselves in. They couldn't tell where it came to an end.

RON FRITSCH

Character List

Spoiler alert: much of the information in this list gives away the plots of the first two Promised Valley novels, *Promised Valley Rebellion* and *Promised Valley War*. If you wish to read about the rebellion and the war before you read about the conspiracy, you shouldn't peruse this list until you've enjoyed all the surprises and reversals in those books.

Valley People

Autumn Wine: Green Field and Gentle Brook's elderly neighbor. Her two grandsons, orphaned in the last war with the hill people, live with her. Despite the unusual number of years she's lived, she's remained vital in both her body and mind. Having suffered profoundly in the previous war with the hill people, she finds it difficult to think well of them. Her older grandson's lover is a young woman whose family are wealthy town people. So was the young woman's unloved husband, who was killed in the battle on the plain in *Promised Valley War*.

Blue Sky: Green Field and Gentle Brook's son and Rose Leaf's brother. He's also the best friend of the prince, Morning Sun. When Rose Leaf, Blue Sky, and Morning Sun came of age in *Promised Valley Rebellion*, the king, Tall Oak, refused to permit Morning Sun and Rose Leaf to marry and have children together. He also declined to explain his incomprehensible decree. That provoked Blue Sky into joining Rose Leaf and Morning Sun in a rebellion against the king and the officials he'd appointed to run the kingdom, many of whom the far more numerous farmers despised. After meeting and consorting with a hill man, Wandering Star—each committing treason by simply befriending an enemy—Blue Sky learned the truth: Rose Leaf was the hill people's kidnapped princess. Green Field and Tall Oak, captured in the war the hill people began and lost during their youth, escaped with the infant princess. Gentle Brook named the child Rose Leaf and raised the hill princess as her daughter. Taking the risk that the valley people might turn against them, Blue Sky led the way in revealing Rose Leaf's provenance to the valley people. After the hill people abducted Rose Leaf and Morning Sun in *Promised*

Valley War, he was one of the few valley people who opposed sending their army, which consisted of all their able-bodied men, to retrieve them.

Early Harvest: Morning Sun's chief competitor in his pursuit of Rose Leaf's consent to be his mate. Although Rose Leaf chose the prince, at a crucial moment in *Promised Valley Rebellion* Early Harvest implored the people not to stand in the way of Rose Leaf's marriage to his rival. He was one of the few valley warriors who survived the battle on the plain in *Promised Valley War*.

East Land: an outspoken farmer who fought alongside Green Field, Tall Oak, and Full Harvest in the previous war with the hill people.

Fair Judge: a special friend of the queen, Rainbow Evening. She's also the teller who was in charge of the education of the prince, Morning Sun, as well as the orphanage where Spring Rain and Many Numbers grew up. The people insist upon calling her Fair Judge. She publicly castigated the first teller, Law Keeper, for his corruption and cronyism. After he and most of the other male tellers died in the battle on the plain in *Promised Valley War*, Green Field, having become the regent in the absence of Morning Sun, appointed Fair Judge their people's first female first teller.

Full Harvest: Early Harvest's father, who fought alongside Green Field and Tall Oak in the previous war with the hill people. He became a wealthy upper-valley farmer and the apparent father of a large number of children born to mates of his brothers who died in that war. Late in *Promised Valley Rebellion* Blue Sky discovered how it came about that Full Harvest and Gentle Brook—the wife of Full Harvest's friend, Green Field—are lovers. In *Promised Valley War* Full Harvest took the lead in welcoming to the upper valley the lower-valley survivors of the battle on the plain.

Gentle Brook: wife of Green Field, mother of Blue Sky, and cousin of the queen, Rainbow Evening. She and Full Harvest, her husband's cousin and friend, are lovers. In the previous war with the hill people, she took as her daughter, Rose Leaf, the hill people's infant princess Green Field and Tall Oak had abducted. In *Promised Valley War* she insisted that women have the right to join in the fighting to defend against the hill people, whose leaders proclaimed their intent to exterminate the valley people. She was instrumental in founding the auxiliaries, whose efforts arguably did more than those of the warriors to keep the hill people out of the upper valley.

Good Harvest: said to be a younger cousin of his best friend, Early Harvest, but more likely his half-brother. He came of age in *Promised Valley War* and fought in the battles to keep the hill warriors out of the upper valley.

Green Field: Gentle Brook's mate and Blue Sky's father. He's a farmer hero who saved the life of his best friend, Tall Oak, then a prince and heir to the kingship, when they were captured in the previous war with the hill people. He accomplished their escape the night before the hill people's king had scheduled their execution. At the end of *Promised Valley Rebellion*, he convinced the farmers to approve the marriage of the current prince, Morning Sun, to Rose Leaf. He and Gentle Brook had led the people to believe Rose Leaf was their daughter, but he ultimately revealed she's actually the daughter and sole heir of the hill people's king. He and Tall Oak took her with them when they escaped. In *Promised Valley War* Green Field became the regent of the valley people, in the absence of Morning Sun, who is the last remaining person above Green Field in the line of succession to the kingship.

Law Keeper: the kingdom's former first teller and Sturdy Limb's submissive ally. The farmers openly laughed at his bumbling attempts to impress them with his authority. He used his position to attempt to separate the physically attractive Spring Rain from Many Numbers and have him for himself. Blue Sky not only mocked and ridiculed Law Keeper but also revealed his scheming to the farmers, who, adoring Spring Rain, expressed their outrage. Despite his age, he fought in the battle on the plain in *Promised Valley War* and died there.

Many Numbers: a young teller who lives with his mate, Spring Rain. Many Numbers was the first to join Blue Sky's rebellion on behalf of the prince and Rose Leaf. Many Numbers had good reasons to work for the downfall of the ill-chosen Law Keeper and Sturdy Limb and their corrupt regime. In *Promised Valley War* he was one of the few who opposed the punitive expedition against the hill people. After the horrifying defeat of the valley people on the hill people's plain, Green Field appointed Many Numbers chief warrior. Many Numbers crucially helped Blue Sky plot the battles that kept the hill people out of the upper valley.

Morning Sun: the prince, the only living child of Tall Oak and Rainbow Evening. He was also Blue Sky and Rose Leaf's best childhood friend. Perhaps as a result of that, he tended to side with the farmers against his father's officials. In *Promised Valley War* Long Arm's abduction of Rose Leaf and Morning Sun led to the war between the valley people and the hill people. Long Arm's people, though, soon took a liking to both Rose Leaf and Morning Sun and began treating them not as captives but as members of their family.

Noon Breeze: a scrawny, boyish, no-apologies, pleasure-loving son of poor farmers. In *Promised Valley Rebellion* he became an unlikely friend of Blue Sky's in the apprentice tellers' encampment. In *Promised Valley War* he survived the battle on the plain and the two subsequent battles defending the upper valley. Blue Sky, Early Harvest, and Good Harvest saved him after he came close to thoughtlessly throwing away the valley people's victory at the end of the last battle.

Rainbow Evening: the queen, Morning Sun's mother, and Gentle Brook's cousin. She despised Sturdy Limb and Law Keeper and spends a good deal of her time with Fair Judge. In *Promised Valley War*, she suffered the abduction of Morning Sun and the death of Tall Oak, the prince-who-became-king she married, as well as the deaths of the three sons of her deceased sister, Sturdy Limb's wife. Rainbow Evening was the only mother her nephews ever knew.

Solemn Promise: a son of a wealthy court family and a friend of the prince, Morning Sun. In *Promised Valley War* he died in the battle on the plain.

Spring Rain: Many Numbers' mate, a young teller the people favor for his lovely tenor voice, patience in hearing their arguments, and pleasing looks. As a teacher in the apprentice teller's encampment in *Promised Valley Rebellion*, he shared a hut with Blue Sky. Spring Rain was the second man—Morning Sun was the first—Blue Sky fell in love with but couldn't have. In *Promised Valley War* Blue Sky, separated from Wandering Star against his will, and discovering Many

Numbers wished to go with others as well as his partner, commenced an affair with Spring Rain.

Sturdy Limb: Tall Oak's brother and chief warrior. Most of the farmers despised him. After the abduction of Rose Leaf and Morning Sun in *Promised Valley War*, he insisted upon leading a punitive expedition against the hill people by the valley people's army, which consisted of all their able-bodied men except those who explicitly opposed yet another war: Green Field, Blue Sky, Many Numbers, and Spring Rain. The hill people killed Sturdy Limb in the battle on the plain.

Tall Oak: the king, Rainbow Evening's mate, and Morning Sun's father. At the end of the previous war with the hill people, he appointed his brother, Sturdy Limb, to be chief warrior, after Green Field, the people's choice, turned down the position. In *Promised Valley Rebellion* Blue Sky, Rose Leaf, and Morning Sun forced Tall Oak into letting Green Field tell the people the truth regarding Rose Leaf. In *Promised Valley War* Tall Oak sided with his brother Sturdy Limb and led his army onto the hill people's plain and a horrifying tragedy for both peoples. Tall Oak died in the battle.

Valley Defender: the oldest of Sturdy Limb's three sons and Morning Sun's first cousin. He also wished to be Rose Leaf's mate. In *Promised Valley War* he was the last valley warrior to die, after Wandering Star and Blue Sky led him and the other few survivors of the battle on the plain back to the valley.

Hill People

Aim Far: Second Brother's oldest son.

Dancing Song: Wandering Star's mother. In *Promised Valley War* she told Blue Sky that the hill people's king, Lightning Spear, is Wandering Star's father.

Dark Cloud: the closest cousin to Dark Storm and War Cloud.

Dark Storm: the older son of Thunder Hunter, the hill people's second most powerful chieftain.

Deer Tracker: a hill boy whose father and grandmother died in the battles with the valley people in *Promised Valley War*.

Evening Shadow: a young hill teller-warrior. His lover is Night Whisper.

First Brother: the older of Long Arm's two surviving brothers, who chose to change his name after he helped Long Arm abduct Rose Leaf and Morning Sun.

Heaven's Voice: the hill people's first teller.

Lightning Spear: the hill people's king. Rose Leaf, abducted by Green Field and Tall Oak in the previous war with the valley people, is his only legitimate child.

Long Arm: a skillful hunter who spied on Wandering Star and Blue Sky, committed the abduction that started the most recent war with the valley people, and immediately became a hero.

Night Whisper: a young hill teller-warrior. His lover is Evening Shadow.

Rose Leaf: a young woman who grew up believing she was Green Field and Gentle Brook's daughter and Blue Sky's sister. Morning Sun, Early Harvest, and many other young valley men wished to be her mate. The king, queen, and her parents warned her she couldn't choose Morning Sun. In the previous war with the valley people, Green Field and Tall Oak, escaping from their captors and correctly guessing she was Lightning Spear's only child, abducted her, intending to kill her. When they realized they couldn't kill a child, they took her back to the valley with them. Upon seeing her, Gentle Brook wished to raise her as her daughter.

Second Brother: the younger of Long Arm's two surviving brothers, who chose to change his name after he helped Long Arm abduct Rose Leaf and Morning Sun.

Thistle Dew: the hill people's queen. After Rose Leaf's abduction, she refused to appear in public.

Thunder Hunter: the hill people's second most powerful chieftain, after his cousin, their king, Lightning Spear. Known for his brutality, in *Promised Valley War* his warriors forced the other chieftains' warriors to keep fighting. His sons are Dark Storm and War Cloud.

True Hunter: a teller cousin of Dark Storm and War Cloud. He's physically attractive and probably the hill people's finest warrior.

Wandering Star: a hill man who became Blue Sky's lover, both of them aware they were committing treason every moment they spent together. In *Promised Valley Rebellion* Wandering Star told Blue Sky that Rose Leaf is the hill people's princess. In *Promised Valley War* he led the survivors of the battle on the plain back to the valley.

War Cloud: Thunder Hunter's younger son. He's as physically seductive as True Hunter and a warrior as worthy as True Hunter and Long Arm. He begs his father and Lightning Spear to let him carry out executions prolonged to maximize the pain.